THE
CAT'S EYE
CHARM

THE CAT'S EYE CHARM

A WITCH CATS OF CAMBRIDGE MYSTERY

CLEA SIMON

For Jon

Praise for The Cat's Eye Charm

"A treat for anyone who loves warm, sensitive, caring characters determined to do what's right for both animals and humans."—Vicki Delany, bestselling author of the Tea by the Sea, Sherlock Holmes Bookshop, Lighthouse Library, and Year-Round Christmas cozy mysteries

"*The Cat's Eye Charm* is catnip for the mystery-lover's soul, with just the right mix of suspense, magic, furry mayhem…and cats, of course. Highly recommended!"—Amy Shojai, CABC, author of the September & Shadow Thriller Series

"*The Cat's Eye Charm* surprises and delights as witch detective Becca hunts for a lost cat while her cats at home work their own magic."— Marty Wingate, author of the *London Ladies' Murder Club*

PRAISE FOR THE SERIES

"(A) delightful series launch…You don't have to be a cat lover to appreciate this paranormal cozy's witty observations, entertaining dialogue, and astute characterizations."—*Publishers Weekly* on *A Spell of Murder*

"An otherworldly fun trip…I couldn't figure out which group provided the most fun: the clueless humans or the ever-so-sly cats."—*Mystery Scene* on *A Spell of Murder*

"Simon expertly casts suspicion on one member of her tiny human cast after another…for readers who want all cats, all the time."—*Kirkus Reviews* on *An*

Chapter One

"Bast be thanked," Becca said to no one in particular. "I mean, blessed be."

It was a rainy August morning, the day as dreary as could be. But for the young woman with the curly brown hair, it was as if a ray of sun had broken through the pall of clouds. Even her momentary self-correction spoke of relief, amending her invocation to the Egyptian cat goddess to the more general Wiccan blessing. Not that the usual customers at Charm and Cherish, the little shop where she worked, were all practitioners of the earth-centric religion, but Becca was not only a practicing Wiccan, she was, as far as she knew, Cambridge's only witch detective. Besides, she truly was grateful, and it couldn't hurt to say it out loud.

"Blessed be," she said again, letting out a sigh of relief. The Bast statuette had been found.

Charm and Cherish might feel like home, but Becca was only an employee. The sole employee, if she didn't count Elizabeth Cross, the owner's sister, who had a tendency to waft in and out, though she could be relied upon to cover when Becca wasn't available. That meant the loss of one of the shop's showpieces would be doubly disastrous, not only to her reputation but likely to her paycheck as well. The black cat goddess had been sitting guarding the store's old-fashioned register since Becca's first day in the crowded storefront, watching over the cash flow and also the small collection of semiprecious stones that sat beside it, promising various healing and protective powers. Until, that is, the figure went missing.

Becca had opened the store only an hour before, but once she'd hung her rain jacket and hat in the back, she'd focused on the window display, which tended to collect dust. It wasn't until she retrieved the cash tray for the register and slid it into place that she noticed the cat statuette that usually stood right nearby was gone, a blue miniature of the Hindu goddess Kali in its place.

"What the...?" She'd been on her knees in a second, peering under the edge of the sales counter and then the floor below. Charm and Cherish didn't have a resident cat—not a warm, furry one, anyway—but because Becca cohabited with three of her own felines, she automatically assumed when something went missing that it had been knocked to the floor. When she couldn't find it on the faded linoleum, she began an increasingly frantic search of the store—from that dusty front window to the display area, two round tables where Becca had arranged a few candles and a bundle of purifying sage smudges that would be in high demand once the students started moving back in, as well as some larger crystals poised to catch the light. From there, she moved onto the bookshelves that began right in front of the register, four freestanding cases facing the front of the store that held both scholarly volumes and more light-hearted works.

The shelves were deep enough that Becca had been able to place various statuettes and knickknacks in front of the books—at least, the ones unlikely to be browsed. Moving the Kali to the first shelf in a fit of pique, Becca strode by each case, naming the figures as she passed: "One Minoan snake goddess, a 'Venus' of Willendorf, a clowder of winged cats, the two Moon Goddesses." She reached up to stroke the goddess's crescent-shaped horns, removing a swipe of dust. "A world tree, a Hecate..."

Only when she paused to catch her breath and doubled back did she see it, peering down from the top of the first bookcase and prompting her exclamation of gratitude.

"How'd you get up there?" Grabbing the stepladder, she reached for the figurine, ready to return it to its accustomed spot.

"I put her up there." Becca whipped around to see a tall, lean figure waltz into the store. Clad in a purple and turquoise caftan that only accentuated her hawk-like features, Elizabeth Cross smiled over at Becca. "I wanted her to be able to see everyone who came in this morning. For their own protection, of course."

"Of course," Becca responded without thinking. With Elizabeth, that was often the best idea. "Should I take her down now?"

"No, no." Elizabeth's caftan shimmered as she waved off the suggestion. "She'll be fine where she is for the time being."

Becca knew better than to question the older woman. Elizabeth rarely spoke about magic, but she had an unnerving habit of saying things that proved, if not prophetic, then strangely on the mark.

"I didn't see you on the schedule," she noted instead as she climbed back down and found herself looking up at the towering gray-haired woman. "Did you want to switch a shift?"

"I just wanted to say hi." Elizabeth's craggy face lit up as she spoke. "And wish you luck."

"Thanks?" Becca's voice reflected her uncertainty. But by then, in a swirl of color, Elizabeth was gone.

Shaking her head, Becca went back to setting up. More New Age shop than classic botanica, Charm and Cherish sold everything from books to biodegradable glitter, with at least a dozen cat figurines in among the candles and incense. After closing the night before, Becca had put some of the pricier pieces, such as a crystal ball with an intricately carved stand, in the back. Now she brought it out to that front table, wiping it with her sweater so that it caught whatever light the clouds let through.

She'd only just placed the crystal ball, stepping back to admire her arrangement, when the bells over the front door rang once more. Expecting Elizabeth again, Becca turned and found herself face to face with a young woman of about her own age. Slimmer than Becca, who had what her friends considered a healthy figure, the newcomer's dark hair fell about her pale face, her pallor and slight breathlessness suggesting something of a rush—or, Becca decided upon taking in a certain wide-eyed look, a crisis.

"May I help you?" Becca thought about offering the distraught woman tea, but before she could say anything more, the pale newcomer had grabbed her upper arm.

"You're Becca Colwin, right? The witch detective?"

"Yes." Becca nodded a little warily. Despite her waifish build, the newcomer's grip was strong.

"Thank the goddess." The speaker's shoulders seemed to relax a little, and some color came back into her face as she released Becca's arm. "I was hoping I'd find you here."

Becca couldn't help feeling a bit self-satisfied. Clearly, this woman was in distress. Still, it was nice to have her powers recognized—even if she wasn't entirely sure how much of her few successes had been due to witchcraft and how much to plain old sleuthing and common sense.

"Well, you did." She eased into a smile, hoping it might calm the woman. "How do you think I can help you?"

"It's my cat," the stranger answered, letting out the breath she'd apparently been holding since she walked in. "He's gone." And with that, she burst into tears.

Chapter Two

"I'm so sorry." Becca raced around the counter to take the weeping girl in her arms. Although her current cats were alive and well, she could well remember the aching grief she felt over her first feline's death. As a devoted pet lover, she could recall only one antidote to the fresh waves of devastation that had surprised her at the most inopportune moments, and that was to lose oneself in memories. "Would you like to tell me about your late kitty?"

"Late? No." The visitor pulled away, shaking her head and reaching into her pockets. Becca responded by grabbing the tissue box she kept behind the counter and holding it as the visitor plucked out half the box. "He's just lost. He got out, somehow, and now I can't find him."

"Ah." Becca took stock. "Well, I don't know if you need a witch detective for that. But I do know something about finding lost cats, and I'd be happy to help."

"You would?" Visibly brightening, the visitor held out the hand that wasn't clutching a handful of moist tissue. "I'm Trina, Trina Cruces. And my kitty is Mr. Butters."

"Okay, that's a start." Becca reached behind the counter for a paper and pen. She'd learned to take notes at the start of any case, and although a lost cat was a mystery of a different sort, she knew jotting down the essentials could prove useful later on. "Why don't you tell me what happened?"

"That's just it. I'm not sure." Trina shook her head, reaching up to push away the hair that had stuck to her damp cheek. "Mr. Butters is an indoors-only cat, and he always greets me at the front door. I was out doing errands early this morning, and when I came back, he wasn't there."

Becca, who had some experience with "disappearing" cats, turned a skeptical eye on her potential client. "And you checked everywhere? Under every piece of furniture and on top of all your appliances as well?"

Laurel, the most agile of Becca's cats, had once wedged herself between the top of the refrigerator and the cabinet above it—most likely in response to a particularly noisy gathering of Becca's coven. But as she started to tell Trina about this, the other woman broke in.

"No, he's not anywhere. I looked behind my shoes in the closet and on top and behind everything. I—we—live in a small apartment. There's just no place to hide."

"We?" Becca cut in. "Do you mean you and your cat?"

"No, well, yes. I—we—also have a human roommate, Shira, but she was at work all day yesterday. She left before I did—and before I'd fed Mr. Butters—and she didn't come home until after I did, so I know she didn't let Mr. Butters out. All I can think is he slipped out somehow, like, maybe when I was locking the door?"

"It's possible." Trina seemed to want a response, but Becca was already moving on. "At any rate, let's assume he got out. You do know that most housecats who get outside are frightened and respond by hiding right near where they got out, right?"

Trina shook her head, prompting Becca to tear off a clean sheet of paper. *First things first*, she wrote on top. *Search near your building*. On the next line, she wrote, *Make up signs*. At that, she paused, pen poised.

"First off, what does Mr. Butters look like?"

"He's a ginger tabby. A big boy with orange and white stripes and a nice white bib." Trina's voice warmed as she described her pet. "Big pale orange paws and the bluest eyes."

Becca jotted down these details. "Does he have a collar with tags?"

"He's microchipped." It was a non-answer, and Becca had to work very hard not to roll her eyes. "But he does have a collar. It's light blue, and I've hung a little blue charm from it."

Becca inhaled to keep herself from chastising the worried woman. It was too late now, anyway. "I'm sorry he isn't wearing a tag with your address or your phone number," was all she said, keeping her voice level.

"I know, I should have added a tag." Trina sounded genuinely contrite. "It's just that he's always been an indoor cat, and I didn't think it was necessary."

"I get it." Becca couldn't help but feel for the other woman. "What does the charm look like?"

"Oh, it's just a little painted ball, like a Christmas tree ornament. It's blue, but it's got this black stripe through its middle, like the pupil in a cat's eye. That's what drew me toward it."

"Did it come with the collar?" Becca kept writing. Any detail, she knew, might prove useful.

"No, I found it at a flea market." Trina shook her head. "It's not fancy or anything, but it's pretty. And it goes so well with the collar."

"I'll write it down as an identifying detail, but keep in mind, Mr. Butters might have managed to get rid of his collar."

"I know. I just want him back." The sadness in Trina's voice could have broken Becca's heart, making her glad she hadn't lectured her about collars and ID tags. "So do you think you can help me find him?"

"I can't tonight, I'm sorry. But here's a list of things you can do now." With Trina looking on, she added to her list. "Check behind any trash cans that are around your building, and if there are basement window wells. Also, even if your building is right up against a fence, check the space between the building and the fence. You might need a flashlight. Cats can squeeze into the tiniest places.

"If you don't find him right around the building, try putting a piece of your clothing outside." Becca checked off another item on her list. "Some people think a familiar smell will draw a kitty out. And you should make up fliers with photos of Mr. Butters and a way to reach you. What is your phone number, anyway?"

Trina recited it, and Becca jotted down her own before handing the to-do list over. "Will your roommate help with this?"

"Definitely. Shira loves Mr. Butters almost as much as I do."

"I'm glad to hear it." Becca visibly relaxed. Some people, she knew, didn't take to cats, and she had been quietly weighing the possibility that the roommate had done something to get rid of Mr. Butters. "You also might call Animal Control and see if they have humane traps you can borrow, but maybe that won't even be necessary."

It was going to be wet that night, but Becca stopped herself from mentioning that. The poor woman was scared enough as it is. "I'm hoping you get home, and he greets you just like normal," she said instead. "Cats do have a way of surprising us after all."

"Thanks," Trina sniffed as she stared at the floor. Despite the list of actions Becca had given her, the pale young woman didn't seem eager to get started. Or, to be honest, leave the little shop.

"Is there something else?" Becca spoke as gently as she could. Clients, she had learned, came to her as much for reassurance and emotional support as for practical answers or any real detecting.

Trina shook her head, but Becca waited. Finally, the other woman began to speak. "I just wish I knew what had happened. How he got out." Dark eyes darted up to meet Becca's. "I'm super careful. I know how dangerous this city can be. And…"

Another shake of her head, and she was staring at the shop's dark linoleum floor again.

"What is it, Trina?" Becca didn't want to play therapist, but clearly something was bothering her visitor. Besides, now that she'd found the Bast statuette, there was little for her to do until another customer came in.

A sigh, as she looked up again. "I guess I was hoping that you could, you know, cast a spell?"

Becca smiled. Since she'd set herself up as a witch detective, she'd become accustomed to such requests.

"We'll find her. I'll do what I can to help," she said, trying to convey more confidence than she felt. It could do no harm to prop up this sad girl. "But we'll find her faster if you get to work."

Chapter Three

"*Oh, Bast! Not again.*" Even as Becca was advising the worried Trina, Harriet, the oldest and largest of Becca's three cats, was dealing with a situation on the home front. Only two months earlier, Becca had rescued a tiny tortoiseshell kitten, an oddly marked little beast with bright green eyes and one peach-colored toe on her left front paw, and although she frequently spoke of rehoming the newcomer, the unnamed kitten was still living in Becca's one-bedroom apartment. And while Harriet's two littermates, the tawny Laurel and calico Clara, had pretty much gotten used to the interloper, the fluffy marmalade clearly felt her territory had been infringed upon. *"What were you thinking of, you unpleasant little beast?"*

The tortie, whom Harriet firmly believed to be an idiot, didn't respond. But Clara did, gently pawing at the shards of a small china bowl with one white paw. The kitten had pushed it off an upper shelf, seemingly only to watch it shatter on the floor below. Becca, Clara knew, was not going to be happy about that. The bowl had been a pretty thing, with a white and blue pattern that reminded the calico of the clouds in the summer sky.

However, Harriet's dismay, she suspected, sprang from an altogether different grievance. Her problem wasn't that the kitten had knocked the bowl to the floor. Kittens will be kittens, they all knew. And sometimes things just have to be pushed off surfaces.

No, what bothered Harriet, at least according to what Clara suspected, was that the little tortie hadn't jumped up to that shelf to nudge the bowl off its perch. When the piece fell, the kitten had been sitting on the back of the sofa, several feet below. But that she had been responsible, none of them doubted. The three older cats had all seen her raise one paw—the one with the peach-colored toe—and move it through the empty air, almost as if she could feel the bowl start to slide, which it did with cataclysmic results.

No, more than the crash, it was the kitten's seeming ability to move an object without physically touching it that bothered Harriet. It wasn't simply that the tortie apparently had some psychic ability. Like her sisters, Harriet had magical powers. After all, it was Harriet's particular ability to conjure items out of the ether that had mistakenly convinced Becca that she was, in fact, a witch. It had been bad luck that Becca had been trying out a conjuring spell one afternoon when Harriet, lazy as always, had decided to summon a pillow rather than move, and the ill timing of that small bit of feline magic was what had started Becca on her path to pitch herself as a witch detective.

No, Clara knew, it was that her oldest sister had written off the kitten as a talentless feline. Because even though all cats have the ability to do some basic magic—when Becca reminded Trina of how well cats can hide, she was very near a bigger truth—Harriet and her sisters were descendants of feline royalty, blessed by the great goddess Bast herself for service to a beleaguered young servant at her ancient Egyptian temple. For this kitten to have similar advanced powers appeared to make light of this divine lineage. Or—to Harriet—worse, Clara suspected. Could it be that this nameless kitten had some other source for her power?

"Don't even think it," Laurel, Clara's middle sister, snarled. As sleek as some unknown Siamese forebear, Laurel had a bit of an attitude. She was the one, after all, who had dubbed Clara "Clara the Clown," pointing out that, unlike her own symmetrical good looks, her baby sister had an orange patch over one eye and a black one over the other. Now she looked from her calico sibling over to the tortie. *"She just got lucky, Clown. With that silly little peach toe!"*

Clara held her tongue and, more important, tried to still her thoughts. Most cats have some mind-reading ability, but Laurel, she knew, was quite adept at picking up what her sisters—her littlest sister especially—was thinking. Clara didn't know if this was linked to Laurel's special talent, the ability to suggest emotions to humans, but it could be unnerving. Especially now, when she found herself disagreeing with her seal-point sister. There was something uncanny about the kitten who had recently joined their household.

The tortie's arrival had been less than auspicious. Becca's rescue of the kitten had involved her chasing the kitten down an alley after seeing the mottled little beast darting across two lanes of traffic right outside Charm and Cherish. That the kitten had settled beside the dead body of Becca's ex complicated the rescue. Since then, the kitten—still nameless, but significantly larger—had resided with Becca's original three cats. It was an uneasy truce, at best. And one that the tortie's antics weren't helping.

"It would help, I think, if we knew what to call her." Clara spoke softly, out of respect for her sisters—and in the hope that Laurel wouldn't read her true thoughts. *"Maybe we could encourage her to behave."*

At that, the kitten looked up at her, green eyes bright against her caramel swirl fur.

"Call me?" The words sounded in Clara's head.

Clara blinked. This wasn't the first time she thought she'd been getting something from the kitten. Only whenever she did hear what seemed to be a communication, it disappeared just as quickly.

"Call her annoying, that's what." With a thud, Harriet jumped from the sofa to the floor. The big marmalade had been partially responsible for the kitten's continued presence in the apartment, grooming her in a familial fashion when one potential adopter had come to visit. *"Well, I couldn't let a cat go to just* anyone." From the look she shot Clara, the calico could tell that her big sister had accessed the same memory. *"I mean, even if it is just a dumb kitten."*

"I'm not sure she's so dumb." Clara held out a paw, and the kitten rose on her black-stockinged hind feet to bat at it, until she overbalanced and landed on her side.

"Ha. Look at it." Laurel had joined them, her tail still twitching with annoyance. *"Not an ounce of feline grace."*

"We were all kittens once." As Clara watched, the tortie righted herself and

began to wash.

"*Speak for yourself, Clown.*" Laurel wasn't going to be appeased, and it hit Clara. Laurel, the best jumper of the three, was likely to get blamed for anything knocked off a high shelf. "*When it was clearly an accident or the wind or something.*" Laurel, picking up on Clara's thought, grumbled. That this contradicted her earlier deduction that the tortie was responsible didn't seem to faze her. Cats, after all, are not known for their logic.

"*Whatever is going on, we might all benefit from a conversation,*" said Clara, ever the peacemaker. But it was too late. Laurel's tail was lashing again, and Harriet had gone to sleep.

Chapter Four

"Oh, no." Becca's voice woke Clara, who had also curled up for a nap. Hurrying through her usual yawn and stretch, the calico jumped from the sofa to comfort her person, who now held the two largest pieces of the blue porcelain bowl in her hand. "Oh, kitties."

Laurel, the calico noticed, had made herself scarce. But Becca wasn't looking for any particular feline—or to lay blame, her pet hoped—and instead was gathering up the shattered pieces. Fitting them together like pieces of a puzzle, she seemed distracted for a moment.

"This might work," she muttered to herself. "I wonder if there's a spell…"

"She needn't bother." With a thud, Harriet landed beside her sister. Still blinking off sleep, she gazed up at Becca. *"That would be easy enough to replace."*

"Better to let her repair it," the calico suggested. The last thing any of them needed was Harriet summoning a new bowl out of the air. Becca was confused enough about her powers—or lack thereof—as it was. *"At least, she'll feel like she was able to do something,"* Clara offered the explanation, earning a scoff that sounded suspiciously like a hairball to her sister.

But Becca had already put the pieces aside, tucking them deep into a shelf, before heading into the kitchen. The four felines followed—the kitten appearing out of nowhere to tag along—eager for dinner. Even after their dishes were laid out, however, Becca kept moving, pulling out several plates and filling the tea kettle that always sat on the stove.

"She isn't…" Harriet, who had already finished her can, looked up.

Clara didn't respond. She didn't have to. She and Laurel exchanged a glance, knowing what was coming next.

"Blessed be." The doorbell had already rung by the time Clara had finished her dinner, and she had to trot to catch up with her siblings at the front door.

"Blessed be, Ande." Becca leaned in to embrace the tall woman who had just arrived carrying a bakery box that had Harriet sniffing at the air.

"Is Marcia here yet?"

"You're the first." Becca took the box and retreated to the kitchen, leaving Ande to hang her jacket by the door.

"The first?" Ande's eyes widened as she followed her host. "Did you invite Larissa and Trent?"

"Yeah." Becca's voice betrayed her ambivalence. "They did found our coven, after all."

Ande nodded, reaching for one of the almond cookies that Becca was arranging on a plate. Harriet, meanwhile, was circling, her mouth open in anticipation.

"I was thinking we could use more collective power," Becca continued, seemingly oblivious to her eager cat.

"Something bothering you?" Ande, almost as empathetic as Clara, leaned against the counter.

"I'll explain when Marcia gets here. Larissa and Trent are still 'away.'" Becca made air quotes as she summoned a smile. "Maybe it's just as well."

"What's going on?" This time, it was clear that the question came from the tortie kitten, who emphasized her query with a nudge.

"Becca's coven." Clara glanced down at the smaller cat. *"Mind their feet."*

"What's a coven?" Like all children, the kitten was full of questions.

"They eat cookies," Harriet broke in, even as she maneuvered to catch a crumb.

"They get together and try to do magic," Clara, a little more sympathetic to the small beast, explained.

"Why don't they—" The kitten began, as the doorbell rang again.

"Marcia." Becca ushered in the third member of their coven as she shook out her Red Sox hat. "Is it raining again?"

"Just starting." Marcia brushed her dark hair back from her face and, after a moment's thought, hung the cap beside Ande's wrap. "What's up?"

"It's just been a while." Becca led her guest into the apartment and went to get the tea.

"Something's bothering her." Marcia's aside to Ande was clearly audible to the cats.

"I know." Ande looked back into the kitchen.

"What's bothering me is a lack of cookies." Beneath the table, Harriet began to grumble. And while Becca wouldn't dare try to silence her older sister, Laurel swatted at the fluffy marmalade, one chocolate paw landing on the orange spot on her back.

"Hey, watch it." Harriet whirled around.

"You'll get more treats if you can keep quiet." Laurel retreated, hissing.

"What is it now, kitties?" Becca's head dipped below the table, her concern clear in her voice.

"You hush!" Harriet sat, curling her tail around her front paws in a model pose, ignoring Laurel's side-eye.

"Have they been fighting a lot?" Ande's face appeared beneath the table, too.

"More than usual." Peace restored, at least temporarily, Becca sat up. "I'm wondering if introducing the kitten into the mix was just too much."

Ande and Marcia exchanged a look. "Four cats are a lot," said the shorter woman, keeping her voice soft and even.

"I know, but…" Becca sighed. "I thought they were getting along. Almost like family."

"Huh." Harriet coughed, and Clara eyed her with alarm. But the bigger cat simply licked her chops and resumed her position by Ande's chair.

"Is there something else bothering you?"

"Why don't we get started first?" said Becca, her voice determined. With that, the three took each other's hands and began their slow chant, welcoming the forces of nature from all points of the compass as the tortie, who had jumped to a chair back, looked on. "I'd like to focus on clarity. On seeing clearly."

"Scrying?" Ande suggested.

"Yes, exactly," Becca agreed with a decisive nod.

Curious, the kitten lashed her tail. *What are they trying to do?*

"Summon power." Clara didn't mean to be sharp. She did, however, want to keep an eye on Harriet, who was liable to do anything when cookies were involved.

"Silly." The tortie jumped down, and although Clara had more questions—specifically about what had happened with that blue bowl—she focused on the humans seated above her.

"I'm sorry, I'm just not able to focus." Becca was apologizing to her friends, who looked on in concern. "I just feel so useless."

"Becca…" Marcia reached for her hand again, but Becca shook her off.

"I wanted to try the scrying spell because I had a client today. A woman whose cat has gone missing. Mr. Butters is an indoor cat who got out." Becca spoke in stiff, broken sentences. "I should be out helping her in a practical way. But, instead, I'm here. She came to me in the hope that I could perform some magic, and that's just what I can't do."

"We're more powerful together." Ande started to speak.

"But that's just it. We're not." That shut Becca's friends up, and with a deep sigh, she continued. "We—I—haven't been able to do anything since that initial summoning. It's just so frustrating."

"Is there something else you'd like to try?" Ande spoke gently.

Becca's eyes darted around. "Maybe," she said. "I know it's silly, but my cats broke a bowl today. It was just a pretty thing my mom had given me, and, well, I was going to try to glue it."

"We could try a mending spell." Marcia sounded positively enthusiastic, and Ande chimed in. "Yes, let's."

Buoyed by her friends' optimism, Becca fetched the shards of the blue bowl and, after some discussion, covered them with a white napkin, while Ande thumbed through her phone.

"Here we go," she said, passing the phone around to her friends. "It looks simple enough."

And with that, the three joined hands once again and began to chant.

* * *

"It's no use." Fifteen minutes later, Becca was more downcast than before as she stared at the shards before her.

"The spell might take some time to work," said Marcia, only to be elbowed by Ande.

"It was worth the attempt," the taller woman offered. "And it did feel good to come together tonight."

"That it did." Becca managed a wobbly smile. "I don't know what I'd do without you guys."

"You do have Charm and Cherish." Marcia, always perky, chimed in. But Becca only shook her head.

"I don't know, Marcia," she said. "Foot traffic is off, and the online teaching is only going so far—and do you know the Craft Shop? It is—was—another New Age botanica up in New Hampshire. They closed. They'd had a couple of break-ins, so maybe that's why the owner gave up. But I wouldn't be surprised if Margaret decides to close us down too and turn the place into a crafts store in the fall."

"Let's not borrow trouble," said Ande, taking the teapot into the kitchen. "But speaking of, would it be okay if I gave Harriet a cookie?"

Chapter Five

The rest of the evening passed peaceably enough, thanks in part to Ande's generous distribution of broken cookie pieces to the cats. Even Laurel indulged, although she quickly withdrew to groom her silky coat as if to draw attention to her particularly svelte lines. The tortie kitten had her own approach to the treats, batting a crumb around the apartment until she lost it under the sofa, necessitating an intervention from Clara.

"We can't leave food under the furniture." Although petite, the calico still had to squash herself flat to retrieve the crumb. This, perhaps understandably, made her a bit short with the kitten. *"There are rules."*

"Huh." Although she heard the soft kitten grunt, once she emerged, the little beast was nowhere to be seen.

By that point, Becca had picked up the rest of the apartment and retired to the sofa with her laptop. "No messages," she said to herself, as Clara jumped up beside her. Becca's new boyfriend, Jerry Keller, was off at what Becca called a "veterinary conference," a concept that gave the calico shivers. He'd been good about calling, however, and something about his voice made Clara think of his warm hands and gentle ways, even with vaccinations. No, if Becca was looking for a message, it wasn't from Jerry, she realized, her thoughts going out again to that pale young woman and her missing cat. As the thunder rumbled once again, she cuddled closer to her person, grateful for her presence in their lives.

If only Becca could be as content. But as the calico felt her eyes close, she was aware of her person's wakefulness. Worse, Becca was still clicking away at the computer and softly reciting invocations. These were pointless, her adoring pet knew, and yet she persisted. And as the calico drifted off to sleep to the sound of her person's voice, Clara found herself thinking of a desert landscape and another lone young woman, desperately seeking a way to undo the damage done.

* * *

Perhaps it was those images and the strangely troubling dreams they produced, but Clara nearly overslept the next morning, only waking as the tortie bounded over her.

"*Kitten!*" Clara sat up with a start. She, along with her sisters, had jumped onto the bed when Becca had retired, but now she was alone, the little tortie having already bounced out of the room.

"*There you are, Clown.*" Laurel looked up from her dish, licking her chops, once Clara had made it to the kitchen. "*We were beginning to be concerned.*"

"*Speak for yourself.*" Harriet's voice rose from her dish, where she was chowing snout deep. "*I'd know if either of you were ill.*"

"*I feel fine.*" Clara dipped her head, acknowledging both Laurel's concern and Harriet's claim of greater knowledge. In truth, the fluffy marmalade had taken motherly care of her two siblings when they were first in the shelter, a protective quality she had since hidden behind her more seemingly selfish qualities. "*Where's the kitten?*"

"*Been and gone.*" Laurel continued her toilette. "*Becca's almost ready to go out, too.*"

"*Already?*" Clara peered back into the living room. Sure enough, their human was gathering her laptop into her bag.

"*You should grab a few bites.*" Harriet surfaced long enough to nod toward Clara's dish. "*After those dreams of yours, I think you should follow Becca today.*"

* * *

That had been Clara's intent all along, although she'd never have said so to Harriet. And so she ate quickly and then joined her sisters as they accompanied Becca to the door. The tortie, Clara noticed, joined them belatedly, and she looked at the kitten with interest—the open questions still on her mind. Those, however, would wait for another time. As soon as Becca had closed the door behind her, the calico crouched down and wiggled her butt. Passing through solid objects could be a bit of a challenge after a meal, especially one so hastily scarfed down. But this was her person, and, besides, both Laurel and Harriet were looking at her expectantly. And so, with one more wiggle and a deep breath, she leaped, making it through the door and halfway down the first set of stairs before Becca even reached the building's front door.

Using her magic to carefully shade herself, the calico caught up to Becca and was soon following her down the sidewalk. Playing on her markings, as well as the dim light of another cloudy morning, the little cat was able to blur herself into a gray haze that she knew was nearly invisible. To humans, at least. Two sparrows harangued the little cat from a shrub as they walked. And a chihuahua did stop to stare as Becca—with Clara beside her—as he waited on a street corner, only turning away when his person called.

The pair reached Charm and Cherish before the rain began again, to Clara's relief. But although the damp morning seemed likely to be a quiet one, Becca was clearly agitated. Even as she opened the storefront, retrieving that tray of gems and powering up the register, she checked her phone.

"Nothing from Trina," she said to herself, as her shaded pet looked up with concern. "Maybe I should try that scrying spell again."

As her pet looked on, Becca reached for a volume on an upper shelf and soon was reciting, her voice taking on a resonance that even the damp air couldn't explain. Not that Becca seemed to notice. As soon as she was done, she looked around and once more checked her phone. With a sigh, she put the device away, replaced the book, and returned to her routine, dusting the older books and wiping down a glass candlestick that had gotten a bit tacky from constant handling.

Clara wasn't surprised by Becca's actions. Even before Trina had shown up, Becca had been thinking of attempting the spell, a rather complicated invocation she'd found in one of those thick, older tomes. Scrying—seeking, more or less—was a basic skill, and Becca had long opined that if she could master that one spell, her practice would take off. When she had first noticed the missing Bast statuette, she'd considered trying it, her cat knew, an idea that had grown increasingly attractive as her search grew more frantic. But then Elizabeth had appeared, putting an end to that particular mystery, and, not long after that, Trina had come in.

Despite her brief panic over the black statuette, Becca kind of regretted the simple reasoning behind the Bast's disappearance and its subsequent reappearance. It would have been encouraging if she could have cast a spell that worked. If Elizabeth hadn't swanned in when she did, that bright caftan swirling around her, she might have located the piece using her powers. Being able to "uncover the lost" would be a good skill to have, especially now that she had a case.

It was frustrating, she admitted to herself, to not have at least one good working spell on hand. Despite her previous success with various cases—and the unalloyed support of her small coven—at times Becca doubted herself. That one pillow had been so long ago. If only she could claim one spell that reliably worked.

Worrying about what she couldn't do wasn't going to help anyone—including herself. Becca knew this, and yet her mood darkened by the minute, as if to match the lowering clouds outside. But although Becca might have been expecting thunder, her thoughts were interrupted instead by a jolly tinkle as the bells on the store's front door announced an arrival.

"Welcome to Charm and Cherish." Becca's mood brightened at the appearance of possible customers and almost immediately fell. The two men who had entered couldn't look less like the store's usual clients, and as they strode in, Becca had a moment of concern. Clad in T-shirts and jeans, both appeared to be in their twenties. But in addition to being taller than her and large in their own ways, the two men didn't have the look of clients. The first man in, a sandy-haired stranger, had the rangy look of an underfed dog, while the other sported a dark mop, with a pot belly that stretched his Varitek T to its limit. The Sox shirt was nominally black, or had been a few dozen washings ago, but neither fit either the typical Goth style of Charm and Cherish's regulars, or the latter-day flower child aesthetic that would best explain Elizabeth's wardrobe. Still, Becca did her best to put aside her preconceptions. She wouldn't want to be judged on her looks, especially on an off day. Besides, it was rather miserable outside, which meant nobody was at their best.

"May I help you?" She summoned her best smile.

"What? No." Blondie was chewing on a toothpick, which moved around as he spoke. "I mean, you have any jewelry in here?"

Doing her best to remain calm, Becca stepped out from behind the register. "Yes, we do. A wide selection." *A present for a girlfriend*, she thought, even as she blamed herself for stereotyping the two. *Or a boyfriend.*

Shaking her head at her own presumptions, she led the taller man over to the small case beneath the register that held several sterling silver charms. His colleague had stepped back into the store, seemingly to peruse the bookcases, and Becca steeled herself not to follow. She had, she told herself, no reason to be concerned.

"Nah," said the toothpick. "I'm looking for something, you know, better."

"Oh." It was hard to hide her disappointment, but Becca wasn't going to give up. "Perhaps you'd be interested in one of our semiprecious gemstones? We have several lovely ones, with literature about their properties."

"Semiprecious? No. Thanks," he added, seemingly as an afterthought.

"Nothing here." His companion emerged from behind the shelves.

"Well, thank you for coming in." Becca held her smile even as the two exited, the store's bell no longer sounding quite so jolly. It was only common sense that sent her back in the stacks, but as far as she could tell, the rounder of the two visitors hadn't touched anything. He hadn't even disturbed the dust on any of the books. Clearly, the pair had mistaken the kind of wares Charm and Cherish offered.

Of course, Clara could have told her that. She had picked up on Becca's nerves when those men had walked into the store. And while she was enough of a wily observer not to worry overmuch, she did sense something amiss. Not that they were dangerous, per se. Although Clara had been wrong about such things before, she could usually smell the combination of fear and desperation that led to aggressive acts. Nor, it was clear from Becca's quick perusal of the store's shelves, had they been considering robbery.

Maybe it was the weather, Clara mused. No cat likes rain, and a summer thunderstorm could be irritatingly loud, too. But before the little cat could mull over the strange feel of the day, Becca's phone rang, interrupting her thoughts. It was Trina.

"Hi, Trina." Despite the weather, Becca felt a surge of optimism. "Any news?"

"No. Shira and I went out last night, but we couldn't find him." The sadness packed into that one syllable killed that spark of hope. "And he's definitely not in the apartment. I was hoping he'd come out at dinnertime, but no Mr. Butters. And, yes, I've looked everywhere—even over the fridge and under the radiator."

"I'm sorry. Did you make up posters?"

"Shira's doing that now. I was hoping—well, you know."

"I do." Sometimes, Becca knew, it was hard to accept that bad news was true.

"Anyway, she's going to put some up on her way home," the other woman continued. "They have my cell number on them, and I keep checking, hoping someone has called. Or that, maybe, if you did try a spell…"

Becca was staring out the window, and Clara suspected she was thinking about that cat. The weather was warm, but so wet. No pet deserved to be out in this. "Look," said Becca, interrupting the other woman's hopeful musings. "I'm working until six tonight, but I can come by after and help you look."

"That would be so great." The hope in the other woman's voice could have broken Becca's heart, but Clara sensed something else. Relief. *That spell.* The realization hit the cat like a sunbeam. *She's grateful that girl didn't follow up with her request for a spell.*

"I'll be out looking," the voice on the phone continued. "Just text me when you get here."

Becca rang off and went back to dusting, with Clara, as always, keeping watch.

"At least she's not using the vacuum cleaner," the little calico said to herself, with a shiver. Clara and her siblings had a healthy fear of the evil-sounding machine. Stuck here alone with their person, she was grateful that the worst thing Becca availed herself of in the shop was a foul-smelling cleaner, which did, she had to admit, make the windows shine. However, knowing her person, her cat wasn't surprised as her efforts stalled once she'd pulled over a stepstool to that bookcase again. Instead, she looked on with interest as Becca removed a large, leatherbound volume from the top shelf, this one seemingly older than the tome she had consulted earlier. Cradling the big book in the crook of her arm, she began flipping through pages, all the while murmuring to herself.

"Sealing, seeing..." Suddenly, she stopped. "Seeking, this is it." With that, she began to read aloud a series of syllables, some seemingly Latin, some Greek, before pausing about halfway through. "Oh, basil. Of course!"

Placing the book on the counter by the register, she took a quick photo of the page and was soon ready to go. "Basil," she kept repeating to herself. "Of course, a little catnip wouldn't hurt either."

Becca had just replaced the oversized volume when the bells alerted her to yet another visitor. Despite the dismal weather, Charm and Cherish was attracting a surprising amount of foot traffic.

"Hello," she called out, climbing off her ladder to face a slim, dark-haired man who had stopped in the doorway to fold his umbrella, his open raincoat revealing a charcoal gray suit and blue tie. Although he didn't look much older than Becca, his short straight hair circled a shiny bald spot, and as Clara watched, he reached up and brushed a hand over it, as if aware of her scrutiny. Although this man didn't fit Becca's experience of a typical Charm and Cherish customer any more than the two men who'd come in earlier, Becca felt none of the anxiety those visitors had provoked. The man could be a professor at Tech, down the road. Or, Becca thought, as he beeped the alarm to a black late-model Jaguar parked out front, a venture capitalist visiting one of the many startups the institute fostered.

At any rate, he looked friendly as well as prosperous, she mused. And rather cute, despite his receding hair. "May I help you?" she asked, her smile lifting her voice into a lilt.

"Hello." The man returned her smile, his narrow face wrinkling up pleasantly. "Possibly," he continued. "I'm wondering if you have any antiquities, particularly among your statuary."

"Our statuary." A professor, then. Becca's initial cheer dipped as she realized that none of the figurines in the store were likely to interest an academic. Charm and Cherish's books might hold intellectual interest, but none of the little figures that lined the shelves were particularly old or—she had to admit—valuable. Still, he had said "statuary," and so Becca led him to the figurines on display on those front tables. While some were purely fanciful—Becca was particularly fond of a winged cat who wore a bejeweled headband—others, like the many iterations of Bast, were more classical in design. She wasn't sure she'd ever have called them statues. Still, the man was a possible customer.

"I'm not sure we have any antiques, but here is a good sampling of what we do have." She did her best to sound cheery. Optimistic, without overselling the pieces. That was what Margaret would want, she reminded herself. Or, no, to be honest, the Charm and Cherish proprietor would want her to push this man to buy…ideally, the most expensive piece in the shop.

Maybe, Becca thought to herself, she didn't belong in Charm and Cherish after all.

As her person began explaining the mythology behind one of the figures—a replica of a Sumerian goddess—Clara circled the man for a good sniff. *Wet wool,* she thought, as he gazed over the store's display. *Books, too.* She flicked her tail, recognizing the musty scent from the shelf where she'd been about to nap. But although she associated this scent with Becca, it came across differently on this visitor. Maybe it was his clothes, she thought. Although his outfit, despite its formality, didn't seem that different from what she sniffed every day on the street, it was subtler, somehow. More refined.

"This man has money." The thought struck her, and because the average Charm and Cherish client did not, she set herself to watch as he followed Becca around the store.

"We also have a few smaller pieces," Becca was saying. She started to led him to the back shelves, where figurines—including that winged feline—fronted the books behind them, but he had already paused.

"Ah, I see." His smile widened as he lifted the small Kali that had taken the Bast's place by the register. He turned it around to examine it, as if checking out the blue diety's multiple arms, but Becca squirmed as if she were the one under his scrutiny. She was self-conscious, Clara realized. She, too, had picked up that this man wasn't the shop's usual clientele. That didn't mean Becca had to feel inferior, though. In fact, she should be proud, the calico reasoned. A Hindu goddess or a flying cat were perfectly reasonable purchases for anyone interested in magic.

"We do have some occult artwork," said Becca, her formal diction only making her pet want to rub against her shins. "As well as a decent collection of crystals and geodes."

"Really?" Giving the blue goddess one more look, he replaced her on the shelf and followed Becca to the back cabinet, where the store's few pricier pieces were stored.

"Here, let me get the key." Becca raced back to the register. As she did, Clara continued to observe the man. To her surprise, he had backtracked, once again picking up the goddess figurine.

"This is not an antique, is it?" He raised questioning eyes to Becca, who had retrieved the key.

"No, I'm sorry." Clara looked up, wondering why she was apologizing. Something about the man's demeanor, she suspected. "Would you like to see the geodes?"

"Yes, please." Once again, he put the figure down, and this time let himself be led. At Becca's urging, he picked up one of the geodes, a palm-sized piece whose open interior revealed dozens of shiny facets. "This is quite gorgeous," he said, running one finger over the crystalline interior, almost as if he would pry one of its sparkling pieces loose.

"Oh, please be careful." Worry creased Becca's brow, but even as she spoke, she stepped back. "I'm sorry. It's just that that's one of our better pieces."

"I understand." With a smile, he handed over the sparkling rock. "Though you should know a good geode is not going to come apart from a little touching."

Becca did her best to return his smile, but it was a weak attempt. "I'm sure. It sounds like you know about geodes? Are you a geologist?"

The smile became broader. "No, but they fall under my purview." To Becca's upturned face, he continued. "I'm the curator at the Fallenburg Museum. Brian Hallowell," he extended his hand.

"Becca Colwin." They shook, and Clara realized her person was intrigued. "The Fallenburg, that's out in Brookline, isn't it?"

The visitor nodded. "A small private collection. Open to the public, of course."

He smiled, looking for a moment as satisfied as Harriet after a full meal, and Becca relaxed. "I've never been. Are you planning an exhibit on witchcraft?"

He tilted his head so that the bald spot picked up the light. "No, I'm afraid not." The smile became something softer and warmer. "But it is of interest."

"If you do, we do have many items. Not antiques, but…" Her voice trailed off as she looked around the shop. To Clara's dismay, it seemed she was disappointed in what she saw, as if the little store wasn't perfect for its primary clientele—and for Becca herself. "And both the proprietor's sister and I are students of the craft," she said, her voice dropping almost to a whisper.

"The proprietor's sister?" If Becca was disappointed that he wasn't asking about her, she hid it well.

"Yes, Elizabeth. Her sister owns Charm and Cherish, but Elizabeth works here with me. She's an older woman and quite—well, I believe she has power."

"I'd love to meet her," said the man. "And I'm thrilled to make your acquaintance as well."

Becca smiled in earnest now. "I'd be happy to introduce you. She should be in later. But, in the meantime, did you see anything else that interested you?"

"No." His voice grew thoughtful. "That little Kali, though. I'll take that. And I have to ask, you don't have any other items back in that storeroom, do you?"

Becca looked over her shoulder at the door that led to the back room. She'd left it open, which meant anyone could see the worn sofa where she took her break and the metal shelves that held both files and boxes.

"No, I'm sorry. We're trying to get that cleaned up so I can do more online teaching." She leaned forward conspiratorially as she rang up the purchase and wrapped the statuette. "The storage shelving doesn't make the best backdrop. But all we have back there are additional copies of some of our more popular books and candles. We can't leave those out in the sun, you see."

"Of course." He nodded. "No other geodes?"

She shook her head. "I lock our gemstones back there at night, but that's just in case we get a smash-and-grab."

"Gemstones?" His eyes lit up, and Becca looked unhappy to disappoint him.

"Semiprecious," she explained. "I have a chart detailing what protective or curative powers they have—they're *supposed* to have," she corrected herself. "Tourmaline, for example, is supposed to heal and detoxify."

"I'll remember that," he said, his voice warming as he picked up his package and turned to go.

"May I ask you a question?" Becca seemed reluctant to let the man leave, and Clara hoped it was simply because the store had been so quiet all day.

"Of course." The smile was back in place, but the little calico could sense his desire to leave.

"What show are you planning that you're looking for antiques— antiquities," she amended.

"Nothing in particular, I'm afraid." He lifted the package, almost in a salute. "But, hey, maybe I'll be inspired." The visit, as short as it was, appeared to buoy Becca's mood, and she was humming softly to herself as she resumed her cleanup. Clara forgave her the spritz of foul-smelling fluid that she sprayed on the front window, but she couldn't help wondering about her person's ebullience. Any sale was good, the calico knew. But the statuette of the Hindu goddess was not one of Charm and Cherish's pricier items.

As if to accentuate that fact, when Becca returned the cleaning spray and her rag to the back room, she came back holding another of the blue figurines.

"Blessed be." Elizabeth, walking in the door as Becca emerged, bowed her head slightly, making her long gray curls bob.

"Blessed be." Becca beamed up at her boss and mentor. "We're seeing a lot of you these days."

"We?" Although Clara couldn't be sure, she thought the older woman was looking at her.

"I just meant the shop." Becca dimpled. "When I'm online, I always say 'we,' and I guess it's become a habit."

"Maybe you're wiser than you know." Clara, who had visited both Elizabeth and her sister in their apartment upstairs, eyed the older woman. Resplendent in a green-and-gold paisley caftan today, she dominated the small shop, almost as if she were its main attraction. "Everyone needs a touch of magic sometimes."

Yes, realized Clara. Elizabeth was looking directly at her as she made this last pronouncement. In response, she checked her shading, and then, just to be extra cautious, leaped up on the nearest bookcase, where she positioned herself behind a large cream-colored candle that smelled deliciously of honey. As she checked to make sure she hadn't dislodged the candle—a piece that big falling would be suspicious—Clara was momentarily reassured when she saw Elizabeth nod slightly. Only after the woman turned away did she tuck her tail around her feet and settle down, her fur still quivering at the thought that a human could see her when she was supposedly blurred to a shadow-like gray.

"Speaking of…" Becca, oblivious to the little drama occurring on the shelf behind her. "I just sold one of these."

As she spoke, she raised the figurine.

"Ah, Kali." The smile spread across Elizabeth's face. "And which face of the goddess did your customer want? The creator or the destroyer?"

"I'm not sure." Becca chuckled at the question as she turned to place the statue on the shelf. "Maybe neither, to be honest."

"You think he was here for some other reason?"

"Maybe." Becca paused. "You said 'he'? How did you know?"

Elizabeth only smiled, and Becca, to Clara's consternation, blushed. "I guess my mood is the giveaway."

"Maybe." Elizabeth's partial agreement only made Becca's flush deepen. "But I don't think your client got what he was looking for."

"What? Oh, you mean because the Kali isn't an antique?" Becca paused. "He did say he was looking for antiquities, but we don't have anything like that. Do we?"

Elizabeth shook her head. "A more immediate question is do you want me to take over for you?" She looked around. "I've never seen the shop look better," she said. "But I'm also sure you have other things to do."

Becca beamed her appreciation. Maybe she and Trina could get started early. But she lost her smile when Elizabeth added, almost as an afterthought. "My sister would like you to drop by before you take off. She's up there now, if you want to get it over with."

With a sigh, Becca agreed. "Thanks," she said, even as she punched in a quick text to Trina. "I'm planning to help this woman who came in looking for her cat, but I'll run upstairs first. Whatever it is, it'll be better to get it over with."

"She's more bark than bite," Elizabeth's voice had grown softer. "And you, Becca, have more power than you know."

Chapter Six

Elizabeth's words should have buoyed her, but it was with a sinking feeling that Becca climbed the three sets of stairs that led from the street up to the penthouse apartment the two sisters shared. While Elizabeth took an active interest in Charm and Cherish, Becca knew, her sister—who actually owned the small shop—saw it simply as a chance to cash in on what had once been a hot trend. But although the little shop had its fans, the business slowdown common to every retail business in the summer had hit hard. And Becca's most recent suggestion—the online classes she taught from her laptop at the back of the shop—had drawn only a handful of new clients, at best.

Already, Margaret had started talking about closing Charm and Cherish to reopen the storefront as a craft store, and Becca had no interest in yarn or making her own pottery, assuming the boss would even want to keep her on. Although she tried to take courage from Elizabeth's parting words, it was with a heavy heart that Becca crossed the top-floor landing to knock on the sisters' door.

"There you are," the younger of the two Cross sisters personified their shared last name. Even though Becca had been instrumental in solving the murder of Margaret's husband, the squat little woman always seemed peeved when Becca was around. That might have been because she had also uncovered her late husband's peccadillos, Becca reminded herself as the older woman waved her into the apartment.

"Come in." Turning her back on her guest, Margaret Cross waddled into the living room, leaving Becca—and a shaded Clara—to follow. It had been a while since Becca had been up here, and for a moment, she was taken aback. Overstuffed and overdecorated, the apartment had always reflected Margaret's taste more than Elizabeth's, but Margaret had clearly been adding to the decor. Among the new touches were throws that overlapped each other along the back of the overstuffed sofa and the two upholstered chairs on either side. All six that Becca counted were prints of the kind of paisley that Elizabeth would wear. But these were clearly her sister's work. None of Elizabeth's long and flowing caftans would throw together such clashing colors. Although Clara, like all cats, was somewhat colorblind, she picked up on her person's discomfort and tucked herself under the edge of the sofa where she could watch over her.

"You wanted to see me?" The room was uncomfortably warm, and if Margaret was going to deliver bad news, Becca wanted it over with.

"You heard about the Craft Shop up in Concord? Well, another magic shop has closed—the Witches' Den over in Worcester."

Becca felt like she'd swallowed a stone, but her boss's next question surprised her.

"I wanted to ask you about the computer teaching."

"You mean the online classes?" Becca perked up with relief. "They're going well." Although relatively new to Wicca herself, Becca had been using her online time to teach introductions to the craft and about the healing powers of various stones and crystals. A trained researcher, she loved having an excuse to delve into the shop's books. She also enjoyed the interaction with her students, many of whom reminded Becca of herself a little more than a year ago—contemporaries looking to learn more about an egalitarian and ecologically minded spiritual path.

But that, she knew, was not what Margaret was asking.

"Everybody's paid up for the summer semester, and we're already getting some bookings for September."

"Good, good." Margaret's scowl was permanent, but as she relaxed, her face ceased to look so scrunched. "And you're telling them all to come in and buy things?"

"I make a point of letting the students know that everything I'm teaching them can be found on the bookshelves at Charm and Cherish." Becca was nothing if not diplomatic as she pitched what she hoped sounded close to an affirmative answer. "Also, that they can take their learning further with the help of the store—and that someone is always here to help them choose the books or stones or charms that will continue them on their path."

Margaret snorted a noncommittal snort, but Becca was beginning to relax. If Margaret saw her online teaching as not only a money maker—which it wasn't, not yet—but also a way to drive traffic to the store, maybe she'd begin to believe in the viability of Charm and Cherish.

"Maybe if we had some real publicity," Becca offered. "Some way of catching everyone's attention…" She searched her mind for a viable response. "Maybe we could begin to offer some hybrid classes."

The way Margaret's thick brows bunched up at that made it clear she didn't understand.

"Let students attend in person as well as on the computer," Becca explained, inching toward the edge of the overstuffed chair in her excitement. "The online classes are great because people can log in at home and also go back and listen to the lectures on their own time. But some people prefer to meet in real life. Plus, if they come into the store, they might be more likely to buy a book or a stone or candle."

Those brows rose as Margaret considered Becca's suggestion, but then she shook her head.

"That sounds risky, like it might call for extra insurance." Still, whether it was the idea that students in the store might be converted into shoppers or the crestfallen expression on Becca's face, Margaret's own curdled visage softened. "Then again, it might be a good idea. A few seats right up front where people walking by could see that we were busy…I'll talk to my insurance guy."

Becca beamed, her mood suddenly lifted. "And I've been thinking about adding some other classes, too."

Those caterpillar eyebrows inched up again.

"Now that so many people have taken the introductory classes, I thought I could start offering intermediate or even advanced classes." Becca paused, swallowing her nerves. "I thought maybe I could get Elizabeth involved. She would be a natural teacher, and, honestly, she's way more advanced in the craft than I am."

"Elizabeth." Margaret stared off into space, making Becca worry that she had hit a nerve. But the younger Cross only shook her head and exhaled noisily, waking Clara, who had begun to doze.

"I also thought of another class that I could definitely teach." Becca cleared her throat, aware of how tentative she sounded. At least that made Margaret look at her.

"I was thinking I could offer a class on witch detecting." Another pause, during which Becca swallowed, her mouth suddenly dry. "You know, talking about some of the principles and techniques I try to use as a witch detective.

"I know that doesn't directly relate to the store." She rushed on before her boss could cut her off, so animated that she nearly fell off her chair to Clara's dismay. "But I do use—and would recommend—many of the resources the store has to offer. For instance, I would definitely recommend several of the books that offer scrying spells or spells to compel people to tell the truth. Plus, many of our charms and semiprecious stones promote clarity, which is always good for helping us get to the truth."

"That's right. Your little side business." Margaret did not seem convinced.

"I'm doing well." Becca felt a sudden surge of confidence. "Another woman came into the store yesterday to ask for my help. And," Becca paused, reaching for a way to enlist her boss in her business, "she said she'd never been in Charm and Cherish before. She seemed to really like it, too, so I bet she'll be back."

"So tell me, do you have a license for that?"

The question, coming as it did out of the blue, confused Becca. Even Clara looked up at the older woman, puzzling over the way her mouth had pursed into something sour and mean.

"Are you talking about the online teaching?" Becca tilted her head, looking for all the world like Harriet when facing a toy she couldn't reach.

"No, your detecting practice, or whatever you call it." That mouth loosened barely enough to spit out the words.

Becca shook her head. "I don't understand."

Never the most patient, Margaret only grew louder. "A license," she repeated. Her brows now stood as stiff as a frightened cat's fur. "A detecting license."

"I didn't think I needed one." The question, as much as the volume with which it was delivered, struck at Becca's confidence, and she slid back in the chair.

"I wouldn't be so sure." Margaret's eyebrows crept up with the tone of her voice. "I was watching TV last night, and on this one show, they were making a big deal about someone who was acting as a private investigator without a license. They made it sound like a very big deal." She pronounced that last sentence as if it were all caps.

"Well, I'm not exactly a private investigator." Becca suspected that her boss was looking to rile her up—or to get her to focus solely on the shop. "I mean, I'm a witch detective. That's different. I use the craft."

"As a *private investigator*." Margaret did sound pleased with herself, in a nasty kind of way. "And I don't know that the authorities would care so much about the witchy Wicca stuff."

"No, but I do." Becca spoke so softly that only the cat at her feet heard her.

"They said you could be fined or even arrested." Margaret huffed. "Plus, I can't have my business subject to any kind of investigation just because of your hobby."

Becca bit her lip, but Clara, staring up at her, saw the tears beginning to gather. If only she could rub against Becca's ankles, she thought. If only she could comfort her.

"As for the rest, I'll call my insurance guy tomorrow." Without waiting for a response, Margaret braced herself on the chair's armrest and pulled herself upright. "I'll have to think about your hours before you start adding classes, though. The intermediate ones, that is. Unless Bitsy can handle them."

Becca knew she was being dismissed and stood as well. "Thank you, Margaret." She managed to choke out the words. "There really is an audience out there, and I know many of them will end up buying their supplies at Charm and Cherish."

"Supplies." Margaret harumphed again and waved Becca toward the door.

"Well, at least she's not closing the store," Becca spoke to herself as she descended the stairs. She was making the best after the stressful meeting, the cat who trotted down behind her knew. But it was all Clara could do to not press against her shins in comfort as Becca paused on the street-level landing, worry creasing her brow in a way that, just for the moment, evoked her boss. "But is she right about a private investigator's license? Am I doing something illegal just by trying to help?"

Chapter Seven

Back in Becca's apartment, chaos reigned.

"Stop it! Stop it now!" Laurel's distinctive yowl was directed at the kitten, who was lying on the back of the sofa, apparently sound asleep, her paws and tail twitching in some dream hunt.

"What's going on? Clara had raced home ahead of her person to alert her sisters about Becca's latest dilemma. What she found was worse than one broken bowl.

"It's that thing." Laurel's tail was lashing as she glared at the kitten. *"I don't know what she's doing or how, but she's doing* something!"

Clara turned to where the kitten was sleeping. Sure enough, each time the little tortie's tail twitched, an item went flying. Although it didn't look like anything had broken, the floor was littered with books, and a flying cat lay on its back on the rug, its plaster wings intact.

"Enough already." Harriet roared, landing on the sofa with an audible thud. *"Between the two of you, I'm missing my midday nap."*

"It's not my fault." Laurel's voice rose in a whine as her ears went back. *"It's that creature—and the Clown is defending her."*

"I—what?"

Laurel was nearly spitting in fury and frustration.

"Please, I just got home, and I'm trying to understand." Clara bowed her head, then started back as Harriet began to stalk toward the kitten. *"Harriet, please—"*

"Enough!" Harriet's distinctive deep mew would have been loud enough to wake any adult cat. The kitten, exhausted by a morning of play, slept on,

even as the fuzzy marmalade raised one threatening paw.

"It's Becca, Harriet. She's coming home early." Grateful for the vibrations that announced their person's arrival, Clara raced along the top of the sofa and gently nudged the kitten awake. *"She's had a hard day and is going to need us."*

Harriet harrumphed in dismissal, her short Persian-like nose turning the gesture into a snort. *"Of course she does,"* And then, as the kitten leaped down from the sofa and disappeared, *"I wasn't going to hurt the little thing, you know. But she should learn what it's like to be woken up from a deep sleep."*

As relieved as she was by her oldest sister's explanation, Clara was still grateful for the imminent arrival of their human, which had all three adult cats lined up by the door.

"Hello, kitties!" If Becca was surprised to see the three sisters lined up to greet her, she didn't show it. "What have you been up to. And where," she craned to see into the living room, "is the kitten?"

"Told you." Laurel gave Clara a sideways look. *"That thing made the mess, and it's still getting all the attention."*

"Nonsense." Harriet threw her broad body against Becca's shins. *"We're still her favorites. Plus, we're going to get dinner early. And treats!"*

How she could state that with such confidence confused Clara briefly. After all, Laurel was the sister with the power to suggest emotions—and sometimes even implant thoughts—in their human's mind. Harriet's special skill was in summoning objects out of the ether. But all cats can do some rudimentary mind-reading, and Becca was pretty easy to read. The relief in her sigh, for example, as she spotted the kitten, eyes still half closed, coming to join the other cats. Smiling, she hung her bag up and, despite the hour, headed for the kitchen, all three adult cats in tow.

It was only as she passed by the sofa that she paused, taking in the shambles of what had been a tidy room.

"Kitties?" Her voice made them all stop as she reached first for that winged cat and then a book, splayed open on the rug. "Were you playing? Not fighting, I hope?"

She glanced around at her three older cats, clearly searching for something.

"It's that troublemaker," Laurel growled in Clara's ear, as Becca shook her head. Clara felt as helpless as she had in the Cross apartment as Becca sighed deeply once more and then continued picking up, watching as she placed the figurine on its shelf and reached for another book. *"She's making Becca unhappy."*

The kitten chose that moment to reappear, yawning so widely that her eyes closed.

"There you are." Becca scooped up the little tortie, who immediately began to purr.

"Panderer," Laurel yowled, even as she twined around Becca's legs, directing her most adoring blue-eyed glances up at their person. Whether it was her strange-sounding mew or an idea she'd implanted, Becca soon put the kitten down and retrieved the cats' dishes.

"Do you think we should let her know?" Clara leaned into Laurel's chocolate-colored ear.

"I don't know." Her sister tilted her head with unaccustomed uncertainty. *"I certainly don't want to get blamed, but..."*

Clara swished her tail, the feline equivalent of a nod. It would be hard to reveal the nature of the kitten's mischief without divulging their powers. But by then, Becca had filled all four dishes. Harriet's, with its distinctive gold sun design, came first, and the big cat pushed her way in even as Becca laid the other dishes on the mat. Soon, all four felines were enjoying their early dinner as, with another telling sigh, Becca returned to tidying up the living room.

"What the—oh, kitties!" Lifting her head from her dish, Clara watched as Becca retrieved more fallen objects: two candles, several colored stones that had made their own way over the carpet, and a small figurine of an Egyptian cat that stirred something deep in the little calico. "Well, at least nothing is broken."

With that, Clara glanced over to the kitten. That figurine was fragile, she knew from Becca's cry of alarm years before, when, soon after their person had brought it home, Clara had started to push it off a table. In response, the little tortie swung her own tail back and forth, giving Clara the clear impression that the kitten not only understood but was reassuring her that the lack of damage had been intentional. Which could only mean—

"Are you done?" Harriet was already nuzzling Clara's dish, but with this new question on her mind, food was the furthest thing from the calico's mind.

"Go right ahead," she murmured. The kitten had already gulped down her smaller portion, and Clara followed her into the living room.

"How did any of you even get up there?" Becca was standing on tiptoe, rearranging the pieces on the top shelf. The kitten turned toward Clara, her eyes closing in satisfaction. Clara was gathering her thoughts into questions when Becca's phone rang.

"Trina, I'm so sorry." Becca shook her head, as if to clear it of her own concerns. "I meant to come by right after I left the store, but I stopped off at home first."

"Please, don't worry. I'm calling to let you know Mr. Butters has been found." The other woman's excitement made her voice clearly audible to the cats' sharp ears. It also appeared to cheer Becca, and she responded by pressing for details.

"He's been found? Was he hiding? Was he even outside the house? Tell!"

"I don't have all the details yet, but he got out all right. I just got a call that someone's found him, and I'm going to go get him now."

"That's fantastic!" Becca sighed with relief, collapsing on the sofa. "Do you want company?"

"No, thanks. I'll report back, though." From the city sounds behind her, it seemed that Trina had already started out. "I might want some help figuring out how my naughty boy got out."

"I can do that." Becca agreed enthusiastically. "Or at least try. Why don't you give me a call once you're both safely home? And Trina? I'm so happy for you."

"Thanks, Becca. I am, too."

"Well, that's a relief." Becca looked around at her cats, who were all staring at her as if transfixed.

"Why is she bothering with another cat?" Laurel's drawn-out mew made

Clara's ears twitch. *"You don't think she's going to bring another cat here, do you?"*

"No." Clara abandoned her place on the sofa to rub against Becca's shins. She knew her person was loyal to her and her sisters, although her apparent adoption of the tortoiseshell kitten had disrupted their home life. *"At least I don't think so."* She amended her answer to more honestly reflect her thoughts, which, she had to admit, were troubled.

"We'll just have to put our paws down." Harriet, still licking her chops, joined them.

"Like you did with the kitten?" Laurel joined Clara in twining around their person's legs. She had a point, Clara knew, recalling how Harriet had sent off that one woman who had been interested in taking the tortie by grooming the kitten in an almost maternal way. A move, Clara noted to herself, her oldest sister had not bothered to repeat.

"I had a responsibility to make sure the little beast knew how to clean herself," Harriet responded, as she set about washing one big white mitt. *"Now she does."*

"I wish you wouldn't do that." Clara tried to keep her irritation out of her voice—and her thoughts—but it was difficult. Something was off, and Harriet's smugness was only making things worse.

"You shouldn't be so hard to read, then." Laurel smirked, then set about grooming her own tawny fur. *"But you don't have to worry. I didn't pick up anything about bringing another feline home from Becca just now. And I made sure she thought of that other cat as a nuisance. Just in case!"*

"That other cat has a person who loves him." Clara focused on what she knew. Her sisters didn't pay much attention to the phone or the computer, which might have been why she felt so bothered. *"Becca was only helping his person find him."*

"Well, good then," said Laurel, who had to have the last word. And Clara, who could find no other reason for her disquiet, began to bathe.

Chapter Eight

Becca spent the better part of the next hour cleaning up the mess the kitten had made. While she would never yell at her pets, she did glance over at them occasionally, shaking her head in disbelief and disapproval.

Laurel, of course, felt the weight of that gaze. As the best jumper of the three, she was the obvious suspect, considering that Becca was unaware of the tortie's apparent powers. In response, the seal point was acting extra affectionate, rubbing her dark muzzle up against Becca's shins.

"Have you gotten into the catnip again?" Becca paused in her gathering of scattered potpourri to look down at the sleek feline.

"I think you're unnerving her," Clara commented from the back of the sofa. Her bath had calmed her nerves, as well as smoothing her orange, brown, black, and white coat.

"I'm letting her know I'm innocent. Just a super-friendly pet." Laurel closed her eyes, apparently lost in the pleasure of being stroked as Becca reached down to her impeccably sleek fur. In truth, Clara realized, her sister was using her particular powers to implant the suggestion that she was innocent of the living room mayhem. Which, Clara quickly realized, raised another problem.

"Where is that kitten anyway?" Becca looked around, not seeing Laurel's smirk. "I can't believe that little thing could have gotten up there, but…"

A soft peep announced the tortie, who used her sharp little claws to climb up the side of the sofa.

"Oh, kitten." Clara reached out with one paw to pull the tortie down. *"We*

don't claw the furniture."

"She doesn't understand you. She's just a dumb beast." Laurel, still on the carpet, looked on in satisfaction as Becca advanced toward the little creature. *"Although she did knock all those things off the top shelf."*

Clara bowed her head, unwilling to argue with her sister. Still, she kept one paw protectively over the kitten's back even as Becca reached for her.

"What are we going to do with you?" Becca raised the kitten up to her eye level. In the last month, the tortie had been growing by leaps and bounds, but she still fit in Becca's hands. She was too young to be out on her own, Clara knew, and braced for Becca's next words. This wasn't going to be good, she knew. Quite possibly, the kitten's days in the apartment were numbered.

It had been coming for a while. Crossing Laurel, even unintentionally, wasn't a smart move. And although Harriet might have stood up for the kitten once, the longer the youngster hung around, the more her kittenish antics annoyed the stolid older cat. Harriet was not only big, she was set in her ways. Having a kitten noisily knocking items off a shelf was not how she chose to be awakened. And now, watching her person eye to eye with the small creature, Clara was hit by how bonded she had become with the kitten. How much of herself she saw in the mischievous little tortie. How close…

"Oh, come on!" Laurel yawned, showing her fangs. *"Do not compare yourself to a witless animal!"*

"I'm not so sure she's—" But before she could finish her comment, Clara was interrupted by the sound of Becca humming. In fact, their person was amused rather than annoyed, her cat realized, as she brought the kitten close, nearly touching her own nose to the tortie's black leather one.

"What are we going to call you?" Becca was asking, her voice low enough so that even Clara had to strain to hear. "What's your name, little one? We can't just keep calling you 'kitten.'"

Clara stared, her green eyes wide. While she had tried to elicit the kitten's own name from her, it had never occurred to her that Becca would give a name to the kitten. It was definitely a positive sign in terms of the kitten remaining in their household, but it also went against everything the calico knew and held dear. She and her sisters had had their own names, obviously. Long before Becca found them in the shelter, they were well aware of who they were, and although it hadn't been until recently that Clara had learned of their royal—possibly even divine—heritage, she couldn't imagine any cat, no matter how common, not having a name of their own. The fact that Laurel, like cats everywhere, then implanted that name—along with those of Harriet and Clara—in their person's mind was beside the point.

A cat's name, as both verse and lore attest, was a sacred and profound thing.

"Missy?" Becca eyed the kitten, who had begun to bat at one of her fingers. "Simone? No, none of those seem right somehow."

Clara looked to her sisters, but Laurel only stared back, her blue eyes all innocence. Harriet, meanwhile, had gone to sleep. Only the sound of the door buzzer, announcing a visitor in the building lobby, caused her to lift her head and sent all three cats scurrying toward the door.

Becca, for her part, approached the door cautiously. Despite the relative quiet of the summer, Becca had learned to be careful. Even if it were only her annoying downstairs neighbor, Deborah Miles, she had best be on her guard.

To her delight, a quick peek through the peephole revealed a comfortably built woman with cat-eye glasses and shoulder-length brown hair. Becca opened the door to her best friend, and when she saw that she was holding a large bag with a familiar menu stapled to its edge, she was even more delighted.

"Maddy!" She managed a brief shoulder hug, taking great comfort in her friend's ample softness, before relieving her buddy of the bag. "I didn't expect you."

"No worries," Maddy replied. "I stopped by Charm and Cherish, and that crazy old woman told me you'd gone home early. I knew Jerry was out of town, and I figured I'd surprise you. Besides, I couldn't eat all this by myself."

Becca responded by hugging her friend again before taking the bag into the kitchen. Maddy's feelings about Wicca—and, thus, about Elizabeth Cross— were a bone of contention between them. Still, Maddy remained her closest friend, even if the big woman was never likely to join her coven or quite accept Becca's focus on being a witch detective.

That thought made her pause as she unloaded the deliciously fragrant containers. Clara, circling at her feet, could almost read her thoughts.

"Maddy, do you know anything about private investigator licenses?"

"What?" Maddy asked over the clattering of dishes. She was looking down at the circling felines with an expression that wavered between wonder and amusement. "Look at these creatures, Becca. They must know I'm a softer touch than you."

"Yes." Laurel softened her usual Siamese screech to something almost like a normal mew. *"Yes, we do."*

"They do." Becca agreed without thinking. Which could be experience, Clara thought, or Laurel's suggestion.

"Wait." Maddy shook her head, stepping over the kitten to reach for the bowls. "You're going to get a PI's license?"

"No, probably not." Becca shook her head as she grabbed the serving dishes and followed her friend out of the room. "I was just wondering."

But to her cats, it was obvious that the question kept popping into her consciousness, even as the two humans began to eat and Maddy began to unload about her day. Her job, specifically, and its frustrations. Both she and Becca had trained as historians, and although both had once toyed with the idea of going into library science, Maddy was working at a marketing firm that made little use of her skills. It paid better than Charm and Cherish, but as Maddy unpacked the day's aggravations, Becca visibly struggled to keep from pointing out that her friend had been citing the same issues for more than a year now. Instead, she took a big bite of the dumpling she had just dipped in the soy and ginger sauce. Made more slippery by that sauce, she was holding it rather tentatively between her chopsticks anyway and truly needed to focus on the savory treat. But once she swallowed, she made some sympathetic noises.

"It does sound maddening, Maddy. Truly, it does." She took a breath. "But…do you ever think about looking for another job?" This wasn't the first time Becca had made this suggestion, and Maddy responded as she usually did.

"Oh, it's not that bad." She reached for another dumpling as well, having already slipped a chunk of the meaty filling down to Harriet. "I just like to vent."

Becca nodded. Her friend was, at least, self-aware. And with that familiar topic laid to rest, she went back to the frustrations of her own past few days.

"I really wanted to help this woman find her cat," Becca said, having explained her encounter with Trina. "She thought that I could use my skill as a witch detective to locate Mr. Butters. But there wasn't anything I could do."

This time, it was Maddy who was wisely silent, focusing instead on her food.

"I know," Becca responded to her friend's unspoken criticism. "But a scrying spell—that's a spell that finds things—ought to be simple.

"It's not like I haven't had success casting spells before." Becca spoke before her friend could. "I have. You know I have, Maddy. But since that one time…" She paused. Maddy, who loved her dearly, continued to chew thoughtfully, having already snuck another morsel to a waiting feline. "And now I'm wondering if I'm crazy to advertise my services as a witch detective at all. My boss suggested that I was doing something illegal—acting as a private investigator without a license. But I was just going to do the usual things to help someone find a lost cat. Look around her apartment building and put up signs."

"But she found him, right?" Maddy, having swallowed at last, eyed the last dumpling and, in a gracious gesture, used the side of her chopstick to cut it in half.

"Thanks." Becca scarfed it up before continuing. "Actually, someone else found Mr. Butters and called. I guess she got some posters up after all." With that she paused, chopsticks halfway toward the dan dan noodles with their creamy peanut sauce. "I thought she was going to call me once she picked up Mr. Butters."

"She's probably caught up in getting him back and settled in." Maddy had no such compunction and scooped a healthy serving into her bowl, all the while shaking her head "no" to a disappointed Harriet.

"But that's it." Becca took an equally large portion of the peanut noodles, but she didn't seem to be enjoying the mouthful she then sucked up. "She wanted my help in figuring out how Mr. Butters got out," she said, as soon as she had swallowed. "In fact, she promised to call me when she got home."

"Count your blessings. Did you want to go out tonight?"

"No." Becca shook her head and slurped up more of the noodles. "I do think it's odd that she hasn't called, though."

"People are selfish. Which reminds me, I didn't tell you about the whole office-memo kerfuffle. Did I?"

Considering that Maddy had tried to get Becca to come to work with her, Becca was almost gratified to hear of the inter-office sniping that had resulted from a dispute about loading the printer. Working at Charm and Cherish barely paid the rent, but at least she didn't have to deal with petty office politics—or arguments about what caused paper jams. Still, as the friends moved on from the noodles to a spicy lamb dish, she couldn't stop thinking about Trina.

"She was so upset, Maddy," Becca said as she scooped some of the peppery sauce onto her rice. "She really wanted to understand what had happened. She's concerned that Mr. Butters has found a way out and will get out again."

Maddy knew her friend well enough to recognize when she couldn't let something go. "Why don't you call her then? That way, you'll be able to enjoy the moo shi, at least."

Nodding, her mouth full, Becca went off in search of her phone. "Hey, Trina. Becca from Charm and Cherish here. I hope you are home and you and Mr. Butters are settling in after an eventful day. Do you still want me to come over and help you figure out what happened? I could probably come by tomorrow. Even if you're having second thoughts about that, would you give me a call back and let me know that he's home safe?"

She hung up and turned toward Maddy. "Maybe she was getting too many calls. But don't you think it's strange that she asked for my help but let my call go straight to voicemail?"

"People are strange." Maddy shrugged. "Now, why don't you take the first pancake? I know we have more noodles left, but I'm ready to move on."

Chapter Nine

W hen Becca didn't hear from Trina the next morning, she told herself not to worry. The distraught woman had probably been so caught up with the return of her kitty that she let everything else slide. She might not even have checked her messages. After all, why should she, now that her cat was back?

But even though Becca tried to put the other woman out of her mind, her cats knew something was wrong.

"Why does she care?" Harriet, having finished her breakfast, acted as if all was right with the world as she began to groom.

"The other girl asked her for help." Clara, licking her own snowy paw, offered an answer.

"She should be focusing on us." Laurel, whose own toilette was complete, was staring intently at the kitten. In recent weeks, the little tortie had perfected the ability to bathe without falling over. To the older cat, however, her technique was clearly still limited, and with one chocolate paw, she pulled the kitten close and began to lick her.

"Stop it!" The kitten squirmed away from the rough tongue, as the three sister cats looked on in amazement.

"It can talk?" Harriet's golden eyes opened wide.

"'Course I can." The kitten mewed softly and scampered away

Two sets of eyes—one gold, one blue—turned on Clara, accusingly. *"You knew."*

Clara dipped her head, fully aware that her sisters could pick up on her thoughts. *"I did try to tell you,"* she said. *"I thought you knew. That kitten is...conscious."*

It was an inexact word, but the closest she could come to her sense that the little tortie was as alert and intelligent as Clara and her sisters. Even as she struggled to come up with a better way to explain her awareness of the kitten—her certainty that the young feline was, in her own way, as special as she and her sisters—Clara realized a more pressing imperative. Becca was heading out the door, and knowing how distracted her human was, Clara knew she should follow.

Clara didn't really have to explain to her sisters what she was doing. She was the youngest, however, so it seemed only polite to slowly blink at them both, purring out her words. *"I'll see what I can find out."*

That wouldn't satisfy Laurel and Harriet, she knew well. But neither of the two older cats objected as the round calico carefully shaded herself to near invisibility, and then—with a shake of her orange and black behind—jumped through the closed door and raced down the apartment staircase after Becca.

The morning that greeted her was clear and bright, as if the previous days' rain had washed the sky, and Clara paused to glance upward, luxuriating in the warm sun on her fur. Fully solar powered, as all cats are to some extent, catching up to her person was easy. Once she hit the sidewalk, Becca had paused to check her phone again, staring at it for several moments before tapping in a number.

"Hi, it's Becca again." She bit her lip. "I hope you and Mr. Butters are all settled in. I could still come by later today, though, if you want some help figuring out what happened."

"She's going to think I'm a stalker," she said to nobody in particular once she'd put the phone away. "But she did ask me for help."

Clara purred her agreement, even as she trotted alongside her person, well hidden by the early morning shadows. The route to Becca's workplace was familiar to the calico, and with the students gone, the sidewalk was emptier than usual. In celebration of the fine day, she made the outing a game, dashing from one shadow to another between the leafy maples that lined Becca's street. So caught up was she in her playful frolic that she didn't notice when her person stopped walking alongside her. Only when she put her head up, listening for the familiar tread, did she realize Becca had disappeared.

"That's impossible!" Clara froze, a cat's first instinct. But when no sound or scent cued her in to what happened, she flicked her ears and then raised her orange nose, hoping to catch a clue. Panic was beginning to set in when she heard it: a familiar ring from Becca's phone. Faint, but clear, it came from the next block over, and Clara raced back to the last corner she had passed, ears and tail on alert.

Yes! Halfway down the block, she saw her, and a moment later, a warm breeze brought a confirming scent. Soap and some essential essence that made up Becca, the aroma—and the accompanying relief—washed over the small cat like a wave of joy.

"Becca!" Her mew would be lost in the street noise, Clara knew. Still, she couldn't help calling out as she raced up to the person she held so dear, nearly running into her as she stopped on the sidewalk.

"Hey, Maddy. What's up?" Her person most likely would not have noticed the faint orange-and-gray shadow that now circled her, focused as she was on the device in her hand, but she might have wondered if Clara had bumped into her. Or not. At the sound of her friend's voice—or maybe it was the distinctive tune that signaled her call—Becca had perked up, the worry that had clouded her brow earlier in the morning seemingly wiped away. But the longer she stood there, listening to her friend, the more her brow bunched up, until Clara could barely resist the urge to rub against her in a comforting caress.

"No, I just—No." That got Clara's attention, as her person rarely gave such a resounding negative response to her buddy.

Maddy clearly had her own response, but a moment later, Becca began to speak again, sending a chill along Clara's back.

"I know you want me to give up the kitten, Maddy."

Give up the kitten? Clara froze so quickly that she nearly tripped a passerby. Although she was growing fond of the rambunctious newcomer, in truth, the little tortie had disrupted their home. Plus, Harriet and Laurel both seemed supremely ambivalent about the young feline, as Clara had seen that morning. Perhaps it would be best for the kitten to move on. Find a person of her own, who she could watch out for as Clara did for Becca. But to let the kitten go now, before Clara had gotten to the bottom of who she was or how she might fit into the sisters' royal lineage, would be incredibly frustrating. Besides, as far as Clara knew, Maddy already had a cat—a feline diva named Corabelle who wouldn't allow another animal within the apartment. If only…

But Becca was still talking.

"Look, I get it that your office pal is looking for a new cat. I wish her all the best, and I'm sure she'll find a lovely kitty at the shelter." Mystery solved, Clara relaxed. It helped that Becca had stood up straight, her brow evening out as she spoke. A sure sign, Clara knew, that she had made up her mind. "And, no, I'm not becoming a 'crazy cat lady,' Maddy. And, yes, Jerry gets it. I mean, he's a veterinarian. But the main issue is that the kitten has bonded with my cats, and I'm going to keep her."

Clara could have rolled over with relief. That is, until Becca's next words made the fur along her spine stand on edge. "I'm heading over to Trina's place now, Maddy. I just have a bad feeling about all of this."

Chapter Ten

Ten minutes later, Clara's fur still hadn't settled down. If anything, the calico had become more on edge as Becca led her down a busy street and into a small shelter.

"The number one should get me there," Becca murmured softly to herself. And although the words didn't make much sense to her shaded cat, the small feline suspected something horrible was about to happen and braced herself to defend her person by any means possible.

It was the noise that first alerted her. A horrible wheezing, as if a dragon were approaching, heralded the approach of a beast the likes of which Clara had never seen up close before. Huge—larger even than the occasional taxi the cat had been forced to endure—the yellow-and-white creature lurched toward the small crowd gathered on the curb. But instead of fleeing, the people around Becca surged forward, taking her with them and forcing Clara to press almost against her person's ankles as a last line of defense.

"This is a Nubian Station bus," a voice boomed out. "Next stop, Tech Square."

Bracing herself, Clara followed Becca toward the beast and, focusing on her great love for her, she leaped as Becca stepped up—and found herself inside a moving conveyance, not unlike a subway car. As the beast swayed and rumbled, the calico tucked herself under one of the benches that lined the walls. She had almost gotten used to the noisy jilting when Becca rose from her seat. Still, she thanked the great goddess Bast for their deliverance as her person jogged down the stairs to the sidewalk, the carefully blurred cat by her side.

"Becca!" A voice beckoned, and Clara turned to take in Maddy. This morning, Becca's friend was clad in a lighter brown jacket for an ensemble that reminded the cat of Laurel's fur, a resemblance furthered by chocolate brown nail polish that caught the light as she waved.

"Over here," she called, although Becca had already started toward her. "I told Reynolds I had a dentist's appointment. I'm not letting you go to some stranger's apartment all alone."

"She's not a stranger—"

Maddy interrupted Becca's objection. "I know, I know. She's a client. A woman you know nothing about, except that she came into your shop looking to get you to help her. What if it's all a setup and she just wanted to get you alone?"

Becca's skepticism was clear in her glance, but the cat at her feet was heartened by her friend's concern. Although she and her sisters had been responsible for Becca billing herself as a "witch detective" and had helped her out with several investigations, she never stopped worrying about how their human tended to throw herself into the lives—and problems—of others.

"I think it's more likely that you'll get yourself in trouble at work." Becca's smile softened her words. "But it's nice that you worry about me. However unnecessary that may be."

"Whatevs." Maddy fell into pace beside Becca as they walked down the sidewalk, Clara by their side. This far into Boston, the foot traffic became heavier. But even though the calico had to pay more attention to her own path—avoiding the oblivious footfalls of other pedestrians even as she kept pace with two young women—she couldn't help but notice the strained dynamic between the two friends. Usually, the two would be talking nonstop, although the subject of their conversations was often a mystery to the felines listening in.

When Becca broke the odd silence, it was with an even odder pronouncement.

"Three-one-one," she said. "Number 12." She had stopped walking, Maddy by her side. With a glance at her friend, Becca took out her phone. "I'll try her one more time."

"Come on," her friend said after the two had stood in silence for another minute. "Let's get this over with."

After the trauma of the bus ride, Clara found herself hesitating as the two friends let themselves into the building's glass alcove. From outside, she watched as Becca pressed a button, then pressed it again, and the friends exchanged a weighted look.

"Coming in?" A tall young man, his shaggy dark hair at odds with his pinstripe suit, was stepping out of the building. Eyebrows raised in invitation, he held the inner door open for the two friends, and while Becca hesitated like she was about to say something, Maddy grabbed the heavy metal-frame door.

"Thanks." She flashed a smile at the stranger. "Apartment 12, right, Becca?"

"Right." With her own somewhat apologetic grin at the departing man, she followed Maddy into the building, and Clara, with a wiggle and a deep breath, jumped to join them.

* * *

"It had to be the third floor." Maddy was huffing as they climbed the stairs. "And she's not there. I don't know what you're hoping to find."

"I don't either." Becca, two steps ahead, spoke softly. "I just have a feeling that something's wrong, and I'd be remiss if I didn't check it out."

Because her friend was behind her, Becca couldn't see the way Maddy's brows went up at this. Her friend held her silence, though, as the two reached the doorway marked with a brass "12."

"Trina?" Becca leaned in as she knocked, calling out the name through the door. "Are you there? It's Becca Colwin. From Charm and Cherish."

"If she's there, she's dead, and her cat has eaten her." Maddy leaned heavily on the wall as Becca tried again. "And the roommate, too."

"I'd forgotten about the roommate." Becca ignored the first part of her friend's comment. "Maybe she can tell me what's going on. I'm going to leave a note. Do you have something to write with?"

Perhaps as penance, Maddy shifted through her bag, coming up with a

Moleskine and a pen, and watched as Becca scrawled her name and number, shoving the resulting note into the space between the door and its frame.

"She has your number already," Maddy said. This time, it was Becca whose expression would have at least raised the hackles of either of Clara's sisters, the petite calico thought.

"I didn't mean like that." Maddy sounded contrite as she followed Becca down the stairs.

"It's fine." Becca dismissed the slight as she pushed open the heavy front door. "I'd be happy just to hear from the roommate that Trina's okay," she said, her voice falling away as she spoke. But as soon as the friends had descended the three stairs to the sidewalk, Becca paused, reaching for Maddy's arm.

"Did you see that?"

"What?" Maddy craned around, then focused where Becca was staring—at a low shrub that hugged the brick building's stone foundation. "Please don't tell me you saw a rat?"

"No." Becca crept up to the bush, signaling to Maddy to stay back or at least stay quiet.

Her caution wasn't necessary, however, as a large orange-and-white striped cat emerged from the shrubbery and rubbed his head against Becca's outstretched hand, while Clara—still shaded—looked on with mixed emotions.

"Hello, kitty. You're a nice big boy, aren't you? Are you Mr. Butters?" She scooped up the willing cat and maneuvered him with one hand to look at his collar. Sure enough, Clara could see a round blue charm, like a miniature Christmas tree ornament, hanging from the blue collar. While she wasn't sure how she felt about her person lifting the large orange creature, she had to admit, Becca was doing her job. "Yes, you are," she now said. To Maddy, she explained. "This is Trina's cat, Mr. Butters."

"Mr. Butters?" Maddy's brows went up, but Becca only smiled. "So he got out again." Maddy shrugged. "Sounds like either this girl is careless, or her cat has found some means of unlocking a window." She looked up at the building. "Or the door."

"Or Trina didn't make it home with him yesterday." Becca could have been addressing the orange cat, but Clara's own fur perked up. "Which would explain why she hasn't returned my calls."

"I vote for the former." Maddy was clearly ready to move on. "But if you're concerned, let's see if we can get Mr. Kitty here inside the building."

"And just leave him?" Becca looked over at her friend. "Without knowing if anyone is around to take care of him?"

Maddy opened her mouth, but Becca was ahead of her. "His fur is dry, so maybe someone else took him in, or he found a place to shelter from the rain, but I can't see just leaving him. I'm not saying we should take him. But I do want to get to the bottom of this. It's not safe for a housecat out here, even a big boy like him."

"He seems fine." Maddy's voice lacked conviction. "Okay, I give up. Let's try this Trina again."

Becca did, releasing the orange tabby to twine around her ankles with a resounding purr. But when two more calls went to voicemail, she sighed with frustration. "I'm not sure what to do, Maddy."

Her friend bit her lip, her face twisting up in thought. *At least she's taking Becca seriously,* Clara thought. And with that, she approached the orange tabby, nose outstretched.

"Hello." Although she was still technically invisible, she trusted that her voice conveyed her tails-up friendliness. *"I'm Clara. Becca is my person. Who are you?"*

The cat before her sniffed the air, his upturned pink nose clearly taking in Clara's scent. He remained silent, however, even as his tail curled into a quizzical queue.

"I'm right here. Only you can't see me," Clara tried again. Maddy and Becca were deep in discussion, but she still didn't feel she could risk becoming visible. Her person was dealing with enough without that kind of shock. *"Can't you hear me?"*

The tabby sat, clearly puzzled. But Clara got back no thought, no "mew" of comprehension. Nothing. Her sisters had told her about this—that so-called "normal" cats could not communicate as she and her sisters did. She found it hard to believe that a fellow feline could be what Laurel would call "dumb," but she was getting frustrated.

"Here I am," she said. Reaching out to touch her damp nose pad to the other cat's nose, she jerked back as the other cat jumped. There had been a small electric shock, sure, but beyond that, Clara couldn't account for the tabby's continued freak out, which now had him backing, low to the ground, into the shrubbery.

"Hold on." Becca turned and reached for the cat, who jerked away. "Something has spooked him."

"Maybe it's us?" Maddy had the defeated look of a person who has lost an argument.

"Or the traffic, or he senses a predator nearby. Either way, we can't leave him here."

Moving slowly, hand out for the tabby to sniff, she approached the skittish feline. "Come on, Mr. Butters," she cooed, as gently as a purr. Clara, meanwhile, hung back, her ears and tail low as she considered the trouble she'd caused.

"Here we go." With a triumphant grin, Becca hefted the tabby and turned toward her friend. "So, Charm and Cherish?"

"Might as well." Maddy had the grace to acquiesce with a smile of her own.

"What is she doing?" As the friends set out again, Clara followed at a distance, unwilling to spook the speechless tabby further. But when a car pulled up, apparently in response to something Maddy had done with her phone, she had no choice but to jump in. *"What's going on?"*

The tabby, apparently content in Becca's arms, did not respond, not even as the car sped off, turning down streets that Clara, at any rate, had never seen.

"Here we are. Thanks." A few minutes later, the car had pulled up in front of a familiar storefront, slipping into a space by the curb. "Just let me explain the situation to Elizabeth."

With a jangle of bells, Becca entered the store, her friend close behind. Elizabeth was wearing an orange caftan today, its cream stripes echoing those of the cat Becca still held close.

"I can explain," said Becca.

"No need," the older woman said, with a wave of her arm that made her sleeve billow out like a cloud. Clara looked up, expecting the other cat to pull back at the unexpected movement. To her surprise, the big tabby only began to purr again. "We can put down water and a makeshift litterbox in the back room. That should hold him for a while. After that, I believe you have another errand to run."

"Thank you." Becca's entire body relaxed as she led Maddy into the back of the store.

"Did you call her?" Maddy whispered her query as she glanced back at the older woman.

"No." Clara placed the tabby on the room's shabby sofa while she fetched a small bowl for water. "That's just Elizabeth. You get used to it."

"All right then." Her friend shrugged. "This *is* a magic shop."

That earned her a grin from her friend, and with a wave to Elizabeth, the two were off.

Clara by now was thoroughly confused. That her person wasn't working today was obvious, even if she'd have had trouble explaining the concept to her sisters. What Becca was doing was a mystery to her, though. Yes, as grateful as she was that Becca hadn't taken the inexplicably mute—and seemingly uncomprehending—orange tabby back to their apartment, she was glad her person had found a safe space for the indoor pet. As much as she didn't want another feline complicating their lives, Clara loved that her person wouldn't leave a cat in need. It was part of what made Becca so special.

Still, with all that settled, the little calico was hoping her person would return home now. At the very least, she wanted to consult with her sisters.

Chapter Eleven

Her hope that the two humans would head toward Becca's apartment was soon dispelled, however. Instead of turning toward the leafy street where they lived, and where Harriet would undoubtedly be snoozing in the window, pretending to be alert to everything below, Becca led Maddy toward the city center. With no choice but to follow, Clara checked her shading and jogged along, hanging close behind Maddy's fashionable, if clunky boots. If anything could protect her from errant pedestrians, certainly those could, she told herself, peeping ahead to see if she could make out their destination.

While she couldn't see anything, a faint scent soon reached her. A mix of fear and perspiration, it alarmed the calico, and she found herself crouching low to the ground, as if preparing for an attack.

A few minutes later, they arrived at its source. Becca—and Clara with her—had been here before: a hulking brick and stone building reached by a white stone staircase. On this sunny day, people were seated on the stairs, eating their lunches or just soaking up the rays, the smells of baked goods and spicy sauces adding to the aroma of desperation that Clara had first sensed and which eked out from within.

"I think Trina's place is still in Cambridge, not Boston," Becca was talking to Maddy, and Clara tore herself away from analyzing the smells to listen. "At any rate, the Cambridge police will be a good place to start."

It hit Clara then where she knew this scent from. Becca had been here before, sometimes to ask questions and more than once to be questioned, an unpleasant experience her cat associated with that disturbing tang in the air. Looking up at the two friends, she saw that Becca must be remembering something similar. But rather than retreat to the safety of their home, her human simply squared her shoulders and stood up a little straighter. With a determined nod to Maddy, she started up the steps, her buddy and her faithful cat behind her.

"I'd like to speak to someone about a missing person." Becca wasted no time, walking up to the bored-looking man who stood behind the wooden barrier. Tall with an air of fatigue or possibly resignation, he lowered his graying hair to peer at her over his glasses, as well as over the bags that threatened to take over his face.

"Missing person? Hang on." A moment's rummaging under the counter yielded a form. "Fill this out, please."

Becca opened her mouth, but the clerk—he wasn't wearing a uniform—was already looking over her head. "Next?"

Grumbling a little, Becca joined Maddy in one of the benches by the door. "They don't seem to care very much."

"This probably gives them information they'd have to ask you about anyway." Her friend, always reasonable, was clearly softening her tone. "Here, use my pen."

For the next few minutes, Becca scribbled away. Clara, curled beneath the bench, was beginning to doze when a sudden noise startled her awake.

"What?" Maddy sounded like it had woken her as well.

"This form…" Becca was breathless with exasperation. "They want to know when I last had contact with her and what our relationship is. If I say I just met her when she came into my shop, they're not going to take this seriously."

"Maybe you can explain? Tell them she's a client?"

"I don't know." Becca shook her head. "I'm not sure I want to get into that." Nevertheless, she continued writing, filling out the rest of the form with a few deep sighs. As she stood to hand it in, however, she stopped, turning to Maddy. "I'm going to try her again," she explained. "I mean, what if she came home after we left?"

"Well, if she did, it would've been polite to return one of your calls. But…

yeah." Maddy waved her hand, looking on as Becca retrieved her phone from her pocket.

"Trina? This is Becca again." She stared down at the floor, and for a moment, Clara worried that she could be seen. "I'm beginning to really worry. Please call me."

She hung up and started toward the counter when she stopped short. Taking out her phone once more, she paused, apparently frozen with indecision. Finally, she started typing with her thumbs.

Becca again. I have Mr. Butters. Becca muttered the words as she typed. "I should have said something, and I don't want her to worry," she said, using a slightly louder voice, to her friend.

He was wandering around outside your building when I came by to check on you, and I didn't feel it was safe for him. She stopped typing for a moment, a thoughtful expression on her face that gave Clara pause as well. *I knew him by the blue charm you told me about. Please call or come by when you get this. I'll be at home all evening.* Typing in her address, she hit "send," the click of her phone making Clara dig her claws into the worn linoleum for reasons she didn't quite understand. There was nothing about the sound itself. As she shadowed her person, the sensitive feline had certainly heard louder and more frightening noises.

"Maybe it's simply that this Trina hasn't gotten back to her." She gave her whole body a shake to shed that strange feeling. *"Though at least Mr. Butters is safe."*

Clara was still musing over her odd reaction when she realized Becca was gone. Luckily, this time her ears picked up her person's voice, and she dashed across the floor, following Becca and her friend as they were ushered down a hall and into a small, windowless room that held a table and four chairs.

The man who led them there, a stout dark-skinned man whose blue uniform strained at the seams, motioned to two chairs before settling into a third with a sigh.

"So, you're worried because you can't get in touch with your friend." Up close, he appeared as tired as that clerk.

"She's not my friend, exactly—" Becca broke off as Maddy kicked her under the table. Clara withdrew farther under Becca's chair as her person changed tack. "I'm just worried about her. That's all."

The rotund officer nodded, his chair creaking under the weight. "I understand," he said, his voice calm. "But, you see, we don't really know if she's missing."

"We stopped by her apartment, as I noted—"

This time, it was the cop who cut her off. "She's not at home or not answering the door. That doesn't mean she's missing." His kind voice was tightening up, the words coming faster as if to preempt anything Becca might start to say. "She's an adult, and she's free to go off for a day or two. And not answer her phone." He snuck that in, apparently aware that Becca had drawn breath to respond.

"Is Detective Newsom here?" Becca craned her head around. The name evoked a basset hound, but after a bit of thought, Clara connected it to a sad-faced police officer, one who had helped—or at least been sympathetic—to Becca before. "I've dealt with him before, and he knows me."

"This isn't a case that merits Detective Newsom's time," the uniformed cop cut her off. "Bottom line, unless you have more than a few unanswered phone messages, you can't file a missing report until the person in question has been verifiably missing for at least 24 hours. And considering your last contact was barely two days ago, and all that's happening is she's not returning your calls…"

Becca seemed to collapse in her chair. Maddy, however, perked up, drawing in her feet in a swift motion that made Clara draw back.

"Thanks for your time," she said, pushing the chair back. "We'll come back if we find out more or if she doesn't turn up. Come on, Becca," she turned toward her friend. "Let's get some lunch."

Chapter Twelve

Becca was strangely silent as Maddy led her out of the hulking building and into a small café about a block away. "Two cappuccinos," Maddy ordered, after depositing Becca at a table by the front window. "Becca, do you want a roll-up?"

"Sure," Clara's person answered, her voice neutral. She was staring out at the street, but Clara was pretty sure she wasn't seeing the people walking by, or even how the bright sunshine made the leaves of the nearby maple glisten.

"Okay, what is it?" Maddy had returned to the table by then, and, oddly for a human, appeared to be as aware of Becca's mood as Clara.

"Something's not right." Becca shook her head slowly, staring off into the middle distance so much like a cat that Clara's fur stood on end.

"What's not right is that you're obsessing over this girl." Her friend reached up as a server brought their order over. "Maybe you need some caffeine."

Becca sipped the frothy drink and shook her head once again. "You didn't hear her, Maddy. She sounded so happy. And then nothing. Plus, finding Mr. Butters outside was just strange."

"Well, her pet is safe now." Maddy took a bite out of her sandwich and watched, as alert as a mother cat, until Becca did the same.

"As long as Elizabeth is on duty." Becca chewed thoughtfully. "Margaret is not going to be amused, and she's my actual boss."

Silence fell on the friends after that, despite the bustle of the customers and servers around them. They both had had run-ins with Elizabeth's shorter, stouter baby sister, and Becca had told Maddy about her threats to close the

Wiccan mainstay. They could both all too easily imagine what she'd think of a cat in the back room.

"At least that nice big boy will take care of any mice." Maddy was trying.

"I don't think we have any." Becca took another bite of her rollup as Clara silently concurred. "Besides, he's not going to be there long. We're going to find Trina."

Maddy shuffled in her seat, and something on her face must have alerted her friend.

"What is it?" Her voice was almost lost in the noisy café.

"I told Reynolds that I had a dentist's appointment, not oral surgery. I really should get back to work." Maddy paused. "I'm sorry."

"Don't be." Becca sounded exasperated—at herself, her cat realized. "I've been dragging you all over. I'm supposed to relieve Elizabeth at two, anyway."

The friends parted ways outside the café. But to Clara's surprise, Becca didn't immediately head back toward Charm and Cherish. Cats have no sense of time as we know it, though they are certainly aware of the passage of the day, with special attention to meals. She couldn't know, therefore, that her person had more than an hour before her shift began. And that, like Clara, she had begun to have a strange feeling about the day.

"It can't hurt to check in," she said to herself as she turned down her street. Clara couldn't agree more; the sense of foreboding had been growing on her, making her fur feel itchy and strange. When Becca sped up her steps as their building came into view, Clara was more than happy to break into a trot and then a run, eager to pass into their apartment before Becca had unlocked the door.

Her sisters were waiting by the door. *"Where have you been?"* Laurel positively hissed before Harriet silenced her with a quick slap with one wide, fluffy paw.

"We were looking for that girl, Trina. We found her cat. Who's just a cat." Quietly, Clara filled her sisters in, even as Harriet raised another paw in warning. They could all hear Becca jostling with the lock down below and then her rapid footfall up the stairs.

"Where's the kitten?" Clara glanced around, just as the door opened.

"Hi, kitties!" Becca's voice rang with obvious relief as she took in the living room, which appeared relatively intact. That relief was replaced by a note of anxiety as she echoed Clara. "Where's the kitten?"

Laurel and Harriet looked at each other, and for a moment, Clara wondered if they would respond. Becca didn't know how much they understood. She couldn't be allowed to, by all the laws that governed the pet-person relationship, but the anxiety in her voice was clear, and a moment later, Harriet shifted, revealing the tortie kitten, who had been wedged between two of Becca's sneakers and the marmalade cat's big plume of a tail.

"There you are." Dropping her bag, Becca scooped up the kitten, nuzzling her multicolored fur. At her feet, the older cats exchanged looks, and Clara realized that more than jealousy was at play.

"What happened? Why were you hiding the kitten?"

"I was shielding *her."* Harriet pulled her head back into her ruff. This was supposed to make her look more imposing, Clara knew. In reality, it gave her a double chin. *"If you'd been home—"*

"Someone was here," Laurel squeaked in her softest mew, and suddenly, Clara's foreboding made sense. She lifted her particolored nose. Yes, another scent. A man. No, two men, the scent faint enough so that she could tell they were gone.

Laurel nudged her to get her attention back. *"We weren't sure what would happen. They got the door open. I focused on letting Becca know."*

"But that might have put her in danger." Clara, remembering how Becca had suddenly decided to return to the apartment, felt her fur begin to rise in alarm.

"They had gone by then, silly," Harriet chimed in even as she followed Becca, who had let the kitten jump to the floor, into the kitchen.

"How did they get in?" Clara addressed her question to Laurel, who had hung back.

"That awful woman downstairs let them into the building." They'd all had run-ins with Deborah Miles, who was not a fan of pets of any sort. *"Then they fussed with the door."*

"Fussed?" Clara asked, hoping Laurel would elaborate. But the seal point

ignored her, focusing on their person instead. Probably, Clara realized, unable to explain exactly how the human had gained entry.

Still, she followed her sisters, curious for news as much as treats. Surely her person would be able to tell immediately that an intruder had broken in. Except that, she saw as they paraded through the living room, the apartment appeared untouched.

"Exactly." Laurel looked back over one tawny shoulder, her blue eyes closing slowly in agreement.

"Now, you have all had breakfast." Becca addressed them all, but it was Harriet's golden eyes she stared down into. The marmalade cat had been sitting politely at her feet and, in response, stretched upward, reaching for the top of the counter with her paws. "Now, now." Becca took those big front paws in her hand and detached them from the drawer pull. "You know better than that. I hope the kitten isn't getting you into bad habits."

Clara looked down, embarrassed. It was true, the three of them had much better manners than to reach like that. What was next, clawing? Besides, if anything they did made Becca less likely to keep the kitten, she'd know who to blame.

"She's got to look, Clown!" Harriet's usual mew had turned into a high-pitched whine. *"She's got to see."*

"What?" Clara craned around. That scent. The men had been here. In the kitchen, she realized with a jolt. Not the place an ordinary burglar would bother with. And sure enough, Becca hadn't noticed anything out of place. Clara turned toward her sisters.

"Time for something drastic." Laurel lashed her tail and, with a graceful leap, landed on the counter. Becca gasped, but before she could grab the cat, she had leaped again, this time to the top of the refrigerator, where she sat, looking down, as her tail lashed in triumph.

"Laurel, what are you doing?" Becca reprimanded the cat, clapping her hands to make her point.

"Oh, I hate that!" Harriet put her head down and her paws over her ears. Up on the fridge, Laurel winced, fighting to keep her ears from going flat on her head.

"I know, I'm sorry," she squeaked out. *"But she has to notice."*

"Have you tried suggesting that to her?" Clara felt silly mentioning what was obvious, but she could tell by the way Laurel's eyes suddenly crossed that her older sister had briefly forgotten her special skill in all the excitement.

"Not a bad idea, Clown." Clara ducked her head in acknowledgment. The demeaning nickname, she could tell, was simply a result of her sister's embarrassment. When she looked up, she could feel the warmth of her gaze, even as her eyes remained crossed. And with that, Laurel lashed her tail and focused on Becca, her chocolate-tipped ears leaning forward from the exertion.

"Laurel. Get down…" From the distracted expression on Becca's face, Clara thought maybe Laurel's efforts were working. When she reached over to pull a photo from the refrigerator, she was sure. "What's this doing here?"

Becca looked at the snapshot of herself holding Harriet and turned it over, reading the date. "I didn't have this on the fridge," she said, more to herself than to her cats. She then walked over to the small cork bulletin board that hung by the pantry, reaching for a better photo that featured all three of the sisters. "And this one I did."

She shook her head. "Did one of you knock this off the board? But you couldn't have pinned it back up."

In response, Laurel let loose with one of her distinctive Siamese wails. *"No, we didn't!*

Even as Harriet and Clara joined in, butting their heads against her shins to get her to notice the other photos that had been knocked down, she only shook her head. "You girls have been getting up to so much trouble while I'm gone. I wish I didn't have to go to work, but—"

Laurel gave another wail, but it was in vain. Reaching up on her toes, Becca grabbed the slender feline and deposited her back on the floor. Then she picked up her jacket and bag again and headed back out.

"Do you need me to stay?" Clara looked from Harriet to Laurel, who was busy smoothing her already impeccable coat.

"There's nothing here we can't handle." Harriet curled her own tail around her forepaws. *"But those men are still out there, and who knows what they want."*

Chapter Thirteen

That was enough of a spur for Clara, who quickly shaded herself and jumped through the door in pursuit of Becca. Alarmed as she'd been by her sister's report of intruders, she hadn't considered the possibility that the strangers might still be a danger to Becca. Surely whoever it was had chosen a time when her person was out. How those people had managed to enter the apartment was a puzzle, but if Becca hadn't noticed anything missing, perhaps her sisters' presence had acted as a deterrent; Laurel's powers of persuasion sometimes had greater effect on those who don't normally interact with cats.

Still, the calico was on alert as she trotted after her person, hoping that this time she was indeed headed to Charm and Cherish. From what her person had said—unlike her sisters, Clara had a basic concept of "job" and "work"—this seemed likely, which also meant that Clara would have the opportunity to question that strange ginger tabby. But as they rounded the corner at the end of the block, Clara couldn't avoid an unsettling feeling that someone was following them.

Ears alert, she turned around, looking for anything out of place. In the middle of the day, Becca's neighborhood was quiet, and all her cat could spy was an older woman balancing groceries and a black car cruising slowly past.

Nothing smelled out of place, either, she decided, after taking a good long sniff. Summer leaves, the heat releasing their moist green scent. A faint smell of warm human as she drew closer to Becca.

The pair had come to Mass Ave, where the busier traffic had Becca waiting to cross. Clara, at her side, again glanced around. No footsteps other than her person's had followed them here, and everyone on the busy main street seemed intent on their own business, breaking stride only when they too came to the corner.

But even as a series of cars turned, Clara couldn't shake her apprehension. *Could a human shade himself like I do?* The question seemed ridiculous. Everyone knew that cats were the ones with magic powers. Since the arrival of the kitten, however, Clara had come to question everything she believed— including her sisters' teachings that they alone were the heirs of the great temple cat, the beloved of Bast, blessed with special powers.

As she mused, the light changed, and Becca crossed, leaving her feline shadow briefly behind. With a start, Clara realized what was happening and jumped after her, barely escaping disaster as one driver rolled into the intersection, determined to make the turn.

"Watch it!" Another pedestrian called out, and Clara turned to make out an older woman, her scowling face as much a warning to any other offending driver as the cane she shook in the air.

"Oh, no." Becca had turned too, taking in the short, stout woman. "Margaret." With that, she sped up, almost running the last two blocks until she could push open the door to Charm and Cherish, sending the bells into a ruckus.

"Good afternoon." Elizabeth turned to greet her colleague. "Did you have a productive morning?"

"Sort of," Becca answered, clearly distracted. "I thought I saw your sister. Has she been in?"

Elizabeth nodded and raised her hand as Becca began to speak. "She has, and I explained the tabby. It seems we have had some rodent issues in the stockroom, and you helped arrange a temporary mouser to take care of the problem," she said, sounding suspiciously like Maddy.

"A temporary mouser?" Becca repeated in relief, almost collapsing against a display table, even as Elizabeth beckoned her back toward the shelves.

"That tabby has a home to go back to, I assume. But for now, he's a welcome visitor."

"Thanks, Elizabeth. That reminds me…" Whipping out her cell phone, she tried Trina once more. "Straight to voicemail," she said. "And nothing from the roommate, either."

"Seems like Mr. Butters may be spending the night with us." Elizabeth's sweeping gesture took in the store.

"Maybe." Becca sounded thoughtful, then shook off whatever was on her mind. "At any rate, I'm here now, so if you want to take off, feel free."

"Thanks." Elizabeth was speaking to the younger woman, but her eyes glanced down at Clara, who immediately checked to make sure she was still invisible. "Do you want to talk about how things went with Margaret?"

"I don't know." Just thinking about her boss was exhausting.

"You know, not all of her ideas are bad." Elizabeth's voice was gently chiding. "She is looking out for you."

"Great." The PI license. Clara knew that Becca had been worrying about Margaret's comment, even as she tried to focus on other things. "I'm sorry," she caught herself. "That was unfair. I'm sure she is, and I know you are," she ended with a smile.

"Then I cede the register to you," Elizabeth smiled back, before slipping past the bookcases. But even as Becca checked the till, she could hear Elizabeth in the back room. "Everything okay?"

"Very much so," Elizabeth's voice came back. "I just thought I'd catch up on some reading."

"Enjoy." Becca did her best to sound happy, but Clara didn't need Laurel's powers to hear the doubt in her voice. It wasn't that her boss's sister was checking up on her; she wished she could tell her. Nor that the gray-haired woman didn't think she was up to the job, taking care of the crowded storefront as well as any customers who might wander in. No, as Becca reclaimed her duster from behind the register and began to work her way across the top shelf of bound volumes—"Wicca and Nature Rituals" read the shelf talker—Clara had slunk around the edge of the door that opened onto the store's back room. Elizabeth was, in fact, reclining on the break room's tattered sofa, a thick volume with a black leather binding open on her lap. But instead of looking at the pages, she was gently stroking the ginger tabby, who was perched on the sofa's back, murmuring softly to the cat in words Clara could not make out.

"You can join us, you know." Without turning her head, Elizabeth raised her voice, sending the fur along Clara's spine into high alert. Intrigued, she crept forward, keeping her body low to the ground.

"We don't all speak the same language, but we all understand the basics." Elizabeth appeared to be addressing Mr. Butters, who had now relaxed, stretching his long body along the sofa's edge as Elizabeth smoothed his ginger fur with long, gentle strokes.

"And you don't have to talk to me." That froze Clara in her tracks. "I'm very glad Becca has you to watch over her, though. You've seen the trail, right?"

"Trail?" Clara's first thoughts were of the paw marks she left when she stepped into a puddle. But then she remembered the black car. Spinning around, she raced to the front of the store, jumping onto the low shelf by the front window and wedging herself between a sculpture of the moon goddess and the oversized candles that made up the current display. Sure enough, the black car—a particularly square model, with large tires—was parked out front. Its tinted windows kept Clara from being completely certain, but she was pretty sure that someone was sitting in the driver's seat. Whoever it was might be waiting for Becca, she realized, a thought that caused her entire body to shudder, almost as if she had fleas.

She had to keep Becca from leaving the store by its front door, she realized. And with that, she raced back to the break room, skidding to a halt in front of the sofa, where Elizabeth still reclined.

"Help me," she mewed, putting all her energy into sending her plea mentally as well. *"Help us. Please. You can hear me, right?"*

"Of course." Pulling herself into a sitting position, Elizabeth turned toward the calico. One hand, Clara noticed, remained on the ginger tabby's back, her wide sleeve echoing his orange-and-white stripes. "You've known that for a while now."

Clara shook herself; the woman's response was so unsettling. And yet it was true. Ever since the older of the two sisters had been coming into the shop, she had let Clara know that she was aware of her presence with a wink or a smile. This ran counter to everything the little cat believed, everything her older sisters had told her about their magic. If a human could see through her mystical cloaking—could even understand what she was saying—what else could a human do? Did this mean that Becca's efforts toward using magic herself were not in vain? Was there more to their powers than she had known?

With an eye to keeping her person safe, Clara cleared her head of these questions and addressed the woman before her.

"Someone is following Becca. You knew it. You saw." The cat blinked for emphasis, her ears going slightly back as she strained to make herself understood. *"How can we protect her?"*

"We?" Elizabeth's woolly brows brunched up at the question.

"Me, you—and Mr. Butters." Clara hesitated before naming the ginger tabby. But clearly Elizabeth had formed some kind of bond with the mute feline beside her. Even though Clara knew her sisters would reject the tabby as a mere animal, she sensed that a different answer—a more respectful one—was not only required but perhaps deserved.

It was the right answer, she concluded as Elizabeth nodded approvingly. "I've thought of a few things. But we have time. Becca is safe as long as she's here."

Whether that was because of the public nature of the store or because of Elizabeth, whose powers Clara could only begin to guess at, the calico couldn't tell. The gray-haired woman's answer relaxed her, though, and so she returned to the front room, found an uncluttered corner in that front window display and, with the afternoon sun warming her fur, fell into a sound sleep.

"You're still here." Becca's voice woke her, and the calico blinked as she took in Elizabeth striding into the main room, the large tabby perched on one shoulder.

"It's quite comfortable back there," she responded with a yawn, as if she too had been napping. "But I think this little boy is ready to move on."

"Oh, I should check." Becca reached for her phone, which she'd stuck under the counter while she worked. "No, still nothing. I'm wondering if I should go back to the police."

"Didn't they tell you that you didn't have enough evidence that your client was missing?"

"Well, yeah…" Becca's face screwed up, and Clara knew she was wondering whether she had shared that with the older woman.

"I think it's more important that you take this little boy home with you. At least for the night." As she put a hand up to the ginger tabby, the big orange cat gazed over at Becca with what could only be called an imploring gaze.

"Home? I thought he could stay here."

"I'm not sure how long Margaret will accept my explanation. And no—" Elizabeth held up one hand to stop Becca from interrupting. "I can't take her up to our suite. That would definitely result in him being put out on the street."

Becca looked suitably shocked at that prospect. "Okay, then. But my other cats aren't going to like it."

Elizabeth smiled, with a slight rise of her thick brows that Clara suspected was intended for her.

"There's a box in the back that would be perfect for carrying him home," she said, as if she hadn't heard Becca's objection. "Why don't we pack this ginger baby up and send you off? I can lock up."

"Are you sure?"

Elizabeth said something that sounded encouraging, but Clara barely heard it. Instead, she was getting a powerful sensation, urging her to chime in. And so she did, staring at the human she loved and thinking as hard as she could: *Go into the break room. Leave by the back door. Go into the back!* That, she realized, had been Elizabeth's plan all along.

Whether it was Elizabeth's encouragement or Clara's attempt to suggest the same, it worked, and soon Becca was in the break room, placing a suspiciously placid feline in a cardboard box.

"Did you do something to him?" Clara couldn't resist asking Elizabeth as the older woman stood in the doorway.

"You don't think he wants to help, too?"

Clara ducked her head in acceptance and then looked up again once more at the orange-and-white clad woman. Ostensibly, she was watching Becca, but Clara sensed she was also keeping an eye on the black sedan that remained parked out front. Once Becca had stepped out, in fact, Elizabeth strode briskly to the front, where she reached down to stroke a Bast statuette, a smaller version of the one topping the bookcase. A simple movement, the calico decided, designed to draw the attention of the driver. Only after Becca had walked down the block behind Charm and Cherish did Elizabeth flip the store's "open" sign to "closed." And with that, Clara raced to the back, checked her shading one more time, and with a wiggle of her hindquarters jumped through the door and raced to catch up with her person and the ginger tabby she held in a box in front of her, as if he were a big box of treats she was carrying home.

Chapter Fourteen

Thanks to Elizabeth, the walk home was uneventful. Even with the noise of rush hour traffic and the unavoidable jostling he must be enduring, Mr. Butters remained calm in his box, leaving Clara to ponder Elizabeth's comment. Was it possible that Mr. Butters was more aware than she had thought? That even a seemingly simple creature had some sense of what was going on—and, more important—of a cat's place in the world?

These were questions she wanted to bring up with her sisters, even though she knew their first response would be dismissive. At first mention, Laurel would sniff, and Harriet would fluff out her fur at the suggestion that a strange cat could possess some of their own highly evolved senses. But the few months they'd spent with the kitten had begun to break down some of their resistance to the possibility, Clara knew. And if she could explain what had happened today with Elizabeth, they might come up with some answers.

For now, though, she'd be happy with keeping Becca safe, and so as she trotted alongside her person, she kept her ears up and whiskers on alert, glancing back occasionally as well. Whoever was driving that black car knew where Becca lived. Had possibly broken into her apartment. But it was out here on the street that she felt her human was most vulnerable, and she sighed with relief as their own front stoop came into view.

Until, that is, she got inside.

"What's in the box?" Deborah Miles, their downstairs neighbor, had initially been hostile to Becca and her cats. The successful conclusion to an earlier case had brought about a truce between the two, but as the well-coifed brunette scowled, creating lines around her carefully painted mouth, Clara sensed that hostilities could soon return.

"It's a cat." From the way her voice fell, Clara knew Becca recognized this, too. Before the other woman could speak, she tried to head off any objection. "I'm just watching him for a friend. For a day or two at most."

The other woman's frown deepened, the scowl that barely moved her Botoxed forehead narrowing her eyes into something dark and mean. "You should know I've been talking to the management company. We need a regulation limiting the number of animals in the building."

"Perhaps we need a regulation about helping out our friends and neighbors." Becca couldn't resist snapping back. After all, her quick thinking had helped solve the murder of another tenant, a case that had made Becca a local heroine, at least for a while.

"It's a health issue," the other woman sniffed. "General hygiene."

"Cats are very clean animals." Becca felt the orange tabby shift in the box. "Now, if you'll excuse me."

"That woman is a menace." Laurel, a flight above, lashed her tail. The human voices were clearly audible to the cats' ears, and Laurel in particular had a grudge against the woman she viewed as overdressed and overdone. In part, Clara suspected, because she worked so hard to get Becca to care a little more about her appearance.

"Never mind the person. What is Becca holding in that box?"

Clara, who had raced ahead to warn her sisters, turned toward Harriet. Surely, her big sister could sense the tabby's presence. No, her question was larger.

"He's lost. His name is Mr. Butters, and the missing woman is his human." Clara searched for the words that would explain the situation to her siblings. *"This is Becca's latest case. The work she does."*

"Work, humph!" Harriet settled down with a sigh, just as Becca's key sounded in the door. *"And a male cat? A tom? In our house?"*

"Hello, ladies!" Becca greeted her cats, even as she maneuvered the box through the door. "We have a visitor. A temporary visitor."

Clara wasn't sure how much her person knew about her cats. She herself wasn't completely sure Laurel and Harriet understood the meaning of "temporary," but the idea of a visitor surely had some meaning.

"He's not sleeping on my pillow." Harriet wasted no time in wrapping herself around Becca's ankles, the better to assert her dominance.

"And he better not get any ideas about settling in," grumbled Laurel.

The three tagged after Becca as she carried the box into the kitchen, where the kitten was waiting. Once their person had fed them all, Clara's siblings calmed down. But as the kitten finished the last of her food, putting one paw in the wet mix and licking it, Becca pulled out an old saucer for the visiting tabby, and Clara could sense as well as see the fur begin to rise along her siblings' backs.

"He's in trouble. He needs our assistance." Clara tried to hold back the impatience in her own voice. Focusing on her sisters' powers might spur them to help out, whereas a snarl would get her nowhere with her sisters. *"If we can help him reunite with his person, it will be good for Becca, too."*

Laurel bowed her head. *"I hear you, Clown."* It was the best Clara could hope for. Still, as Becca opened the box, she braced for what could be a violent confrontation as the ginger tabby jumped out and looked around, extending his nose toward the two older cats.

"Why, hello."

Clara turned toward her sister, astonished. She had never heard Harriet mew in such a mellow tone before.

"Welcome." Laurel, stepping in front of her older sister, touched her black nose to the orange male's pink one.

"Harriet, Laurel, Mr. Butters." Swallowing her surprise, Clara made the introductions.

"Butter..." Harriet purred. *"I love butter."*

"Yes, well, Mr. Butters' person has hired Becca," Clara spoke up, trying to get her sisters' attention. *"And now she seems to have gone missing."*

The ginger tabby, at least, seemed to be listening, as he tipped his orange head toward Clara.

It was a strangely courtly gesture, and Clara was moved. *"Please don't worry,"* she told him. *"Our person is on the case."*

"And in the meantime, you're welcome here." Harriet stepped forward to insert herself between Clara and the newcomer. *"More than welcome."*

As she ushered the big tabby over to the food dishes, Clara turned to Laurel.

"What is going on?" The Siamese was looking over Clara's head toward the two larger cats. *"I thought you thought all other cats were simply animals."*

Laurel didn't answer, but Clara could see her ears going back.

"Such a handsome color." The big marmalade was very close to nuzzling the tabby's neck, as Laurel slowly bared her teeth. *"But what is that thing?"*

"It's a collar," Clara explained, drawing on her experience of the wider world.

"No, not that..." One big white mitt came forward, and to everyone's surprise, Mr. Butters hissed. As he did, he backed up, the fur rising along his spine.

"Oh, please!" Clara stepped between them, desperate to stop a fight. The shock of the hiss had startled Laurel out of her jealous snarl, but now both the older siblings were staring at the newcomer in horror.

"What's going on here?" Becca had put her phone down and was staring at the cats, aghast.

"Mew!" An unexpected outburst caused them all to turn. The tortie kitten, having finally finished her dinner, had plopped herself directly in front of Mr. Butters. And as she did, the blue charm that hung from the ginger tabby's collar dropped to the floor and rolled over to Becca's feet.

Mr. Butters meowed in dismay, reaching out with one pale orange paw.

"I'm sorry, kitty." Becca stroked the tabby's head even as she picked up the trinket and rolled it over in her hand. "I'm not sure how to reattach it. But I'll return this to your person tomorrow. With you, of course."

Chapter Fifteen

ats may be masterful at napping, but nobody in Becca's apartment slept well that night. Although mealtime had ended without any further disruptions, Becca knew Harriet and Laurel well enough to be concerned that hijinks—if not actual violence—might occur once she had gone to bed. As a precaution, she locked Mr. Butters in the pantry for the night, and although she had done what she could—folding up some towels for a makeshift bed and providing food, water, and a private litterbox—the ginger tabby had made his feelings known, howling as Becca shut the door.

In response, Laurel chimed in with her own distinctive Siamese-style yowl, and soon after Harriet joined in, though more in protest of all the noise than in support, Clara suspected.

The resulting cacophony had Becca on edge. "Kitties, please!" She dashed around, alternating between trying to cuddle the two older cats and silence them by holding them close. She was thinking of the downstairs neighbor, Clara could tell by the way her eyes kept darting to the door. Surely all that talk about regulating the number of pets allowed was nonsense, her pet reasoned, seeking to reassure herself and her human. And yet, from the worry that creased Becca's forehead, she couldn't be sure.

"Please calm down." Clara did her best to quiet her sisters, to no avail. In fact, Laurel used the occasion to nip at her ear.

"Know your place, Clown." She was nearly hissing. *"If we put up with such an affront, who knows what may happen next? It's a question of standards."*

"Standards!" Harriet took up the cry, throwing her head back to howl.

Becca, meanwhile, seemed to be at her wits' end.

"Where is Trina?" Even as midnight passed, Becca was checking her phone. "Do I even have the right number?" This led to a frantic search on social media, which only annoyed Harriet further.

"Unfair!" She howled, which confused Clara further.

"Why have you taken up a stranger's cause?" She should have been more polite, she knew, but she—like Becca—was growing frustrated. *"He's very nice and all, but why him when you don't even believe our kitten is a sensible creature?"*

"Mr. Butters!" Harriet cried out as if she'd never been spayed. And when Clara tried again, she turned on her baby sister with a hiss. *"He's a gentleman, silly! Even a dumb kitten could see that."*

It wasn't an answer, but Harriet's response left Clara dumbstruck.

It was the kitten, ultimately, who brought about quiet, if not exactly peace. Although the little tortie had remained hidden for much of the evening, at around one she appeared suddenly on the back of the sofa. Fearing that she was about to start knocking items off the shelves again, Clara jumped up to join her—only to end up chasing her over to the pantry door. Harriet, hoping that this would mean treats, followed, and eventually even Laurel sauntered over, taking a break from her caterwauling to observe the other felines.

"What is going on with you?" Becca was the last one into the kitchen, her face clouded by confusion.

Clara turned toward her, eager to comfort her person, even if she couldn't offer anything like an explanation. But the kitten acted first. Leaping at the pantry doorknob, she fell to the floor with a soft, awkward plop. But as Becca rushed forward to scoop her up, she began clawing furiously at the door.

"Don't do that." Clara reached down to pull the kitten back, by the scruff of her neck if necessary. But before she could grab the minuscule beast, Becca's hand was in the way and—in an unexpected move that had the other three cats gasping—the kitten raised her paw, claws out.

"No!" Clara yelped as Becca jerked back. But Becca had had enough.

"I can't deal with you guys any longer," she said, exhaustion clear in her voice. "Here." She opened the pantry door. "Work it out yourselves. I'm going to bed."

Harriet and Laurel looked at each other before turning to Clara, once Becca had retreated to her room.

"This is how you welcome a visitor," said Harriet, her voice taking on an unaccustomed gravity as the four cats gathered by the open door.

"I'm sorry," Clara mewed softly. *"And I apologize for not being more welcoming."* That last bit was directed toward the darkness of the pantry. As much as she wanted to pursue her person into the sanctuary of her bedroom, she knew she had to make things right with the ginger tabby—and her sisters—first. *"Please understand that Becca was trying to do the right thing."*

"And you couldn't convince her otherwise?" Laurel stared at her so hard she went cross-eyed, before relenting. *"But she's right, Harriet. Our person only wanted to protect us. I guess we ought to be grateful."*

At that, Clara dipped her head, thankful for her sister's intercession. When she raised it again, Mr. Butters had stuck his own orange-striped head out of the pantry.

"May I come out now?"

The simple question had the three sisters staring wide-eyed.

"I told you," said the kitten, as Clara's multicolored head swiveled between the two adult felines, her mouth open in surprise.

Chapter Sixteen

Clara knew enough to stay silent after that, as Harriet and Laurel peppered the newcomer and the kitten with questions.

"Could you always speak?" Laurel, in particular, seemed to feel the kitten had made a fool of her. *"Why didn't you let us know?"*

"I wanted to figure things out first." The tortie sat before the two older cats, her black-tipped ears erect. *"I was being cautious."*

"Of course you were." Clara nuzzled the kitten. *"But can you tell us where you came from?"*

To a human, this might have seemed like an aside. Truly, Clara wanted to learn the kitten's name, but such things are private, and to ask outright would seem rude. Besides, although they all had heard how Becca had rescued the kitten, neither she nor her pets knew anything about the kitten's origins.

"Never mind that, what's up with you—and your person?" Harriet confronted Mr. Butters. Her voice had an edge to it, which Clara attributed to her own embarrassment over her own over-the-top behavior. Still, the calico thought her sister was being a tad rude.

"We'd like to help you, if we can," she said, hoping to soften her sister's demand.

The orange tabby slumped. *"I don't know,"* he said. *"I'm scared."*

As much as she sympathized with the newcomer, Clara knew the best way to aid him was to figure out what happened. Lowering her voice further, she asked: *"Can you tell us how you came to be outside?"* Mr. Butters might be able to speak, but Clara doubted he could jump through solid barriers, as she could.

He dipped his head, as if acknowledging her assumption. *"But you can read thoughts,"* she added.

"A bit." His blue eyes took in the assembled cats. *"But I can't tell you much of what happened. There was a door open, so of course I walked through it."*

All three adult cats murmured their understanding. Walking through doors was what cats did.

"But then, when I went to go back, It was closed." The tabby shivered, his orange fur rippling, as Harriet drew back in horror.

"Closed?" Of the three sisters, she had the most trouble with solid objects. The handsome male dipped his head, his tail lashing once in confirmation.

Neither of Clara's sisters could hold a grudge then, and before long, all four adult felines were touching noses, the kitten reaching up to be included in the fur scrum.

By then, Becca had fallen into an uneasy slumber filled, if her mumbled words were any indication, with dreams of flying fur and hisses.

"Well, this is a nice surprise." She woke to find all five felines on the bed. And even though this made exiting it a challenge—Becca knew better than to disturb a sleeping cat—she glowed with happiness as she snuck into the kitchen, Clara at her heels.

"Are you looking for a little attention?" Becca bent down to rub the base of Clara's ears.

"Oh, yes, please!" Her involuntary purr wasn't what she intended, but it was hard to resist the gentle pressure. Only, just as her eyes were closing with the pleasure, the petting was interrupted.

"Do you want some attention too?" Becca had turned toward the counter where the kitten had just landed.

"Get down!" Clara hissed. Jumping on the counter was against all the rules.

"Now, Clara, that's not nice," Becca reprimanded her, and she hung her head—only to hear the soft "ping" of something hitting the floor. The bead from Mr. Butters' collar, she saw. The kitten had knocked it down, and Becca bent to pick it up, reaching it just as Laurel was readying to bat the small blue globe,

"Bother!" Laurel sat back, her ears flat with irritation.

"Bother," Becca echoed, unaware of the peeved cat at her feet. Holding the bead in one hand, the human squatted, even as first Laurel and then Harriet circled longingly. To their frustration, she closed her hand around the bead and got down on one knee to examine the floor more closely. As the cats continued to circle, she stuck out a finger, gently dabbing at a touch of color before her. A flake of paint, Clara realized. "Well, Trina said it was a flea market find," Becca said as she got to her feet.

With that, she reached for her phone. Skimming through her messages, she shook her head. "Nothing," she murmured, even as she thumbed in a number.

"Morning, Maddy." Her voice betrayed no hint of the fatigue that shadowed her eyes. "Yes, all's well here in the cattery. Surprisingly peaceful, in fact. I'm off to work, but when I take my break, I'm going back to the police station. Trina hasn't responded to any of my calls or texts, and she's not posting anywhere either. Something is definitely wrong."

Maddy clearly had her own thoughts on this, and Becca stayed on the phone, nodding. As her friend spoke, she picked up the blue bead again, rolling it between her fingers while the ginger tabby watched, the longing clear in his round blue eyes.

"She feels bad about chipping it." Clara, watching them both, felt the need to translate for the visitor. Beside her, the kitten mewed, though whether in agreement or dismay at having her new toy removed, Clara couldn't tell. The little tortie had proved herself brighter than either of her sisters suspected, but Clara didn't know if she was up on how humans—at least, *her* human—thought.

"It's more than that." The little face glanced up to her. Thanks to her unusual tortoiseshell markings—black, brown, and gold mixed hodgepodge around her wide green eyes—the kitten was hard for Clara to read.

"She's trying to be helpful," the calico told herself.

"Trying to make herself important." Laurel's voice rang loud in her head, reminding Clara of her sister's facility in reading her thoughts.

"No, silly." The kitten lashed her tail. *"That's wrong."*

Clara gasped. Laurel took herself very seriously, though neither she nor

Harriet would take being called "silly" lightly. But before fur could start to fly, a faint mew drew all their attention. Mr. Butters had one paw raised, as if he were about to reach for Becca's leg.

"Mine," he said.

Becca, however, was too focused on the object in her hand to notice the tabby's entreaty. Holding it close to her face, she poked at the blue bead and gasped.

"This is not—wait a minute, Maddy." Rushing past the cats and nearly knocking Mr. Butters over in the process, she ran to the lamp in the living room that illuminated her favorite reading chair. "Can it be?" As Clara, flanked by her sisters, tagged after her, she saw that Becca was turning the bead over in her hand and staring intently at the spot that had chipped. To Clara's amazement, she then started chipping more of the blue paint away, pulling as gently as a mother cat grooming her kittens. Before long, Clara could see the entire blue surface had fallen away to reveal a sparkling, multifaceted surface.

"What's that?" Clara looked up, stunned.

"It's our toy." Laurel appeared unmoved. *"Now, if only Becca would drop it, we could have some fun."*

"Sorry, Maddy. I just made the most amazing discovery." During the pause that followed, Becca turned the glittering globe over in her hand. "The bead on the orange tabby's color? The blue paint was covering up something—a blue stone, I think. Blue like a sapphire. And Maddy? I think it's real."

Chapter Seventeen

Much to her cats' dismay, Becca did not put the blue stone away when she got off the phone. Instead, she placed it on the table in front of her as she opened her laptop.

"Can you grab it?" Harriet turned to the lithe Laurel, a glint in her gold eyes.

"Maybe if I yowl, Clown here could." The seal point took in a deep breath in preparation.

"Why don't we let Becca continue with whatever she is doing?" Clara pushed in, trying to mediate. But Mr. Butters, the orange tabby, had already jumped up on the table and was slowly moving in on the sparkling stone.

"It is mine, you know," he said, moving closer. *"I hate to be rude, but my person did give it to me."*

That shut Harriet and Laurel up, as they gazed instead at the handsome stranger.

"Do you think she knew what it was?" Clara watched as the tabby settled by the laptop, seemingly happy to stare at the pretty thing.

"It's pretty, and it's round. Look!" With one paw, Mr. Butters gently batted at the stone, prompting Becca to glance up.

"I'm sorry, kitty. I don't think this is your usual cat toy," she said, stroking the tabby's back. "But I do think the police will want to know about this."

With that, she pocketed the charm and moved toward the door, where she'd dropped her jacket and bag the night before.

"But it's mine." Mr. Butters jumped off the table to follow her.

"Ours," Harriet corrected him. *"It came to our house."*

"We can share it," added Laurel, surprising Clara, who turned and stared at her sister. *"What?"* Laurel responded. *"We've shared other toys in this house."*

Clara could only dip her head, but even as she did, she caught the trace of a thought. Laurel, using her powers of suggestion, was trying to convince Becca that the pretty blue stone wasn't important. In fact, it was so unimportant that she might as well forget about it. In response, Clara glared at her sister.

"Isn't it better that she not be bothered?" Laurel's whiskers perked up in the feline equivalent of a smirk. *"I thought you liked it when she didn't worry so much."*

"I could summon another version of it." Harriet was lashing her tail as Becca donned her jacket, her gold eyes fixed on Becca's pocket. *"I'll summon one, and you three could trip her. Then we could get the real one all for ourselves. She wouldn't know the difference."*

"She would eventually." Clara tried to soften her words. She well knew that Harriet's powers worked best when they had something to form around, and that once she was far from the apartment Becca was likely to reach into her pocket for the gem-encrusted bauble and find only lint…or a well-licked cat treat.

"But it's mine." Mr. Butters was wrapping himself around Becca's shins, gazing up at her with longing. If he could have reached up to her pocket, he would have, Clara sensed. That bead, or whatever it was, was important to him. And that's when the full force of it hit her—the charm had been hung around his neck by Trina, Mr. Butters' human. The woman whom Becca had been unable to locate.

"You miss your person, don't you?" Clara sidled up to the tabby. *"It's been days now."*

"I do." Mr. Butters sat, his head hanging low. The change from covetous kitty to downcast pet was so sudden that both Harriet and Laurel stopped their machinations and moved closer to the forlorn tabby. *"Trina took me from the shelter. She gave me a forever home. You've been welcoming to me, but I miss her terribly."*

"Well, there you go." Clara brushed up against the orange tabby's striped

side to comfort him. *"We have to let Becca take the charm with her—the real one and not a copy. She's looking for Mr. Butters' person, and that thing might hold the key."*

"What are you waiting for then?" Laurel's question startled Clara, who had expected pushback—especially from the strong-willed Siamese. *"Go!"*

What Clara had failed to notice was that Becca had already left the apartment, after placing both the charm and her laptop computer into the oversized messenger bag she carried everywhere. Looking around, she realized that four sets of eyes were focused on her—and that Mr. Butters' blue eyes were particularly bright. And so, with a shake of her hindquarters to give her upcoming jump a little extra oomph, she leapt, clearing the door and finding herself halfway down the stairs before either of her sisters could say more.

Chapter Eighteen

Racing down the street, Clara was relieved to see her person only a short stretch ahead of her. She was less pleased to see why: Deborah Miles, the downstairs neighbor, had apparently buttonholed Becca. From Becca's stance—back stiff and shoulders creeping up to her ears—Clara could tell that the conversation wasn't going well. In response, her own back arched up as she inched forward, ready to defend her person. Despite their brief truce, their neighbor at heart was virulently anti-cat, and Clara didn't dare risk even the slightest scent or tuft of fur setting her off.

"I've been reading the bylaws." The taller woman had a sharp voice that made Clara think of a little dog's yelp. "And they're quite clear: Owners have the right to add restrictions that pertain to quality of life."

"And how," Becca asked, the slight tremor in her voice clearly audible to her pet, "are my cats affecting your quality of life?"

The other woman scrunched up her lips and huffed as if she were about to hack up a furball. "I would think it was obvious. Cleanliness, health issues—"

"I'm clean. My cats are clean," Becca cut her off. "And my apartment is spotless." She sounded a little less forceful on that one, but to Clara's delight, she kept going. "And you seem to be in perfect health."

"My breathing…" The other woman splayed her perfectly manicured fingers over her chest.

"And as an owner, I have rights, too," Becca concluded. "And I also have a job. Goodbye."

"This isn't over," Deborah called. But Becca had already stormed off.

"That woman…" Becca was grumbling to herself as she rounded the corner.

"You'd think she'd already forgotten what my cats had done for her."

Clara, trotting beside her, started purring. Although Becca was under the misapprehension that she was the one with magical powers, it sounded like she did at least recognize her felines' contribution to the cases she had solved. For the calico at her side, this felt as good as a chin scratch, and it was with her tail held high that she continued along her person's side as they took the familiar route to Charm and Cherish.

"No Elizabeth." Becca sounded slightly downcast as she unlocked the shop's door and looked around. "Well, she's not due in today," she continued, as she went into the back to retrieve the small tray of gemstones that usually sat by the counter. After settling these into place and giving a quick polish to the crystal ball that now held pride of place on the front table, she flipped the glitter-bedecked sign that read "Closed" to "Open," and took her place by the register.

She needn't have rushed. Although pedestrians were flooding the sidewalk again, enjoying what promised to be a warm but pleasingly breezy summer day, none seemed interested in coming into the little shop. For Clara, that was a plus. With nothing to monitor, she curled up right by that crystal ball for a midmorning nap. But as Becca started fussing with the window display, she woke and stretched. Her person, she could tell, was bothered. Unfortunately, drawing in customers was beyond even Harriet's powers.

"Maybe if I prop the door open…" Becca hefted a heavy statue over toward the door and then appeared to think better of it. "That might not be great for the Buddha," she said, carrying the stout figurine back to his shelf, where he dislodged a fluff of dust.

That set off a flurry of cleaning that sent Clara scurrying to the back. When she returned, Becca appeared to be done. At any rate, she had slumped against the wall behind the register, a look of exhaustion making even her curls look limp.

As if she could sense her invisible pet's concern, she soon roused herself, returning the dust cloth and the hideous blue spray bottle to the back room. When she returned, she pushed the tray of gemstones closer to the register and pulled her laptop from her bag.

"Image search." The words meant nothing to her cat. But once she jumped silently to the top of the register, Clara could see pictures appearing on the laptop screen. Shapes of various colors, some of which Becca examined more closely. Others of which she quickly dismissed.

After a few minutes—and an increasing number of those discards—Becca reached into her bag for the blue stone. Turning it over in her hand a few times, she placed it by the computer and began to type again. This turned up a few more images, which Becca clicked on.

It was tedious work for the cat watching her, especially since the images that appeared on the screen had no scent to make them interesting, and Clara could feel her eyes beginning to close. Curling her tail close, she let herself drift off into that dream space cats know so well. The warmth of the little shop, heated by the noonday sun, helped transport her to Egypt, where a young woman, a servant of the temple, was kneeling in front of a slender tawny feline.

"You and all your descendants have been favored," the young woman was saying, the bleached white linen of her gown setting off her dark skin. *"Bast has seen your service."*

"All of my descendants?" The tawny cat said, as the woman kneeling before her nodded.

"She can understand her!" Even in her dream state, the thought sent a shiver through Clara's fur. *"I wonder—"*

A sudden gasp interrupted her train of thought. Waking, she blinked up to see Becca staring, eyes wide, at the computer screen. Clara couldn't figure out why: The image on the screen was simply another version of the blue stone she had propped on the edge of the jewel tray. But Becca was transfixed. She didn't even look away as she fumbled for her phone.

"Maddy? Call me back. I think I may have found what all this is about."

Becca was still staring at her phone, as if contemplating another call, when the bells over the entrance of the shop rang out. Startled out of her train of thought, Becca glanced up—and just as quickly flicked the blue stone into the tray of gemstones, burying it under a stack of garnets, labeled as protective charms that were also useful in love.

"Blessed be. May I help you?" Clara thought her person's smile seemed a bit forced, and as her person turned to take in the newcomer, she wondered why.

"Blessed be." The newcomer, a thin woman whose long, lank blonde hair did her gaunt features no favors, returned the smile. "I'm looking for charms."

"I'm sure we can help you there." With something to focus on, Becca relaxed. "When you say 'charms,' do you mean spells for protection or some other purpose?"

"I meant, you know, something I could wear." The blonde tilted her head, tossing her hair back. "You know, like on a necklace."

"Oh." Becca took this in. "We do have some nice pieces of jewelry. Some by local artisans." Coming out from behind the register, she led the blonde over to a small display on the front table, and Clara looked on with interest. One medallion, in the shape of a dragon, had long intrigued her. Something about the milky stone at its center, she thought, though in truth it could simply have been the way the dragon's tail hung, dangling in a tantalizing way past the bottom of the display's velvet backing.

"Would any of these be of interest?"

"No, no thanks." The blonde's smile faded even as her eyes narrowed. "I guess I was looking for something more colorful."

"We do have some stones—mostly semiprecious gems—that may have various powers," said Becca slowly, a questioning expression on her face. "But they're not set, so you'd have to take them to a jeweler. Or create a setting yourself, of course."

"No, that doesn't sound right." The other woman shook her head. "I'm looking for something painted. Something blue."

"I see," Becca said, standing straighter. As if on alert, her cat thought. "I don't think we have anything like that."

"Are you sure?" The blonde stepped forward, her smile fading, and Becca backed up. Clara didn't think the move was necessarily conscious. Nevertheless, when she felt the counter behind her, Becca's hands went up to grasp the edge of the gemstone tray.

"Positively." Despite her defensive posture, Becca once again smiled. Or, thought Clara, showed her teeth. "I'm sure."

For a moment, the other woman didn't respond, a questioning look screwing up her brows and accentuating the frown lines framing her mouth. Clara held her breath. Beside her, she could feel Becca stiffen as well.

"Well, if you don't, you don't." The blonde tossed one hand in the air as if to dispel her earlier threatening behavior. "I did what I could," she said, and sauntered out the door.

"*I did what I could?*" Becca repeated, shaking her head. "What does that mean?"

Clara wished she could brainstorm with her. Not that she understood what the other woman—the intruder, as she thought of her—meant. But there had been something off about the blonde. Some scent or tone of voice that made the calico's fur bristle, and she was relieved that the woman had left.

Or had she? The question rose in her mind, prompting her to leap over to the front window. Sure enough, the blonde was still there, in front of the apartment entrance next door. For a moment, Clara was tempted to duck back down, worried that the stranger could see her. But the woman wasn't looking back at Charm and Cherish, she realized. Instead, she was peering down Mass Ave, as if waiting for a bus.

Or a ride, it hit Clara. Sure enough, within minutes, a car had driven up to the curb. A black sedan like the one she had spotted tailing Becca. Tail lashing, the calico looked on, expecting the blonde to get into the car and be driven away. Instead, she watched as the window came down and the blonde leaned forward, reaching inside. When she withdrew, she held an envelope in her hand, and as the car drove away, she opened it, her haggard face breaking into a real grin for the first time.

"Maddy, you wouldn't believe what's been happening." Back in the shop, Becca had apparently gotten hold of her friend. "I don't know if you got my message, but I found something in the charm. You know, the one with the cat's eye painted on it? The blue globe that hung from Mr. Butters' necklace?"

After a pause, during which she rolled her eyes, she continued. "Mr. Butters is Trina's cat. The creamsicle-colored tabby? Anyway, the reason I was sure he was Trina's cat was because Trina had described the charm on his collar: a blue globe with a cat's eye painted on it. Trina told me she got it at a flea market. I mean, I have no reason not to believe her. But it's not what she thinks it is, Maddy. It fell off Mr. Butters' collar this morning and chipped, and I realized that the paint was covering up something underneath, so I scraped the rest of the paint off."

Another pause, and Becca sighed.

"Yes, I know. But it started as an accident, and when I saw something glittering underneath, I couldn't resist. The center was covered with a bit of clay to smooth it out and painted over. I chipped off the paint and covering, and it looks like some kind of jewel—a big blue stone, cut so it catches the light and really stunning. Anyway, I started doing some research. I'm at work, but it's slow as molasses—or it was, until a moment ago. And I found out that a piece that looks just like this was stolen from the Fallenburg Museum several years ago.

"It's never been recovered, Maddy. I think this is the jewel, and someone disguised it and then lost it somehow."

Becca looked quite pleased to take a break then, and Clara could hear Maddy's voice rising as she responded.

"No, no suspects. One guard was questioned—and fired soon after—but there weren't any charges filed.

"And, yes, I promise, Maddy, I'm going to go to the police. As soon as I close. But it's getting weirder," Clara's person continued. "A strange woman just came into the shop, and, for the life of me, I think she was looking for the charm."

Chapter Nineteen

Clara was so relieved that Becca had also suspected that supposed customer of something nefarious that she almost fell back asleep. When she realized that her human was going to stay in the shop, alone, until closing, however, the calico realized that she'd better not. Becca might be aware that there was one person out there who had some knowledge of the charm's hidden treasure. She had no idea that the woman was working with others, though, and Clara had no way of alerting her to the black sedan that had followed her and, more recently, apparently paid the haggard blonde who had come in to inquire about the charm.

Maddy was also not happy with Becca's decision. To Clara's sharp ears, Maddy's contention that Becca should go immediately to the police sounded quite reasonable. But even as her friend's pleas ramped up in both tone and volume, prompting Clara to flatten her ears back, Becca stood firm. Literally, as she straightened her shoulders. Breathing deeply in a way that calmed her voice, she explained to her friend that she had an obligation to the shop to keep it open and that she was quite convinced that reporting the charm at the end of the day would be soon enough.

"Besides," she concluded, "maybe I'll hear back from Trina by then, and she'll be able to explain everything. But if not…well, Maddy, then I do fear that she's been kidnapped. And I think that sapphire might be why."

Even with her velvet ears lying flat against her head, Clara heard the sigh that followed. Maddy knew Becca almost as well as her cats did. That meant she knew when her friend wasn't going to be moved. But while Maddy was limited by the fact that she was a human, with a job and without any feline magical powers, Clara had options.

The first, obviously, was to stand guard. Shaking off the last bit of her midday nap, the determined little cat took up a pose in the front window. Standing at attention to make sure the urge to snooze wouldn't creep up on her, she surveyed the street in front of her. She wasn't entirely sure what she would do if that black car appeared again. Or that skinny woman, for that matter. That she would do something—anything necessary—was not even a question.

The second was a long shot. Clara was learning more about her sisters' powers—and her own—every day. Recently, she had found that even at a distance, both Laurel and Harriet could often "hear" her thoughts. Sometimes, they—particularly Laurel—could respond. And so now she reached out to her sisters with her mind, carefully summarizing what had happened with the strange lady and what she had seen of the car. Closing her eyes briefly, she visualized both the woman and the vehicle, the better to prepare her sisters should either appear in or near the apartment they all shared.

While she waited for a response, she continued scanning the scene outside. More pedestrians passed by as the day wore on, a tribute no doubt to the warm sun and blue sky that had replaced the rain of the previous days. Most walked by the magic shop's colorful display without a glance, but one or two did look in, either with a smile or the raised brows that signified interest in humans. That cheered Clara. Her sisters might not hold with Becca having a job, no matter that Clara had tried time and again to explain economics and that Becca's job meant the better-quality cans of food that Harriet in particular insisted on were always stocked in the cabinet. The little calico, however, knew that not only did their family need the income, but that Becca got something emotional from her job as well.

That thought prompted the devoted feline to try again, pitching her ears forward as she concentrated on both her sisters, picturing them in her plea for help.

So intent was Clara on reaching out to her sisters that she nearly missed what was happening in the store behind her. With half an ear, she caught that Becca was trying Trina again, even though something she said about a mailbox being full seemed to frustrate her ever further. Staring out at the street, she didn't realize that Becca had retrieved her laptop and opened it until she heard Becca begin to speak softly to herself.

"Dear Mr. Hallowell," she was saying as her fingers tapped gently on the keys. "As the curator of the Fallenburg Museum, you should know that I believe I have, by accident, come upon what might be the Cat's Eye Sapphire, which I gather was stolen more than a year ago. I am attaching a photo for confirmation. Would you contact me?" Becca fell silent as she typed a bit more, ending with the familiar "whoosh" sound that told Clara she was done with her missive.

But if Becca was expecting an immediate answer, she was destined to be disappointed. Even as she went about tidying and rearranging the statuary and candles on display, she kept running back to check the program on her open computer. Each time, she came away with a sigh and returned to her cleaning. The candles tended to attract dust. Finally, after perhaps an hour had passed, she picked up her phone instead.

"May I have the number for the Fallenburg Museum?" To Clara's surprise, the device must have responded because a half a minute later, Becca was talking to a person. "Mr. Hallowell? Oh, excuse me, Dr. Hallowell," she said. "He's not in today? Do you know if he picks up his messages? Okay, thanks. No, I don't think there's anyone else I should speak with. If he calls in, would you ask him to check his email? It's important."

From the look on her face, a kind of scrunched up expression, Becca hadn't been satisfied by her outreach, a conclusion seconded as Becca continued to talk to herself. "I could have asked if he had an assistant or an associate curator or something. But this just seemed like it should go straight to the top. Besides, Hallowell is quoted in all the news stories about the robbery.

"Someone has to know something, though." She stopped, looking around Charm and Cherish as if remembering that last visitor. "Maybe I can smoke them out."

As Becca began to click away again, Clara was intrigued. Perched on the shelf nearest to where Becca had the laptop open, she saw what looked like the front window of the little shop itself. Of course, she could have nipped herself for forgetting the obvious. Becca had been doing some online teaching for Charm and Cherish, what Becca called the "virtual" store. Though the little cat could see no virtue in it, she did understand the basics: that the store where she now sat at attention had a tiny version of itself, stuck in Becca's machine.

That online version couldn't hold much, she reasoned. Still, it seemed to have something Becca wanted, because as the calico looked on, she saw the picture before her vanish as, with a few more taps, another scene appeared, showing a close-up of the bulletin board behind Becca's register.

"'Lost and found,'" Becca murmured to herself. "Or should I put it under 'announcements'?"

Clara couldn't read, but Becca liked talking to herself, so she soon heard that her person had reached a compromise. "I'll label it 'Found,'" she said, and continued to type.

"One adult male ginger tabby, white belly with pale gold stripes, on River Street in Cambridgeport," she narrated. Clara could only wonder how humans focused on the visual, but then Becca surprised her. "Answers to Mr. Butters, this handsome kitty is clearly missing his person, and I'd be happy to bring him to you. He still has his collar on, with a pretty blue charm, but no ID tag. If you recognize this description, please get in touch."

Whether it was the notice or simply the time of day, Charm and Cherish soon grew a little busier. Two teens came in, dressed all in black, and asked about introductions to witchcraft. Becca showed the young women to the second bookcase, which housed several books on the craft, and also told them about her online course. "We're pretty hands-on," she said to the shorter one, who had been nodding along. "And I always take questions at the end of the class. That is, if you attend live. You'd need more power than I have to get through in the archived version."

This prompted a chuckle, and Becca laughed along.

"That sounds great," said the shorter one. "I'm definitely going to sign up. I'm Roe, by the way. This is Greta." She elbowed her companion.

"Lovely to meet you both. I'm Becca." With that, she paused. But the two didn't seem to recognize her. They did, however, buy two books. "You start with that one, and we'll trade," Roe said as they checked out.

"That sounds sensible." Becca sent them off with a smile. "Blessed be."

"Blessed be," the taller of the two—Greta—parroted back, a grin as wide as a jack o' lantern on her sweet young face.

Soon after, a man in his forties appeared, and Clara could feel her person tense up. Could this be the driver of the black car? But he only inquired about the small Bast statuette in the front window and, after some hemming and hawing, bought it.

"He paid with his card," Becca said to herself, once she had carefully wrapped the cat goddess and sent it off with the customer. "If he was involved in something nefarious, he'd have paid cash."

After he left, the store fell quiet again, and as Clara looked on, Becca reached for her phone. But from the way she shook her head and sighed, her pet could tell nothing had come in—from the museum or Trina. Just as she seemed about to make another call, the bells over the front door chimed, and both cat and human looked up to see two figures, one tall and dark, the other short and pale, the brim of a Red Sox hat shading her freckled face.

"Ande, Marcia!" Becca beamed at her coven mates. "Welcome. What brings you to Charm and Cherish?"

"We can't just drop in to say hi?" Marcia pushed her cap back to reveal the rose of a fresh sunburn. "But seriously, Luz and I were about to head out for the Cape when Ande called."

"I saw the notice on the Charm and Cherish board." The tall woman's voice, already deep, rang with concern. "I know we just had a circle, but it sounds like you've gotten yourself involved in something serious."

"You could tell from my listing?" Becca cocked her head. "Did you get a feeling off it?"

"It wasn't anything magical," Ande replied with a shake of her head. "It was your wording. You were signaling. There's something about that charm, isn't there?"

Becca nodded. "It's not what it, at first, appears to be. But there's more." As quickly as she could, she filled her friends in on what had happened since

Trina's first appearance in the shop. "So, I have the cat, Mr. Butters, at my place, and this morning the charm dropped off his collar." Becca paused there, a curious, faraway expression on her face. *"She's wondering* why *it dropped off,"* Clara realized.

"Anyway, it chipped when it hit the floor, and when I picked it up, I saw something sparkle. And I realized that the blue was just a thin layer of clay and paint. Underneath was what looks like a real jewel—a blue one—cut like it belongs in a ring or a pendant. I did an image search, and I'm pretty sure it's the Cat's Eye Sapphire, which was stolen from the Fallenburg Museum a few years ago. There's all sorts of legends tied in with it, too, going back all the way to when it was first unearthed, and the disguise even fits in with that—a blue ball with a cat's eye painted on it. The only question is: How did it end up in a flea market? Unless Trina wasn't telling me the truth about where she got it."

"Do you think she was involved in the original robbery?"

Becca paused to think. "No, I don't think so. She was too casual about the charm, for starters. She only talked about it as a way to identify her cat, and she really did seem much more concerned about Mr. Butters. But now she's gone missing—or, at any rate, I can't get in touch with her. I think somebody is trying to track down the charm, and they think Trina's either got it or knows where it is."

"Okay, you've got to go to the police with this." Ande's dark eyes bored into Becca's, while Marcia nodded enthusiastically. "Definitely," she agreed.

"I'm going to as soon as I close the shop for the day."

Ande took a breath, undoubtedly about to argue for an earlier departure when Becca's phone pinged.

"Hello?"

"Hey, sweetie! How are you doing?"

Becca beamed, turning away from her friends. "Hi, Jerry. Nice to hear your voice."

"I know. I'm sorry," her beau replied. "It's been crazy. I just attended a fascinating panel on feline DNA. Did you know they can trace a cat's lineage back almost indefinitely?"

"I didn't, and I want to hear all about it." Becca glanced back over her shoulder. "But now I'm kind of busy. Talk later?"

"Of course. And I'll be home soon."

"That was Jerry." Becca's cheeks had pinked up.

"Figured," said Ande. "But as we were saying—"

She was interrupted by another ping, and Becca clicked through without a glance.

"Jerry?" Becca asked and then drew a sharp breath. While her friends looked on, Clara could clearly hear a male voice asking about the cat—and its charm.

Becca frowned and shook her head. "I'm sorry, is Trina there?"

"Trina is fine, but she misses her cat."

"And can she come and pick her up?" Becca held the phone away from her ear as her friends leaned in to listen to a deep male voice. Too deep, Clara thought. The caller was trying to disguise his voice.

"Trina can't leave here just yet. She wants to see you—and her cat. If you want to see her, you should come to her."

"Is she back in her apartment?" Becca, Clara noticed, was careful not to give the other woman's address. There was, she knew, the possibility that the caller was bluffing about having Trina.

"Not yet. But you can make that happen."

"Okay, I'm game." Ande was shaking her head, mouthing the word "No." But Becca waved her off as she kept talking. "Who are you, and how can I reach you when I've picked up the cat?"

"So, you don't have the cat with you?"

"You should know that. You sent that woman in, didn't you?"

Silence, and Clara could tell from the worried furrow that had appeared between her brows that she feared she had said too much.

"Get the cat. And the charm." As the man began speaking again, Becca let out the breath she'd been holding. "Be at the Hatch Shell at seven," he said, naming the graceful vaulting bandstand that had pride of place on the Charles River Esplanade.

"Will Trina be there?" But the man had hung up.

"Quick, let me do a search." Ande reached for the phone, and Becca handed it over. Ande's technical expertise was a given among the coven members.

"Are you going to go?" Marcia's red face grew visibly paler with worry. "Shouldn't you call the police—or go to them first?"

"There's no time." While Ande worked on her phone, Becca glanced up at the clock on the wall. "I have to get back to my apartment to get Trina's cat."

"And the charm. Don't forget." Marcia's voice betrayed her growing concern. "Or, well, the sapphire."

"I'm wondering—" Becca glanced over at the tray of semiprecious stones where the jewel lay hidden.

"Bother," Ande broke in before Becca could explain, handing the phone back as she shook her head. "Whoever he is, he's good. He blocked his number, and I couldn't call anything up."

"Maybe it doesn't matter," Becca said, her mouth setting in a firm line that Clara knew only too well. "I'm going to meet him. It sounds like he has Trina, and that's the only way I can think of to get her back."

"Marcia's right," Ande looked skeptical. "You can call the police."

"And tell them what? They didn't even believe she'd been taken," said Becca. Her friends both turned to her then, the question clear on their faces. But Becca had already turned the front door sign to "Closed." When she returned, she grabbed the gem tray. "I was meaning to tell you." She set it down and fished around among the blue tourmalines, pulling out one stone that shone brighter than the rest.

"The Cat's Eye Sapphire," she said, as her friends looked on in awe.

Chapter Twenty

"That's…something." Marcia stared wide-eyed at the gem, which sparkled with blue fire in the light.

"It's stolen property. That's what it is." Ande, always practical, seemed a little less impressed. "We should turn this over to the police immediately."

"I know, and I will." Becca nodded in agreement. "But I can't. Not right away."

"What part of 'immediately' are you not getting?" Ande's tone had an edge that had Clara staring up at the tall, dark woman.

"There's a whole question about my detecting that I can't get into right now, Ande." Becca sighed. "I will go to the police. I promise. But that call I just had? I've got to show up with the jewel—and with Mr. Butters."

"Mr. Butters?" Marcia chimed in.

"Trina's cat," Becca explained. "I suspect that whoever has Trina doesn't know that I know about the sapphire. They're expecting me to show up with a cat with a blue charm hanging from its collar. He won't have the charm, but maybe they won't notice at first—and I can always tell them the truth: that the charm dropped off."

"But won't they expect you to have brought it along?" Marcia looked worried.

"Not if they think this is all about the cat for me."

"You are going to bring the sapphire, though. Aren't you?" Ande's question sounded more like a command. "To bring to the police after?"

"I don't know." Becca looked down at the gem. "It might be safer here."

"Becca?" Ande wasn't taking no for an answer.

"I hear you." Becca reached into the tray. "And now I've really got to go. I've just got time to pick up Mr. Butters and get to the Hatch Shell."

"I'll drive." Marcia fished in her bag for her keys. "The Blue Bomb is at your service."

"But—"

"Don't even try, Becca." Ande was already pulling her jacket back on. "We're coming with you."

* * *

Becca did try to argue as she locked up the shop and walked with her friends to Marcia's rust-marked blue Toyota, Clara trotting along behind. Climbing into the back, in deference to Ande's long legs, Becca pointed out the obvious problems with their plan.

"For starters, they said I should come alone." She was leaning forward between the seats of the beater, oblivious to the shaded calico trying to balance on the seat beside her. "And, besides, there's no place to park by the Hatch Shell."

"We'll figure it out." Ande sounded determined. "We are not letting you go there alone."

Even as she hung on with her claws, Clara started purring. With friends like these, Becca would be okay. Especially, she thought, as Becca's building came into view, with her pets in league to help her.

As Marcia backed into a space a little too close to the corner, Clara leaped out of the car and raced up the stairs, anxious to fill her siblings in on the latest development.

"Becca got a call," she said as soon as she was through the door. *"Someone is holding Mr. Butters' person. She's got to bring Mr. Butters to them in order to get her back."*

"I don't like the sound of that." Laurel, who had come to greet her sister, sat suddenly, her ears going out flat to the sides. *"Why does Becca have to go?"*

"Why does she ever have to go anywhere?" Harriet had clearly just woken

from a nap. As she stretched, she yawned, showing her white fangs. *"She should just stay home."*

Clara worked to keep her own tail from lashing. Her sisters could be so frustrating at times. *"She wants to help Mr. Butters—and Trina,"* she added.

"If there's anything I can do for my person, I need to do it." The ginger tabby joined the sisters, the tortie kitten in tow.

"We could all help," the kitten added, looking up at the older cats. *"From here, I mean. Using our powers."*

"Our powers?" Clara could feel Laurel start to bristle at the kitten's presumption and thought quickly to cut her off.

"She's working for all of us. She wants us all to be safe in our homes," she improvised. But a stray thought was tickling her, almost as if a gentle touch was flicking the fur that extended from her ears. She turned to the tortie. *"What did you mean, we could all help?"*

"Just..." The kitten shook her fur, the feline equivalent of a shrug. *"We could work together. Maybe try to figure out what is going on."*

Clara was intrigued. This, after all, was what she'd been thinking at the shop earlier that day. But now wasn't the time to improvise. *"I think it's too late for that. Becca is about to come through the door."*

Already, the sharp ears of the felines could hear their person running up the stairs. On the floor below, she paused momentarily. Clara could have told her that their annoying neighbor was not home, but by then, Becca was at the door.

"Kitties." Despite the tension in her voice, she greeted the assembled felines with a smile. "I'm afraid I'm just here for a few minutes. Where's—" She looked over to where Mr. Butters sat, on the back of the sofa, posing as if he didn't have a care in the world. Reaching out to stroke him on her way to the pantry, Becca paused. "I hope this works, Mr. Butters."

"We trust you." The ginger tabby looked up at her and blinked, the vote of confidence Becca needed as she went to fetch the carrier.

"Hey, that's mine." Harriet bristled, the hint of a growl in her voice.

"I thought you hated that thing." Laurel's mew held a hint of insinuation. *"The vet and all."*

"I do, but..." As Clara looked on, Harriet hung her head. The cats had recently come around on their vet, in part because of his fondness for Becca. *"I guess it's for the best."*

"She'll bring it back," Clara promised, hoping she was telling the truth. *"I'll go with her to make sure."*

"Here we go." Mr. Butters didn't resist as Becca lifted him into the plastic case, instead hanging limp as Becca tucked his legs inside. "What a gentleman you are."

Harriet nudged Clara at that, giving her a significant look. *"She knows he's a gentleman."*

"She does." Clara resisted the urge to point out that Mr. Butters didn't struggle while being put in the plastic case, unlike Harriet. Instead, she looked over at the tortie. *"So, do you think we can do something together?"*

But the younger cat didn't respond and simply sat, staring at the carrier as Becca snapped it shut and headed out the door.

Chapter Twenty-One

The three human friends didn't seem to have any more idea of a plan than Clara did. As Becca raced back to Marcia's car, Ande stepped out to let her in. "You should take the front seat," she said, folding herself into the back. "That way you can get out quickly, before anyone sees you."

"I could be taking a ride service," Becca posited, as Ande rolled her eyes. But the taller woman did get back into the front of the little car.

"Where to, ma'am?" Marcia tried to keep things light as she pulled away. "Seriously, where should I drop you?"

"I'm thinking I should get off across from the Esplanade," Becca spoke slowly, as if visualizing a plan. "Then maybe you could come around and pull in behind the Shell."

"I think that's for park personnel only," Ande chimed in. "And the police."

"Works for me," said Marcia, pulling her Sox cap lower over her eyes. "I'll keep the engine running. Just let them try to catch me."

The friends fell silent after that, as Marcia crossed the river and doubled back, melding into the heavy traffic along the Storrow Drive as it ran along the Charles River, when the bandstand came into sight—along with a horde of pedestrians.

"Looks like everyone and their sister is clearing out." Marcia slowed as a daring party raced across the road.

"Fire on the waterfront?" Becca was joking, but a certain tightness in her voice betrayed the anxiety beneath. "Shark in the Charles?"

"Storm, more likely." Ande tilted her head to gaze up at the sky. "I think we're going to get soaked."

"Great." All the air seemed to go out of Becca. "I was hoping there would be a crowd, for safety's sake."

"It's not too late to call this off." Ande leaned forward again. Beside her, Mr. Butters shifted in his carrier. "We can go to the cops instead."

"She's not going to go." The ginger tabby murmured to Clara, who, unbeknownst to the humans in the car, sat right beside the carrier. *"She's going to give up."*

"No, she's not," Clara mewed softly, butting her head gently against the plastic carrier. *"Becca's not like that. Don't lose hope."*

"I think this cat senses the storm coming," said Ande, reaching over to the carrier as if to comfort the feline inside. "I hope he doesn't get car sick."

"We're almost there." Marcia craned to check her rearview. "I think I can pull up here," she said. And with a bump, the blue car was up on the curb.

"This is not legal." Becca's eyes had gone wide.

"No, but it works." Marcia flashed a smile at her friend. "Now, go! I promise, we won't be far behind."

With a swift nod, Becca wrapped her arms around the cat carrier and let herself out onto the grassy edge of the Esplanade. Marcia had pulled up far enough that Becca was out of sight of the arching bandstand, a small grove of broad-leafed trees shielding her from the concert area. Usually, Becca knew, these trees would provide a welcome bit of shade, a cool area that ran from Storrow Drive to the edge of the river, a few even flanking the Hatch Shell.

Now, however, the trees' broad shadows were swallowed up by the growing darkness as dense storm clouds gathered overhead. Already, the air was growing cooler, and Clara's acute nose picked up the scent of the oncoming rain. As she followed her person over to the bike path, Clara stayed close. It wasn't just the looming storm—or the strange, electrical smell of ozone that had already begun to infuse the air—it was the crowd. All around them, the exodus continued, as families packed up strollers and blankets, some already readying umbrellas for the coming deluge.

"Come on, kitty." Becca lifted the cat carrier, holding it close to her body as the crowd surged past. She was speaking to Mr. Butters, Clara knew, but she might as well have been addressing her calico as the little cat lifted her head and began to trot beside her person. They were coming up behind the back of the bandshell, the wind picking up with each step. Already, small branches were flying past, causing Becca to duck, her arms around Mr. Butters' carrier. At her side, Clara's whiskers were on full alert as she readied for whatever might come.

"We can work together." Maybe it was the wind, but for a moment, Clara thought she could hear the tortie's soft voice. Wishful thinking, she told herself. Although Mr. Butters was being as brave as possible, hardly mewing at all despite the inevitable jostling of his carrier, Clara knew that she and the ginger tabby were essentially alone with Becca. And while she didn't doubt Becca's courage, the idea of her person facing some unknown villains—people who had already nabbed one cat's human—filled her with dread.

"We should make a plan," Clara mewed as loudly as she dared, knowing her voice would be drowned out by the rattle and hiss of leaves.

"What can we do?" Mr. Butters' cry held an edge of panic. *"I'm stuck in here."*

"I know," Clara acknowledged, kicking herself for not having questioned the tabby earlier. For all she knew, the gentlemanly feline possessed magic of his own. *"Is there anything you can do? Anything you can control?"*

It was too much, probably, to assume that the tabby had any powers that could equal hers or her sisters'. Despite the shock of hearing the newcomer speak, the ginger tabby was otherwise an apparently ordinary feline.

"I can try." The soft voice, emanating from within the carrier, made Clara hang her head in shame. The ginger tabby might not share the royal lineage of Clara and her sisters. That did not mean he was in any way a lesser cat—or that he wouldn't do what he could to help save his human.

"I know you will," Clara purred back, doing her best to project a sense of calm and competence. *"Together, we'll figure this out."*

Chapter Twenty-Two

Clara was still thinking of follow-up questions, eager to get a sense of anything the tabby might be able to do, when she realized Becca had come to a halt, sheltering under a mature plane tree as the rain began to fall. Looking to her right, Clara saw that they were at the side of the bandstand, from which a curving brick wall extended. Inside of the curve, she could see a metal door—apparently leading beneath the hulking structure. A parking area marked off for police vehicles lay in front of them, its black pavement already beginning to darken with the first drops. To their left, about twenty yards off, traffic on Storrow was racing by, its hum adding to the whir and strain of the wind in the trees.

"Okay, where are you?" Becca's head swiveled as she peered around, and Clara followed her lead. With so many odors whipped up by the coming storm—the air a heady mix of leaf mold, food wrappers, and, somewhere nearby, a discarded diaper—she was unable to make out the signature scent of any particular single human.

"Can you smell anything?" She looked up at the carrier, which Becca still held fast.

"Yes!" Inside, Mr. Butters was up and pacing, his mew rising in excitement as he rocked the plastic crate in Becca's arms. *"It's Trina! She's coming closer."*

Clara looked up at her person, willing her to be aware. But if Becca sensed anything, her cat couldn't tell. To her relief, Becca did keep craning around, looking for any movement.

"You came. Good." The low voice, barely audible above the wind, caused Becca—and the virtually invisible cat at her feet—to whirl about. As Clara hunched down, readying for an attack, she saw a husky man step out from the curve of that brick wall. "And you brought the cat."

"I did." Becca choked out the words before swallowing. "Where's Trina?" she asked, her voice gaining strength.

"Soon enough," said the man, glowering at her. "I want to see the cat."

"Trina first." Becca backed up, holding the carrier close.

"I don't think you're in a position to bargain," he said, his wide mouth turning up in a smile that was somehow more menacing than his scowl. Clara, her senses suddenly alerted, whirled around a moment before Becca did the same—just in time to see a rangy taller man behind them. In his hand, he held a large hunting knife, which he raised as he took a step toward Becca.

"No!" Clara looked up at the second man even as she hunkered down, readying to jump. A sudden attack would confuse Becca, but it would be better than letting her person be hurt.

But before she could leap, she heard a howl. Mr. Butters, his face pressed against the case's grill, was caterwauling like a siren. The two men, momentarily distracted, shifted their focus from Becca to the carrier—and Becca stepped forward once again.

"Come any closer, and I'll open this case," she said, her hand on the carrier's catch. "This cat is clearly agitated, and I bet he'll jump out and run for it. You'll never catch him."

"Good girl!" Clara held her pose—the tall man was close enough, she should be able to leap straight up and claw his arm, perhaps even make him drop that evil-looking knife. But Mr. Butters' actions—and Becca's—had clearly given the two men pause, and so she waited. Despite the plane tree's broad branches, the calico was growing increasingly wet as the storm grew stronger, a feeling no cat likes. She was warmed, however, by the burgeoning hope that her person had a plan.

"I want to see Trina," Becca said again, as the wind whipped her hair across her face.

In response, the heavy-set man nodded at his companion, who stepped past him to duck behind the wall. When he emerged, he was holding Trina, her hands tied together, and a look of sheer panic on her face.

"Trina, are you okay?" Becca stepped toward her, but the taller man pulled his hostage to his chest, raising the knife to her throat.

"Show us the cat." The big man took a step toward the plane tree.

Trina looked from Becca to her captor. "I don't understand," she said, tears—or perhaps it was the rain—brightening her eyes.

"It's not Mr. Butters they want. It's the charm you hung on his collar," said Becca. Hugging the carrier close, she raised one hand to push her hair back. "It wasn't just some flea market find, Trina. That blue clay was covering up a jewel—a stolen jewel. The Cat's Eye Sapphire."

"What?" Confusion was beginning to replace the blanched fear on the other girl's face.

"*Good,*" Clara thought to herself. If they were going to get out of this, Trina needed to be functional. Mewing softly to Mr. Butters, she began to outline her plan.

"Crazy, isn't it?" Becca seemed to be stalling.

"*She's giving Marcia and Ande time to get here,*" Clara realized.

"Enough chatter." The hulking man must have had the same thought. He motioned for his partner to bring Trina closer. "You're so smart, you know what we're here for, then. Let me see it."

"You mean my cat?" Trina might not know what was going on, but she'd picked up that Becca was playing for time. Her captors ignored her.

"Come on, bring it here." The bigger man gestured, beckoning Becca toward him.

"*Don't get closer.*" Clara didn't have Laurel's powers, but she did her best to project the thought onto her person. It didn't work, and Becca took a step forward. Desperate, Clara thought of the cats she had left in the apartment— Harriet, Laurel, and, yes, even the tortie kitten. "*Sisters!*" Clara concentrated so hard her ears went flat out to the sides. "*We need your help. Can you—*"

A booming rumble, followed by a bright flash, broke her train of thought. The storm was upon them, and in his carrier, Mr. Butters wailed again in dismay.

"Come on." The big man made a fetching motion, urging Becca forward.

"Open the box."

"I'm not giving you the cat." Becca's voice was barely audible over the rising wind.

"Get the collar off it then," said the man. "You know what I want."

In response, Becca shifted. Unlatching the carrier, she reached inside.

"My collar doesn't have the charm on it." Mr. Butters' caterwaul only heightened Clara's fear. *"Not any longer!"*

"She must have a plan," Clara mewed back, no longer concerned about being overheard. In truth, she had no idea what Becca had planned—or what she hoped to accomplish—and held her breath as Becca pulled her closed fist out of the carrier, pushing the latch closed with her wrist.

"Show me." The big man nodded at her while his companion pulled Trina closer.

"Here," said Becca, opening her fist to reveal a flash of blue.

"It's a tourmaline." Clara gasped. *"A different stone,"* she translated for Mr. Butters' benefit.

"Bring it over here."

Clara's heart sank. Her keen eyes could make out that the blue stone in Becca's hand was not only smaller, it was a different shape than the sapphire that had been hidden in the cat's charm.

"Let Trina go," Becca said, raising her voice to be audible against the wind.

"Sure. Just give me the jewel."

It was a standoff, and as Clara watched—her tail stiff with dread—Becca took one step, then another, pausing as a gust of wind blew one of the plane tree's leaves in her face.

She was taking too long. Even as she reached up to brush the broad green leaf away, the big man lunged, grabbing Becca by the arm.

"No!" She pulled back, still hugging Mr. Butters' carrier close, as Clara leaped, sinking her teeth into the man's arm.

"What?" He jerked back, and Becca pulled free. But even as he did, his companion jumped forward, abandoning Trina and brandishing that wicked-looking knife.

"Trina, run!" Becca yelled, as another peal of thunder threatened to drown her out. Clara had hit the wet ground and was scrambling to ready herself for another leap when a louder crack split the air.

"Becca!" Trina yelled, her wet face staring upward as one of the plane tree's thick boughs shimmered and then fell, knocking over the knife-wielding man and splashing on the ground between Becca and her assailant's companion, who stumbled backward.

"There you are!" Clara looked up to see Ande appear from beyond the brick wall, Marcia close behind. "Let's get out of here."

"Come on." Becca, still holding the carrier, dodged around the tree limb, grabbed Trina's arm and ran, Clara, still unseen, hard at her heels.

Chapter Twenty-Three

"Do you think he's dead?"

Marcia raised her eyebrows but kept her eyes on the road, now littered with wind-torn leaves and small branches. Ande, by her side, leaned back and appeared to ponder Trina's question.

"I don't think the branch was big enough," she said. "But he is going to have a headache."

"Serves him right," Marcia muttered, even as she swerved around a traffic cone that had blown into the road. "I'm sorry it didn't hit them both."

Clara, who had leaped into the car just as Becca slammed the door, shared their driver's sentiment. She also had her own thoughts about the timely branch.

"Do you think that was an accident?" It was easy enough for her to mew softly. Marcia's car rattled rather noisily, and she had turned on the heat, which added to the din.

"It wasn't my doing." Mr. Butters shifted in his carrier. *"Could it have been your sisters?"*

"I'm not sure." Clara was remembering how the tortie kitten had wreaked havoc in the living room, sending high-up items tumbling to the floor.

Becca, her arms still around Mr. Butters' carrier, stared out the rain-lashed window, oblivious to either the cat at her feet or the chatter of her friends. "Who *were* those two men, anyway?"

"Thugs," said Ande. From the frown on Marcia's face, she would have used a harsher word.

"I don't know." Trina grew thoughtful as she looked at the carrier. "May

I?"

"Of course." Becca slid the carrier over and watched as Trina opened its top, reaching in to pet the purring tabby. *"My person,"* he said, in tones only audible to Clara. *"I knew she'd come back to me."*

"I'm sorry," Becca interrupted their reverie. "With everything going on, I never asked. Are you okay?"

"Yeah, I am." Trina sounded thoughtful as she continued to stroke the ginger tabby. "I mean, at the end there, that was pretty scary. But I'm okay. They mostly left me alone. I don't know how you even found me."

"They found me," Becca said, relating the events of the last day. "But we still don't know what happened."

Trina sighed, looking down at her pet, who stared up lovingly. "It all started with Mr. Butters," she said, after a moment's pause. "I still don't know how he got out. I was frantic. You know."

She looked up at Becca for confirmation. "The last thing I heard was that you were going to meet someone who had him." Becca filled in the blanks. "Am I right?"

Trina nodded. "It was a woman on the phone. She told me she was parked by the Weeks Bridge. Said she had seen an orange tabby by the river and then seen one of my posters. She said she had grabbed Mr. Butters and had him in her car. I ran over after leaving that message for you. There was a white van parked on the grass, right by the footpath, and I thought, 'That's got to be her.' I walked around to the driver's side, but I didn't see anyone. I was going to bang on the back, thinking maybe she was in there. But then someone grabbed me.

"The next thing I knew, someone was shoving a bag over my head, and I was being lifted up. Into the van, I guess. I could feel an engine start and the van bump as it drove back onto Memorial Drive. I know it turned a few times, but I lost track. I was just so scared."

Becca reached over to put a wet but sympathetic hand on Trina's shoulder. She didn't stop with her questions, however. "Did anyone in the van say anything?"

Trina nodded, pushing her own damp hair back from her face. "Yeah, as soon as we were on the road, one guy started asking me questions."

"One? How many were there?" Clara, grooming her wet fur in the backseat footwell, approved of how Becca was taking charge.

Another nod. "Two men. I think the same ones who brought me to the Esplanade, but the short one did almost all of the talking. As far as I could tell, there was no woman."

Becca looked thoughtful, as if remembering the brief standoff by the Hatch Shell. "I might know who made the call."

Trina's face perked up. "You do?"

"Sorry, it's probably not a big deal." Becca shook her head. "Someone came into the shop, obviously looking for the charm. A woman and she—well, she looked rough. I think I saw her get paid by someone in a car with tinted windows."

At this, Ande twisted around further. "You didn't tell us about this, Becca. This is beginning to sound more and more complicated."

"Yeah, maybe." Becca still looked thoughtful. "But Trina, go on."

"There's not much more to tell you." She shrugged. "They kept asking me where my cat was, and I kept telling them he'd gone missing. I mean, that's why I put up the posters."

"Jerks." Marcia was maneuvering around a double-parked delivery van, and so it wasn't immediately apparent to whom she was referring.

"Where did they take you?"

Trina only shrugged and shook her head. "I can't tell you much. It was a room without windows. Concrete walls. It was clean, at least. I remember them pulling me out of the van and then walking me down a hall or across a big space, and I heard a door closing behind me. I can tell you, I was terrified. But all they did was ask me about Mr. Butters. Like, if I let him go out, and if he had a favorite place to hang out. I kept telling them he was a house cat."

She shook her head again.

"Then they left me. At least they took the hood off. After a while, one of them—the taller guy—opened the door and pushed in a bag and a bucket. The bag had a cheese sandwich in it and a bottle of water. It took me a while, but I figured out what the bucket was for after that."

"Can you tell us anything else about the room?"

Trina shook her head again, and Clara had the thought that the last two days were catching up with her. "I'm sorry, I can't. It was square-ish and clean. It was so dark, I can't even tell you what color the walls were. Though I did see one thing."

Every face turned toward her. Even, Clara was a bit startled to note, Marcia's.

"When the tall guy opened the door to toss in another bag, it let in some light. I saw marks on the wall."

"Like, from other prisoners?" Ande's voice had gone tight.

"No, stripes."

"Like from shelves?" Becca offered.

"Yeah, maybe. White marks in the paint. I think the paint was gray."

"That's something. That could be helpful." Becca's confidence wasn't catching, however.

"Really?" Marcia, glancing back over her shoulder. "Shelves on a gray wall?"

"It sounds industrial," explained Becca. "That's something we can work with."

"Something we can work with?" Ande parroted her words back, her brows rising in surprise.

"Yeah," Becca confirmed. "We can start looking at warehouses or storage spaces. There's that one place, on Mass. Ave. for instance. Though I don't know how they'd be able to walk a woman with a hood over her head into the building."

"No. Just—no." Ande sounded stern. "You are not investigating this yourself."

"You're all with me." Becca smiled, making Clara—at her feet—want to purr with pride.

"No, we're not. It was wrong to go to that rendezvous, and it was sheer luck that we got away. Now, even before we change into dry clothes, we're going to the cops, like we should have done from the start."

"Not 'going,'" said Marcia, as she put the car in park. "We're here."

Chapter Twenty-Four

"No." Becca's outburst caused all the small car's inhabitants to turn toward her.

"Excuse me?" Ande stared at her in disbelief.

"We can't go to the police yet. Please, Marcia, keep on driving."

With a shrug, the short woman put the car into gear, driving slowly to the corner where she once again stopped. "What are we doing?"

"Let's go back to my place," Becca offered. "Please, just until we can sort this out."

"What is there to sort out?" Ande was shaking her head. "Trina, don't you want to report your kidnapping to the police? You were grabbed, blindfolded, and held prisoner."

"Becca helped me when nobody else would," she replied. "Whatever she thinks, I'm backing her."

"I want to tell the police everything. Honest," Becca began her pitch. "But how am I going to tell them that I went off to meet kidnappers without alerting them first?"

"You were scared?" Ande offered. "You were under duress?"

"And what am I going to say about the sapphire? That I found a gemstone and realized it was stolen and didn't turn it in? No, I'm already at risk—my boss pointed out that I'm acting as a private investigator without a license. I want to figure this out, but what if I end up in jail because I tried to help?"

The moment of silence that followed answered that question. But as Marcia started to drive once more, Trina spoke up, her voice tremulous.

"Becca, the stone you showed those men—was that the sapphire?"

"No," Becca admitted. "It was a tourmaline from the shop. I thought, maybe, they would go for it and release you."

"That was a huge risk for you to take," Ande scolded, but Trina continued as if she hadn't heard.

"I wondered," she said, her hand still on the purring tabby. "But you do have it, right?

Becca nodded, freeing a drop of water to roll down her face. "Yes."

"Good." Trina looked down into her tabby's eyes. "Because I wouldn't want its power to fall into the wrong hands."

All eyes turned toward Trina, including Marcia—who quickly glanced over before returning her focus to the road. "Power?" Ande voiced the question on all their minds.

Trina nodded. "I've read about it. The Cat's Eye Sapphire is more than just a valuable gemstone. It's got protective powers that shield its bearer from harm."

"I read that too," Becca jumped in. "That's why it was set into the crown of—what was the kingdom? Not Burma, some smaller country in Asia."

"Which we've probably never heard of because it no longer exists." Ande oozed skepticism

"After the sapphire was stolen from the crown." Trina, warming to her subject, continued eagerly. "Kind of like what happened to that other guard."

"Wait, what?" All eyes turned to Trina.

"One of the museum guards—Matt Robbins—had a heart attack like a week after the robbery."

"Poor guy. It couldn't have helped that it was such a stressful period. Had he been a suspect?"

Trina shrugged. "They questioned everybody, but I don't think he was on that night, and I never heard his name mentioned."

"So it probably had nothing to do with the sapphire," Ande cut in. "And these supposed powers are why we're not supposed to go to the authorities?"

"I didn't say we wouldn't *go*." Becca emphasized the last word. "Just not yet."

"Well, anyway, we're here," Marcia announced as she pulled into a space by the curb in front of Becca's building.

The four emerged, soggy but relieved, especially Trina, who was leading the way and holding Mr. Butters' case close. After jumping to the curb herself, Clara watched, wondering what the ginger tabby had thought of the discussion. She was about to question him when she realized that Ande had drawn her own person aside.

"Becca, I'm worried." The taller woman kept her voice low, bending slightly to keep her thoughts confidential.

"I will go to the police. I promise." Becca turned toward her building. The storm had ended as quickly as it began, but they were all wet, and Becca dearly wanted to change. Ande's hand on her arm stopped her, drawing her attention back.

"It's not that. It's this girl, Trina." Ande's face was shadowed with concern.

"You can't think she had anything to do with the theft of the sapphire." Clara wasn't sure if her person was making a statement or asking a question, but Ande was shaking her head.

"We can't rule it out," she said. "Maybe not for its value as a jewel, but she seemed awfully interested in its purported powers. I mean, what do you know about her, really?"

"I know she came to me because her cat was missing." Becca spoke firmly, if softly. "And, yes, I do believe she was truly concerned about Mr. Butters, not the charm she'd hung around his neck."

"Maybe the cat wasn't supposed to go missing. Maybe that was an accident, or she had a fight with her partners."

"*Partners?*" Becca raised her voice just enough so that Marcia and Trina, waiting by the door, looked over. "Are you forgetting that she was kidnapped or taken hostage or—"

"So she says." Ande glanced over at the waiting women. "All we know is what she's told us. She certainly didn't give us any useful information."

"Actually, she might have," Becca ventured, and Clara leaned in closer to hear. But whatever she had been about to say was interrupted by Marcia.

"Is there something wrong? Cause, if not, I'd love to use the bathroom."

"Sorry, coming!" Becca strode toward the door, key in hand, leaving Ande to follow, a pensive frown making it clear that it was more than wet sneakers bothering her.

Chapter Twenty-Five

"Where have you been?" Harriet met Clara at the door the moment the calico jumped through it. *"It's been hours."*

"And did you get our message?" Laurel eyed her sister, one paw raised to groom her chocolate-brown ear.

"Your message?" Clara, who had started to groom her damp fur, paused.

"That you should jump." Laurel went back to cleaning, apparently unconcerned about her youngest sister's still-damp fur—or the danger their person had been in.

"I knew I should," Clara responded, a bit put off by her littermate's nonchalance. *"Becca was at risk."*

"She was never in any real danger." Laurel had moved onto the base of her tail, twisting her slim body around.

"No?" Clara had heard Ande's insinuation. But her sister, she soon realized, wasn't talking about whether Mr. Butters' person was other than she appeared. *"You mean because you two were involved?"*

"We three!" A high voice piped in. The kitten—who was looking more like a cat every day—had come racing around the corner. *"I knocked the branch down all by myself."*

Laurel broke off washing to stare cross-eyed at the kitten, but it was Harriet who corrected her.

"Nonsense," said the marmalade. *"While we appreciate your contribution, all felines have the power to knock things down. I, personally, was responsible for creating some of those flying leaves. A good distraction, don't you think?"*

"A great one." Clara bowed her head to her senior sister, all the while

wondering just how the flying leaves had helped.

"They distracted!" Harriet, miffed, responded to her thoughts, rather than her words, just as the assembled felines heard the approaching steps.

"Hello, kitties." Becca beamed down at the cats as she opened the door and stepped aside to allow in Marcia, Ande, and Trina, who still held Mr. Butters' carrier in her arms. "I know, Harriet. It's late for your dinner."

"She loves me," the big cat purred, before trotting off to the kitchen.

"She loves us all," Laurel corrected her. But because she kept her typical Siamese caterwaul to a minimum and because her sister was distracted, she got no response.

"Can we help with anything?" Marcia called out as the four cats streamed by, Clara, in the rear, hanging back to observe the humans in the living room.

"No, I'm good. Hang your wet things anywhere you can find a space, and, please, feel free to grab some towels from the bathroom," Becca called back. "I've got to deal with these gals first, or I'll never hear the end of it. Trina, do you want me to feed Mr. Butters, too?"

"That would be great." The newcomer made as if to follow her hostess into the kitchen, only to be restrained by Ande's grip on her arm.

"You can let the cat out here." The tall witch spoke in an urgent voice just above a whisper. "You and I have to have a talk."

"Excuse me?" Inside the carrier, Mr. Butters shifted, though whether in response to the growing tension between the humans or the enticing aroma of canned food that was emanating from the kitchen, Clara couldn't tell. "Hang on." Lowering the carrier to the floor, Trina opened it. And as Mr. Butters jumped out, she rose, not noticing that her cat hadn't raced after the others but instead stood, staring, as his person turned once more to face Ande.

"What's going on?" She looked from Ande to Marcia, who was toweling her short curls dry.

"You tell me." Ande's dark eyes had gone hard. "For starters, why do you know so much about this sapphire?"

"The Cat's Eye?" Trina appeared honestly perplexed, but Clara had already figured out that reading people wasn't her strong suit. "It's kind of a long story."

Ande kicked off her wet shoes and sat gingerly on the edge of a chair, facing the newcomer. "I'm listening."

"Maybe we should wait." Marcia looked toward the kitchen. "Becca should hear this, too."

"Becca?" Ande called to her friend.

"Coming!" Becca called back, even as the cats circled her, waiting for their meal.

"Laurel, are you getting anything from this girl?" Waiting her turn, Clara directed her thoughts toward Laurel.

"I'm getting that you're going to forfeit your dinner if you don't come soon."

"And it will be your own fault," Harriet chimed in. *"You know we wouldn't let anything happen to Becca."*

That wasn't exactly what she had asked, Clara thought. But this was clearly going to be a bigger conversation, and so she joined her sisters just as her own special dish, with its gold and black pattern, was lowered to the floor.

"What am I missing?" Having fed the cats, Becca came back into the living room, wiping her hands on a towel.

"Are those your familiars?" Trina leaned back on the couch to peer in at the felines.

"They're just pets." Becca's face lit up as she gazed down at her cats. "Though sometimes I wonder…"

Clara froze at that, and she and Laurel exchanged glances. *"Do you think she knows?"*

"Can't." Harriet spoke around a mouthful of cat chow. *"Nice girl, but…"* She paused to swallow. *"Human."*

Clara didn't dare contradict her eldest sister, despite her growing suspicions that Becca had begun to notice their machinations. Besides, she realized, she was missing out on the conversation in the living room.

"They do seem, well, aware of what's going on with me," Becca was saying as Clara sauntered back into the room. Doing her best to look like she had no interest in what was being said, the calico leaped to the back of the sofa and immediately proceeded to bathe.

"Fascinating." Trina looked around, opening her arms as Mr. Butters jumped up into her lap. "I feel that way about this big boy, sometimes." She stroked the red-striped head. "Almost as if he could talk to me."

"What does she know?" Even as she licked one immaculate white paw, Clara silently queried the tabby.

"About us? Or about my charm—?"

"Never mind," Clara cut him off. It was too important right now to listen.

"That's why I bought him that charm," Trina was saying. It sounded to the cat like she was finishing her answer, but her ears twitched at the thought that she had missed something important. Something that might help Becca.

"Speaking of the charm…" Ande began, a coolness creeping into her voice.

"Ande's right," Becca butt in, her tone noticeably friendlier than her coven mate's. "I would like to hear more about how you found it—and what you know about what was really inside it."

"I don't know anything. Didn't, I mean. Honest." Trina's head swiveled, taking in the women around her. "I already told you that I found the charm at a flea market out in Worcester. I like to go to flea markets and thrift stores, and the ones outside the city tend to have better deals. I wasn't looking for anything in particular, but this piece seemed to call to me. This was soon after I adopted Mr. Butters. I already had a blue collar for him, and all I could think was how striking the charm would look, especially against his white chest fur."

"So, you didn't know what was inside the charm?" Ande was staring at her in a way that reminded Clara of Laurel. Almost, she thought, as if she could get inside the other human's mind.

"I didn't," Trina answered with emphasis. "But I do remember hearing about the theft. I mean, it was called the Cat's Eye Sapphire, so how could I resist reading about it? I certainly never imagined that a two-dollar charm would be hiding a stolen jewel. I just thought it was a pretty bead. If I did, would I have left it hanging on Mr. Butters' neck for more than a year?"

"She's got a point." Clara looked at Ande, who didn't seem convinced.

"Speaking of," Trina spoke up, "can I see it?"

"Yeah, I want to check it out again, too." Marcia had spread the towel on

Becca's one big, upholstered chair so she could safely collapse back in it. But now she scooched forward to listen.

"I don't have it here." Becca turned toward her friends. "I meant to take it when we stopped by Charm and Cherish. But at the last moment, I grabbed one of the blue tourmalines instead. I thought if I could save Trina and the sapphire, why not?"

Ande started to answer, but Becca had already turned toward her guest. "I'm sorry. I know that put you at risk. I guess I just wasn't thinking."

Trina shook off her concern. "No, I get it. I wouldn't want anyone evil to have access to its powers."

Becca gave a half-hearted nod, and Ande began to speak once again. But Trina wasn't finished.

"I confess, I had some fun with the idea. I mean, Mr. Butters' charm was blue, and it had a cat's eye painted on it. I used to joke that it *was* the sapphire and that it was keeping me and my kitty safe. But I never thought I was telling the truth."

"That makes sense to me." Becca locked eyes with Ande as she spoke, and her coven mate responded with a nod, if a bit reluctantly.

"But I'm curious. You said you used to joke about the charm?"

"Yeah, but just among friends. I can't imagine anyone thought I was serious."

"Maybe not." Becca looked thoughtful. "Unless you were overheard."

Trina shook her head. "Everyone I told about it knew I was talking about a painted charm. A bead. I mean, I know what a gemstone looks like."

Ande's brows rose quizzically.

"Shira and I were actually at the Fallenburg Museum a few weeks ago. They still have a pretty impressive exhibit there. In fact, they have a big sign up about the Cat's Eye Sapphire, giving some of its history and explaining that it got stolen." She leaned in, her voice dropping. "Supposedly, the police have no leads at all."

"And you were talking about the charm there?" Becca ignored her last statement.

Another nod. "Yeah, I was joking about it—but I know I said something about the cat's eye 'being painted on.'"

"That's it," said Becca, sitting back in satisfaction.

"What is?" Marcia voiced the question in all their minds.

"How the thief—or thieves—found out about it." Becca looked at her friends, her eyes lit up with glee at having solved at least one of the puzzles before them. "Someone overheard her talking about the charm and knew that the charm held the sapphire. Whoever was behind the theft must have disguised it like that to hide it or smuggle it or something. And then, somehow, they lost track of it—and it found its way to a flea market where Trina bought it. But when they heard Trina talk about a blue bead with a cat's eye painted on it, they knew they'd found the sapphire again. Someone at that museum is behind the theft."

Chapter Twenty-Six

"Anyone could have been at that exhibit that day," Ande, the voice of reason, broke into the general cheers greeting Becca's pronouncement. "Maybe the thieves were planning their next heist and were scoping out another target."

"I know it's a leap, but it would explain a lot," said Becca. Focusing again on Trina, she continued her questioning. "Can you remember who else was there that day? Besides you and your roommate?"

Trina sighed. "I'm sorry. I don't remember. I do remember that it seemed pretty empty. Just one or two people and the guard." She paused to survey the room. "The other visitors moved on, but it seemed like the guard was stationed there permanently."

"One of the guards was initially a suspect." Becca filled her friends in. "He was never charged, though. Maybe they had the wrong guard?"

Trina leaned forward as if she were about to speak, but sat back as Ande responded.

"Or it was one of those 'one or two people,'" she said.

"What we do know is that somehow they found out that Trina had the charm—and that it was on her cat's collar." At that, all eyes turned to Mr. Butters, who lay curled in his person's lap.

"Don't respond," Clara, faking a doze on the sofa's back, murmured softly.

"Not to worry," Mr. Butters replied in an undertone too quiet for human ears. *"Not to…"*

"He's snoring. How cute." Marcia beamed at the ginger tabby, who had fallen asleep.

"You think that it was someone at the museum?" Trina had laid her hand on her prone cat but kept her eyes on Becca.

"Or someone else who overheard you. My point is that whoever stole the gem also disguised it. I bet they've been looking for it. In fact…" Becca bit her lower lip. A sign, Clara knew, that she was thinking. "I think I can guess what happened. You say Mr. Butters has never gotten out before, right?"

Trina nodded.

"I bet the thieves broke in, looking for the bead. But while they were there, Mr. Butters got out, and they couldn't find him—or the charm. Then they must have seen one of your 'lost cat' posters. The ones I told you to make," Becca continued, with a regretful sigh. "That's when they hatched their plot. They called you, pretending to have Mr. Butters, and kidnapped you, hoping someone would be willing to exchange him—or, at least, the charm—for you."

"But there was no sign of anyone breaking in." Trina shook her head.

"And who?" Marcia perked up. "I mean, you posted that you had Mr. Butters, but why would they have grabbed Trina before they knew that?"

That wasn't a question Clara or her sisters would have asked. In truth, Clara knew, her sisters didn't credit humans with much ability to reason. But hearing Marcia pose the question, the little calico had to give it credence. Becca had reached out to the kidnappers, but not until after they had grabbed the dark-haired woman.

"Maybe they thought Shira had Mr. Butters?" Trina offered, her voice as tentative as her speculation. "I mean, if they thought he was in the apartment all along, only they couldn't find him, it would make sense that my roommate would have access to him."

"But didn't Shira know you were kidnapped?" Becca seemed to be asking herself the question. "Would she have noticed that you weren't at home? How close are you two?"

Trina sucked in her cheeks as she considered the question. "We're close enough, I guess. But we're not friends. She answered an ad after my old roommate moved out, and she's been dealing with some stuff. She's nice though—and she does really seem to like Mr. Butters. Plus, she's got a steady job."

Dealing with some stuff? Clara looked up at her person, but Becca seemed reluctant to follow up.

"You said she was out at work the day Mr. Butters went missing." Becca was building to something. That much was clear, although Clara couldn't figure out what exactly.

Trina nodded. "I tried to reach her, but she's not allowed to have her personal phone on her when she works, and she works a ton. Which makes her kind of a great roommate, honestly."

Nobody argued with that, but Becca had more questions. "Where exactly does she work?"

"She does security for Mass General, and since she's the low girl on the totem pole, she always gets called in when they need someone."

"Low girl?" Becca was questioning everything, Clara noticed.

Trina nodded. "Because she's new. Relatively new. I mean, she just moved here a bit over a year ago."

"Where did she come from?"

"One of those suburbs to the west of the city. Natick, I think. She wanted to be closer into town, but rents being what they are, she couldn't afford her own place here. I can't either, so it's worked out well."

"And you're friendly, if not exactly friends?"

"Yeah, definitely." A vigorous nod. "When she's not working, she's fun to hang out with."

"I'm wondering if we should talk with her," Ande chimed in.

"Yeah, maybe." Becca mulled over the idea. "I know the police will want to." Turning back to Trina, she asked, "Would you give her a call? Maybe she can come over."

Trina shook her head. "No, I'm sorry. I mean, I can call her, but she's at work, so she won't pick up."

"Does she have any idea what's happened?"

A shrug. "I doubt it. Like I said, she's always working. I think she's hoping that if she does well enough, she might get her old job back."

"Her old job?" Becca tilted her head. To Clara, she looked strangely like

CHAPTER TWENTY-SIX

Laurel at that moment.

Another nod. "Yeah, even though it's a drive."

"Wait…" Becca held up a hand, even as a smile of disbelief began to spread across her face. "When you said you went to the museum, did your roommate go with you?"

"Yeah," Trina agreed, seemingly unaware of the track of Becca's questions. "That's where she used to work as a security guard."

Becca turned to Ande, who only shook her head. Even Marcia muttered something that sounded like, "I can't even…"

"What is it?" Laurel might be expert at influencing humans, but that didn't mean she was any good at interpreting their various social clues.

"They look like they just found a mouse." Harriet, to the best of Clara's knowledge, had never had an actual encounter with a rodent, or any prey larger than a moth, for that matter. But her comment, from her perch on the gold-tasseled pillow that she had made her own, still struck a chord with her youngest sister.

"Why are they talking about Shira?" Mr. Butters woke from his nap and looked around. *"I like her."*

"What?" Trina looked from one set of human eyes to another, seemingly perplexed by the silent agreement between them.

"I think it's pretty obvious." Becca spoke softly, as if she were speaking to an invalid or a child. "Your roommate is involved in the theft and probably your kidnapping as well."

Chapter Twenty-Seven

"That's not possible." Trina sounded perplexed rather than angry. Her voice had gone up a notch, which the humans as well as the cats in the room noticed. "She's not like that. And, like I said, she was gone the day Mr. Butters went missing, and that's when this all started."

"It started long before then, really." Becca maintained her conciliatory tone, even as Ande glowered. "Maybe she didn't have anything to do with someone breaking into your apartment, but she very well might have told someone about the charm. And she was in a position to know what the charm hid."

"But it's been over a year—"

"She might just be very good at playing the long game," Ande interrupted Trina's attempt to explain. "Or she's been waiting for the right time for some reason. At any rate, I think we now know enough. It's time to go, and I don't even think we should stop to pick up the stone. Becca?"

"I think you're right. It's been safe at Charm and Cherish so far." Becca rose and held out a hand to Trina. "I'm sorry, Trina, but Ande's right. It's time to go to the police and tell them everything. And that means everything about your roommate, too."

"I don't understand," Trina rose, dislodging the ginger tabby, who jumped to the floor. "I mean, I see what you're saying. But you don't know Shira. She's not like that. Just on the most basic level, if she wanted Mr. Butters' charm, she could have just taken it. She's been alone with him a lot. Why not just slip it off his collar and then pretend she didn't know what happened to it?"

"I don't know," Becca admitted. "I don't know who she's working with or what constraints she might be under." Ande shot her a look at that, but Becca shook off her friend's warning. "For all we know, she might have been under duress. What we can't ignore is that she worked at the museum where the gem was stolen. And then she brought you to the museum—and, right after that, someone grabbed you in an attempt to get the charm. I mean, the Cat's Eye Sapphire."

Even as she spoke, heads bobbed in agreement. Ande turned to Marcia to whisper something that sounded suspiciously like "I told you." Only the cat at Trina's feet looked up in dismay, mewing so softly that nobody but Clara heard.

"But I like Shira," the ginger tabby mewed, even as he lifted one creamsicle paw to gently dab at Trina's shin. *"Shira's my friend. She would never do anything to hurt us."*

Chapter Twenty-Eight

Clara had no time to question Mr. Butters further. Becca was already standing. Trina was ushering Mr. Butters back into his case, and Marcia had her car keys out.

"Can I ask a favor?" Trina looked at Ande before swinging around to include Marcia and Becca. "Can we stop by my apartment so I can drop Mr. Butters off?"

"I don't see why not," Becca responded. Ande, off to the side, began to grumble, prompting Becca to explain. "There's no reason to take a cat to the cops, and the poor thing hasn't been home in days."

"Okay, but no lingering." Marcia, as the driver, laid down the rules. "Trina, you can run in and let your cat out. And Becca, maybe you should go with her."

"I really don't think that was necessary." As the women filed out, Becca leaned over to whisper in Marcia's ear. The short woman raised her brows till they disappeared under the Sox cap.

"Better safe than sorry," she said. "Besides, maybe the roommate will be there."

"Good point. At the very least, I want to meet her and set up a time to talk." Becca pulled the door shut, checking to make sure it had locked behind her.

Clara couldn't help but agree—and as she jumped through the closed door, she directed a silent plea to Laurel. *If that other woman is there, can you help?* The calico wasn't sure what exactly her half-Siamese sister could do long-distance. Implanting ideas in humans' heads was different from reading their thoughts. Still, it couldn't hurt to ask, she figured, even as she bounded down the stairs just in time to wiggle beneath Becca's feet as Marcia drove off.

"When I drop Mr. Butters off, would you mind if I grab something to eat?" Ostensibly, the question was directed to everyone in the car, but Mr. Butters' person turned toward Becca as she asked. "It's been a while since I had that last sandwich those men gave me."

"Oh, you poor girl!" Becca nearly exploded, heading off whatever Ande had been about to say. "I should have offered you something." Becca shook her head—and then, paused, a faraway look in her eyes. "Wait, can you tell us anything more about the sandwiches? Because, if so, it might mean they were in an apartment or someplace with a kitchen."

"No, they came from a deli or something. They were wrapped in paper and cut through into two sections."

"Even better." Becca scooted forward on her seat, the better to turn and face the other woman. "Was there anything on the paper?"

Trina sat back, thinking. "Yeah, I'm trying to remember. There was a name printed on the paper, over and over. Something like Matt's Big Boys. Or maybe Mike's?"

"Hang on." Becca pulled her phone out of her pocket and was soon busy thumbing in words. "Success! There's a Mal's Big Boys on Huntington Ave. Just past the Museum of Fine Arts, on the way out to Brookline." She looked up. Ande was leaning over the back of her seat at that point, and she and Becca locked eyes for a moment. "Another museum connection."

"Where did you say your roommate works again?"

"Shira? At Mass General, but you can't think…"

Ande, still facing Becca, rolled her eyes.

"We will need to talk to her—and the police probably will, too." Becca kept her voice gentle, as if she were reassuring a cat, Clara thought. "She might have some information that she doesn't even know she has. Like you telling us about the sandwich wrapper."

It was a stretch, and Trina seemed to shrink in her seat, jostling the carrier. *"Shira is my friend,"* Mr. Butters mewed, woken from his nap. *"Trina's too."*

Clara, crouched down on the crowded car's floor, didn't dare give an audible answer. In truth, although she usually trusted feline perception to be much more reliable than human, she wasn't sure what to believe about the mysterious roommate.

"But maybe she knows something." She did her best to project her thought to the ginger tabby. *"And don't you want to find out who took your person?"*

"I do," said Mr. Butters, and with a soft, sad mew, shuffled inside the carrier. Although Clara could hear that he was lying down, one paw over his head, she doubted the other cat was going to be able to nap. Cats, she knew, had long ago outgrown worrying about the future. Still, to have one's person—even one's secondary person—being scrutinized for possible malfeasance would have to be unsettling.

"This is your building, right?" Clara had been so focused on Mr. Butters that she hadn't noticed the car slowing until Marcia spoke up.

"Yes," Trina, perking up, answered. "You can pull up into the visitor slot."

"Gotcha." Clara leaned against the wheel well as the car turned, but the movement still threw her into Becca's leg, and her person looked down, confused.

"That's crazy." She might have been speaking to herself, but Ande and Trina turned.

"A new thought?" Ande sounded hopeful.

"No, sorry." Becca shrugged, as if to shake off the evidence of her own senses. "It was just that for a moment, I could swear I felt fur against my ankle. It made me think of how Clara, my calico, likes to rub against me when I get home."

"Mr. Butters does that, too." Talking about her pet perked Trina up and, facing Becca, she managed a shaky smile. "I think that's how they tell us they love us."

"Or mark you as their own," countered Ande. "But I think in this case, it's stress. I mean, Becca, you've been going all out on this. And it does involve a cat, so…"

"Yeah," Becca acknowledged. "I mean, it's not like Clara would have followed us, right?"

At her feet, the little calico stayed as still as possible, claws dug into the car's carpeting in case of any further jostling.

"Anyway, we're here—and the sooner we drop off Mr. Butters and go to the cops, the sooner I'll be home with my own cats. Trina?" Becca nodded toward the door.

"Maybe I should join you." Ande reached out for her own door handle, pausing as she looked back at Becca.

"No, please don't." Becca softened her words with a smile. "We're just going to run in, let Mr. Butters out, and grab something from the fridge. If Shira is in, we'll ask her to come with us."

What she didn't say, Clara realized, was that the group had no way to compel the other woman to come with them to the police. Though if she refused to, that could be revealing in its own way.

"She'll be happy to see Mr. Butters, if she is. And it might be nice for Mr. Butters to have some familiar human company," chimed in Trina as she stepped out of the car.

"I have some questions for her, too," Becca repeated, addressing Ande sotto voce, as she followed the brunette out of the car.

Clara remembered the layout from Becca's previous visit to Trina's apartment and trotted behind the two. Becca paused to take down two posters about Mr. Butters' disappearance as they walked to the front of the building.

"No point in making people worry," she said.

Trina, holding the carrier in her arms, nodded. "I'll get the rest of them down later. Shira was a real help posting them all over the neighborhood."

Becca smiled in response. Clearly, the other woman was trying to cast her roommate in the best possible light. But neither Becca nor the shaded cat at her feet were reassured when they reached Trina's apartment to find the door closed but unlocked. Even Becca's inferior human hearing, Clara thought, must have been able to hear someone walking around inside.

"Anyone home?" Trina stuck her head in. "Shira?"

"There you are! I was getting worried." A short dark-skinned woman about Becca's and Trina's age stepped out of the kitchen. Still wearing a blue uniform jacket, she was in the process of pulling out a hair tie and releasing a mass of blond curls. "I was looking for a note or something. Oh, hey, Mr. Butters." She came forward to smile into the carrier. "Welcome home! So that phone call paid off?"

Becca bristled, standing a little taller as she faced the uniformed woman. "In a way," she began. "When did you and Trina last speak?"

"Trina texted me that someone had found Mr. Butters, and she was going to pick him up." Shira sounded so matter-of-fact that Becca began to relax. "I'd been asked to cover a graveyard shift and took a quick nap in the staff room. But when I came home and neither Trina nor Mr. Butters were here, I started to get worried. I texted you." This was to Trina. "But you didn't respond."

"You did?" Trina set the carrier on the floor and gently opened its lid. Mr. Butters stood, looking around and—Clara could tell—sniffing for any changes or potential dangers before stepping out and trotting deeper into the apartment.

"I checked the litterbox, too." Shira smiled as the sound of scratching carried into the foyer. "That's when I began to suspect that Mr. Butters hadn't been home."

"There's your text." Trina, meanwhile, was checking her phone. "We were on our way over."

"Yeah." Shira nodded. "I started to worry when I got home. I did think it was odd that you didn't text me when you picked up Mr. Butters, but I figured, well, I'm not always the most accessible. Besides, you were probably making up for lost time with some kitty love or having him checked out—he is okay, isn't he?"

"I think so." Trina reached down to stroke her cat, who had returned. "He was outside overnight, but he looks good, and he's certainly eating well. And I figure he must have found some place to shelter during the storm, which is probably why we didn't find him when we first went out to look. The rain had stopped by the time Becca found him."

Shira's eyebrows went up. "Wait, are you the woman who made the call?"

"No. It's a long story." Becca held out her hand. "Becca Colwin."

"The witch detective!" Shira beamed, apparently delighted. "Trina said she was going to ask for your help."

"I didn't really—"

"Yes, you did," Trina cut her off. "But it was all a lot more complicated than we thought."

Shira turned her puzzled gaze from her roommate toward Becca.

"We were hoping that you could help us straighten it out." Becca eased into the topic with a grin. "Would you tell me about the day that Mr. Butters went missing?"

"Yeah, sure." Shira stared at the space above Becca's head, as if her memories could be seen up there. "I remember that day because it was one of those stormy days we've been having, and I thought I'd lost my raincoat. I'd left my keys and phone in the pockets—we can't have personal phones on the floor—and so I didn't know that Trina was calling me until much later."

Becca made a quizzical squeak that would have done Laurel proud.

"We have lockers at work," Shira explained, turning to face her directly. "But I didn't want to shove my wet raincoat in there, so I hung it on the rack in the staff room. I was meeting a friend for lunch, and when I went to the rack, everybody had hung their coats there. I was digging through, looking for mine, and starting to get worried when he showed up. His time was limited, and so we just went up to the cafeteria. At the end of the day, the pile had thinned out and, sure enough, my coat was there."

Becca nodded, gnawing on her lip as she did when something was tickling the back of her brain. After a few moments of silence, she appeared to shake it off and moved on.

"Trina says you used to work at the Fallenburg Museum?"

"Yeah." Shira drew out the syllable. Almost, Clara thought, as if she were expecting to be interrogated.

"That sounds like there's a story in there." Becca laughed to lighten her query, but the other woman only shrugged.

"There was some weirdness with my boss." She tossed her hair as if to shake the question off.

"Oh?" Becca was on it. "Actionable?"

"Well, sort of." Staring off into the distance, she shrugged. "I was let go."

"Were you given a reason?"

"I wasn't following the assignment sheet, the implication being that I was trying to pad my hours." She shook her head again. "It was just as well; the place was going downhill."

At that, Trina started to speak, but with a gesture, Becca silenced her. "Shira, did your firing have anything to do with the break-in at the museum?"

The other woman nodded vigorously. "We're not supposed to speak about it. I had to sign an agreement to get my severance. Management is afraid that if anyone finds out how the museum was robbed, it could happen again. But…"

She paused.

"What?" Becca urged her on.

"It just wasn't fair what they did." Shira was shaking her head, her smile flattened out into a grim line. "They implied that the robbery happened in part because I wasn't following protocol, but I was filling in for another one of the guards."

"So, you weren't alone in the museum?"

"No, that's what's so unfair. I was trying to help out."

That gave Becca pause, and as she wrestled with what to ask next, her phone rang. "Ande?"

"Is there a hold up?" Clara's sharp ears made out the other woman's voice. "Do you need any help?"

"No, sorry." She shared her apologetic smile with the room. "Trina's roommate, Shira, is here, and we got into a conversation."

"Is she going to come with us?"

"I was just about to ask." Becca looked up. "That's my friend. They're waiting downstairs. We haven't had a chance to fill you in on everything that's happened, but, well, with everything going on, we're going to talk to the police."

At that, Shira straightened up. "The police?"

Becca nodded. "We were wondering if you'd come with us?"

"You don't have to," Trina broke in. "You just got home from work, and honestly, I'd love it if you could stay with Mr. Butters for a bit."

Becca looked at her, confused. "You sure?"

Trina nodded, and Shira chimed in. "I'm happy to sit with my favorite ginger," she said. "Good to meet you, Becca."

* * *

"What was that about?" Becca grilled Trina as they returned to the car. "Why didn't you want her to go with us?"

"It didn't seem right, dragging her into all of this." They'd reached Marcia's car by then, and Becca quickly brought her friends up to speed. "She's already paid her dues."

"I understand she feels she was treated badly." Becca chose her words carefully. "But I want to know more about what happened that day. Even assuming she wasn't involved—" She put up a hand to stop Trina from interrupting. "Even if she's not actively guilty," she continued, "she still might know something."

Trina made the kind of nodding shrug that seemed to pass for assent.

Ande blew her lips out. "And she wouldn't come to the cops with us?"

"I didn't push her," Trina admitted. "I didn't think it was fair."

"Fair?" Ande barked back. "You were *kidnapped.*"

"Yeah, and you think my roommate had something to do with it." Trina didn't exactly bark back, but there was an edge in her voice the others hadn't heard before.

"Maybe." Becca alone didn't seem to notice. Speaking slowly, as if she were still working things out in her head, she continued on as if the little squall hadn't happened. "At any rate, I think I know how Mr. Butters got out. I may be wrong, but I think he got out because someone else came in."

Trina shook her head. "You said that before, but there were no signs that anyone had broken in. The door was even locked when I came home."

"That might be because they had Shira's key." Becca quickly explained to Ande and Marcia about the 'lost raincoat.' "We know there are two men working together. What if that lunch was an excuse to grab Shira's keys?"

"But that would mean Shira's friend was involved, too, and he's gone out of his way to help her."

"Returning a favor?" Ande's voice dripped with acid.

"That's not what I meant." Trina turned to answer it.

"Okay, let's all calm down." Becca turned from one woman to the other. "It's been a crazy day for all of us. The main thing is that you're safe—and Mr. Butters is safe too."

Ande huffed in a way that made Clara think of Harriet but held back on further comment.

"We're going to the police," Becca responded to the unspoken complaint. "There's just too much going on here for us to deal with."

"I don't know." Trina smiled weakly at her. "I don't think I'd have gotten away—and gotten Mr. Butters back—if it hadn't been for you."

"Thanks," Becca said quietly. "But this really is beyond us now."

"Anyway, we're here," said Marcia, pulling up to the curb. "Why don't I drop you guys and then try to find a place to park?"

"I'm coming with." Ande reached for the door, following Trina out onto the sidewalk. Reaching for Becca's arm, she spoke in a stage whisper. "You do realize how odd this all is, right? There's something not right about this girl. And probably her roommate, too."

"I know, Ande." Becca sounded disheartened. "But we'll turn it over to the police, and they'll get to the bottom of it."

Clara didn't like hearing her human sound so discouraged and looked up to see if she could read her face. But Becca's lips were closed tight, her brows knit with worry as she followed Trina and Ande up the granite stairs and into the looming brick building. And in the back of her mind, the calico heard the echo of the ginger tabby's plaint. *"Shira's my friend,"* he had said. *"She would never do anything to hurt us."*

Chapter Twenty-Nine

Trotting alongside Becca, Clara was acutely aware of how odd the little troupe must have seemed: four young women traipsing into the Cambridge police department, their faces set in varying modes of gravity and concern.

"I'd like to speak to Detective Newsom." Becca took the lead, approaching the front desk, where a bald man in uniform was busily shuffling papers. "It's about a kidnapping."

That merited raised eyebrows from the bald officer. "A kidnapping?" He parroted back.

"Yes." Becca paused. "We rescued her, but we still believe we ought to report it. It's a serious crime, and the culprits got away."

"So an *attempted* kidnapping?" The bald officer seemed to be having trouble following her.

"No, they nabbed her—Trina, with the dark hair." Becca gestured behind her to where Trina, Marcia, and Ande stood. "But we got her free. We believe she was kidnapped because of the stolen Cat's Eye Sapphire."

"The Cat's Eye—I see." The officer didn't seem entirely convinced. "Alrighty, then. This sounds like a discussion worth having. Would you—and your friends—come with me?"

"I'd already started speaking to Officer Brooks," Becca broke in, even as the officer motioned them to a side corridor. "I had reported Trina's disappearance as a missing person. Or I tried to. She hadn't been gone twenty-four hours then."

"Follow me, please." Clara could have been wrong, but she thought he was shaking his head as he led them down the hall.

*　*　*

Twenty minutes later and the officer, whose name was Mike, was still shaking his head.

"So, you—Trina Cruces—were grabbed because you had possession of a stolen jewel."

Trina nodded vigorously. "I didn't realize it at the time. It was hidden inside a charm that I had bought for my cat's collar."

"And the kidnappers grabbed you because they couldn't find the cat?"

"Exactly," Becca chimed in. "Mr. Butters—the cat—was lost, and that's why Trina reached out to me."

"And you're some kind of professional pet finder?"

Becca winced, and Clara remembered her concerns about the legality of her new profession.

"She's a witch detective." Trina had no such compunctions. "I knew she'd find Mr. Butters—and she did!"

"A witch detective?" The bald officer pushed his chair back. "Would you wait here a moment, please?"

"Now they're going to take us seriously." Trina was beaming as the officer closed the door gently behind him.

Becca, on the other hand, had folded into herself. "I wish you hadn't told him that," she said.

"Why?"

Becca could only shake her head. "They—I—well, I may be accused of practicing without a license."

"Wait, because I was kidnapped?"

"No, it's worse than that, Ande broke in. "It's pretty clear they're not taking you being grabbed off the street seriously. Since you walked in with us unharmed, I think the cops are going to consider the high-value jewel theft the priority."

"And if I turn it in, they're going to wonder how I got it." Becca was shaking her head.

"*If?*" Ande turned toward her, but Becca raised her hand.

"These girls have quite a story." The bald officer's voice carried as he approached the room, clearly in conversation with someone else.

"Becca Colwin?" A familiar gruff voice made Clara's ears perk up.

"That's Detective Newsom," Becca whispered to her friends.

"Your friend?" Trina piped up before Becca could shush her.

"She seems to be some kind of private investigator. She's calling herself a 'witch detective,'" the other man began to explain. Until, that is, Detective Newsom cut him off.

"Yeah, yeah. I have some acquaintance with the young lady." The pause that followed had Becca looking around at her friends. When the voices picked up again, they were quieter. So quiet, in fact, that even Clara had to strain to hear. "She's got a knack for finding things out," the cat heard. "But she's going to get herself in trouble."

"I heard him say 'you're going to get in trouble.'" Trina's whisper was so loud that Becca shushed her again.

"What I want to know is how did they get their hands on a stolen gemstone?"

Becca and Ande turned to each other, and Becca slowly shook her head.

What followed next was spoken too quietly for even Clara to make out. Becca, sliding quietly out of her seat, made her way to the door, and her pet looked on in concern as she pressed her ear against it.

"Witch detective." That came through loud and clear, as did the laugh that followed.

"Don't let her leave." That was Newsom again. "I'll start the paperwork."

* * *

"I knew it." As the footsteps receded, Becca spun around to face her friends. "I'm sorry, but I've got to get out of here."

"You don't know what they're talking about." Ande held her hands up as if to stop her.

"I don't need to know any more." Becca began pacing. "You said it yourself, Ande. They don't take the kidnapping seriously, and they're wondering how I came by the sapphire, especially since I'm acting as an unlicensed private investigator. I just—I'm afraid they're going to want to detain me, and I can't risk that. I'm leaving."

"Okay, then." With a sharp nod, Marcia stepped up to the door. "I'm parked over on Pearl Street. I'll distract them. Meet me by the Blue Bomb."

With that, the short Sox fan pulled open the door and loudly addressed the officer standing there. "Excuse me, where's the restroom?"

"Down the hall. Make a right."

"Down this way?" Inside the room, they could hear her walking away.

"No, no. Miss?" More footsteps as he hurried after her.

"Now," hissed Becca, with a glance behind her as she led Trina and Ande—and the shaded Clara—quickly down the hall, into the lobby, and out of the building.

The three walked quickly, heads down, until they'd reached the corner. Then, as if by some unspoken agreement, they all collapsed in laughter.

"I can't believe we just did that." Trina wiped her eyes.

"I feel like a fugitive." Becca stood up, suddenly sober. Ande nodded toward her.

"There's Marcia." Trina took off down the block, but as Becca made to follow her, Ande put out a hand to restrain her.

"Hang on a minute." Ande leaned in. "I just want to say, I don't trust this Trina for a moment. Between her and her roommate? They're deeper into this whole robbery than they're letting on."

"We've been over this, Ande. Trina couldn't have known about the sapphire." Becca hung back. Ahead, Marcia was waiting. "If she did, she would have taken it off Mr. Butters' collar sooner."

"Maybe not," said Ande, as the two began to walk again. "After all, it was the perfect place to hide it."

* * *

Clara, who slipped in by Becca's feet as the door was closing, mulled over Ande's words. The tall Wiccan had a point about the sapphire. Disguised under Mr. Butters' charm, it had been safe for more than a year. But Becca had a point as well: Trina truly seemed unaware of its existence. Add in that Clara's sympathies automatically went to her person, and she was at an impasse.

"Maybe Laurel will be able to sense something," she thought to herself as the blue beater pulled into traffic once again. Between her faith in Becca and her gut instinct that Mr. Butters, with his superior feline perception, was speaking the truth about Shira, Clara was at a loss.

With everything on everyone's mind, the drive over to Charm and Cherish was surprisingly quiet. Even Trina seemed subdued as Marcia began to pull up to the storefront.

"Hang on." Becca broke the silence, sitting upright in one startled motion.

"What is it?" Marcia looked over her shoulder at her passenger.

"That car. There." Becca pointed, and Clara sat up to take notice as well. Sure enough, the black car she had seen tailing Becca was parked outside Charm and Cherish. Or not parked, she noticed, but waiting, its engine still running.

"That's the car I saw before," said Becca, and then went on to explain. "This woman came into the shop looking for the sapphire. She didn't say as much, but it was clear. And when she left, I saw her lean into a black car like that, with dark-tinted windows. I think whoever was inside paid her."

"Whoa." Marcia braked, just a few spots away from the storefront. "What do you want to do?"

"Don't go in there," said Trina, as Ande nodded vigorously.

"But Elizabeth should be working," said Becca. "And, besides, don't you all want to know what's going on?"

"Well, I can't stop here." Marcia, looking over her shoulder at a Kia that had already begun honking, started rolling slowly.

"You can pull around the back," said Becca, leaning forward. "Take the right, and you can park in the alley."

"Becca," Ande's warning didn't need words.

"I'm sorry, Ande. I know you're concerned. But I need to get the sapphire anyway. And if they're waiting outside for me, I can be in and out before they notice."

As much as Clara agreed with Ande that going into the shop was a risk, she understood Becca's point as well. It was time they got some answers.

Chapter Thirty

As Marcia eased around the block, Becca leaned forward.

"Maybe you should pull over before the alley," she said. "Just in case they have someone inside the shop."

"If they do, it doesn't matter which door you use. It's not safe," Ande interjected, before Marcia could.

"No, I think it will be," Becca countered. "They want the sapphire, and they don't know where it is."

"They grabbed Trina." This time, it was Marcia who pointed out the obvious, even as she pulled up to the curb.

"But Elizabeth will be in there. And Charm and Cherish is open to the street."

Ande and Marcia exchanged a look, but Becca was already getting out of the car, with Clara close behind.

Using her key to unlock the store's back door, Becca stuck her head in. "Elizabeth?" She called, keeping her voice low.

"I'm here," the older woman called back from the front of the little shop. "I believe you're in the clear."

Becca wasn't sure how to respond to that, but she did walk up to the break room door. "I'm in the clear?" she asked.

Elizabeth turned toward her, today's ochre caftan swirling around her, and waved one hand toward the window. "For now, dear," she said. "They can't see in."

"Ah." Becca took this in. "The afternoon light reflecting off the glass."

"As you will." Elizabeth grinned, and for a moment, Clara was sure she was smiling down at her. "At any rate, it's safe for you to be in here."

"Great." Becca exhaled, even as she glanced out the shop window at the black sedan still idling at the curb. "I can't remember how much I told you, but it's been a crazy day."

Elizabeth's smile grew wider. "I can imagine," she said. "But we can catch up later. I think you came by to pick something up?"

"Yes." Becca could only shake her head at the other woman's awareness. "I tried talking to the police—"

"But they're not the ones who you truly want to question."

"No." Becca spoke with a new firmness. "You're right." And with that, she scooped through the gemstones by the register, fishing out one particularly large, bright blue stone. Almost as an afterthought, she then opened the register, retrieving a card from the cash drawer.

"Thanks, Elizabeth," she called as she made for the back door. As her person turned, Clara was almost certain Elizabeth looked down and winked.

* * *

"I've got it," said Becca, getting back into the car. Opening her palm, she displayed the sapphire, its clear blue seeming to gather the light.

"That's something," said Ande. Trina reached forward to touch it, only to draw back.

"I can't believe how much trouble that stone has caused," she said.

"Back to the cop shop?" Marcia asked, drawing away from the curb.

"I don't think so." Becca's response drew a double take from Ande.

"Becca," she said, a warning in her voice.

"I know, Ande." Becca acknowledged her friend. "But they aren't taking us seriously, and I want to get to the bottom of this. Without getting arrested, if that's possible."

Before Ande could respond, she continued. "I'm thinking we should contact the curator directly. After all," she offered up. "There's a reward for the sapphire, so why shouldn't we be the ones to collect it?"

Ande wasn't happy about it, but Becca would brook no dissent. "I have a plan," she said. "Or the beginning of one, anyway."

The idea she outlined was simple. "I'm going to call Mr. Hallowell, and, if he's going to be around, go out to the museum tomorrow or Friday. That way, I'll get to speak with him and also see where the theft took place."

"I don't know." Ande was the first to disagree. "Can't you wait for the weekend? That way I could go with you."

"Same here," said Marcia. "I'd be happy to drive, but I can't take another day off without notice."

"I'd love to go with you," added Trina. "Maybe I could get Shira to come, too."

Becca shook her head. "Thanks, everyone. But this is just going to be a fact-finding mission. I promise, I'll share whatever I learn as soon as I get home."

* * *

"She's planning something." Fifteen minutes later, Clara was racing in ahead of Becca, as she called out to her sisters.

"Of course she is." Laurel, who had sensed their approach, was already sitting by the front door, giving her already perfectly smooth coat a final tongue bath.

"Couldn't you do something?" Harriet lumbered into view. *"She's been out more than in recently, and if you aren't willing to take charge…"*

Before her oldest sister could finish her threat, they heard Becca's key in the lock, and all three sat up to greet their human and her two coven mates.

"Hello, kitties." Becca beamed down at them. "Where's the kitten? Oh, there you are," she added, as the tortie tumbled into the foyer.

"Make yourself at home," she called back to Marcia and Ande, heading into the apartment. Pleading exhaustion, Trina had asked to be dropped off, to Becca's relief. "I've got to feed these little guys."

"Not a problem," Marcia collapsed on the sofa as she pulled out her phone. "How do you feel about pepperoni?"

Becca's cats all perked up at that. Until, that is, they realized that Marcia was planning for a human food delivery.

"What have you been up to?" Clara turned an inquiring gaze on the kitten.

"Research," came the reply, but before Clara could follow up, Becca headed toward the kitchen, and all four cats followed suit.

"So, what is she planning?" Harriet spoke through a mouthful of chicken cuts, her favorite flavor. *"And why can't she do it at home?"*

"She needs to talk to someone." Clara was still waiting patiently for her own can. *"I think she wants to see where the blue stone came from."*

"But we can tell her where it came from." Laurel's voice was muted as she dipped her brown muzzle into her own dish.

"We can?" Clara turned from her own dish, which Becca had just placed on the mat.

"Don't you want that?" Harriet looked over, a scrap of food on her chin.

"Yes, I do." Clara nibbled at her dish, her thoughts on her sister. *"What do you mean, Laurel?"*

"She's just talking." Harriet disliked not being the one in charge.

"No, I'm not." Laurel was pushing her sister, Clara knew. As she ate, she eyed her sisters, wondering if Harriet would erupt as Laurel sat back and began washing her face. *"You know too,"* said the Siamese finally, dipping her head to her marmalade sibling.

"I don't understand." Clara was at a loss.

"Why do you think they call it the Cat's Eye?" Laurel turned toward the calico, her own blue eyes wide. When Clara didn't respond, she crossed her eyes—her version, her little sister knew, of rolling them in disbelief.

"I don't know," Clara admitted. Clearly, she had missed something. *"Does this have to do with Mr. Butters?"*

Harriet made a hacking noise. Although Becca turned, concerned, the marmalade immediately sat back and licked her chops. There was no furball, her youngest sister knew. This was simply Harriet's way of scoffing at her question.

"Don't blame the Clown." Laurel blinked slowly at their oldest sibling. *"She still hasn't heard all our family history."*

That made Clara's whiskers tingle. After all, she thought her sisters had not only told but shown her their family's semi-divine origins, as temple cats in Egypt. *"There's more?"*

Now it was Laurel's turn to cough, although she was quiet enough so that Becca didn't notice. *"Tons,"* she said, raising one paw to her ear.

Clara looked from her to Harriet, knowing her oldest sister would want to be the one to speak.

"You remember what we've shown you, yes?" Harriet's tone made it clear that her question was rhetorical. Clara dipped her head in assent anyway. *"You know that we were gifted with powers because of our service to the young priestess."* Another nod of acknowledgement. *"Well, that young priestess had duties beyond gathering the sacrifice."*

With that, a haze descended. In it, Clara saw a dark-skinned young woman, a tabby cat by her side. It was a scene she had witnessed before, with the tabby's skill as a mouser saving the young woman's basket of wheat. Only this time, the priestess wasn't carrying a woven basket. Instead, in her hands, she held a necklace made of bright blue stones.

"Not many remain of the Cat's Eyes." Harriet's voice broke through the vision. *"The stones that protected the temple and all who worshiped therein. But when one surfaces, it is our responsibility to keep it safe."*

"Our?" Clara turned to Laurel, whose tail swiped once in confirmation.

"Our family," she said, her voice rumbling into a purr.

"As I said," the little tortie chimed in, *"research."*

Chapter Thirty-One

"I 'm wondering if we should try another circle." Ande was helping herself to a slice of mushroom and olives, one of two small pies that had just been delivered, when she brought up the coven. "A full one, this time. We could use the clarity."

Becca, her mouth full, didn't respond. Or maybe, her cat thought, that's because she didn't agree with her sister witch.

"We did just meet," Marcia pointed out. "I know Trent and Larissa are going to be back soon. But do we want to involve them in all of this? It's not exactly coven business." While the unlikely couple were no longer the center of the coven, they had begun participating again, joining in a circle to celebrate the solstice a month before. "Besides, after what happened with the bonfire…"

She didn't have to finish her sentence. Litha, the midsummer celebration, had been the last time the full coven had come together, convening in the park beside the Charles River for what was planned as a holiday celebration, as well as a kind of low-key party to acknowledge the return of the prodigal couple. The highlight had been a very modest celebratory bonfire in the park, specifically in an area where grilling was allowed. However, the fire department had not agreed with the group's interpretation of the rules, showing up in force. Becca suspected an unsympathetic onlooker—perhaps, even, her neighbor Deborah—had called the authorities. Whatever the reason, the arrival of a pumper truck, along with several yellow-suited firefighters, had resulted in a hasty summation of the celebration.

"We were lucky not to be ticketed," Becca conceded, looking down at her half-eaten crust. She wasn't really seeing it, Clara knew her mind was far from last month's disaster. While her friends were talking about the coven's founders, Clara suspected Becca was more occupied with the question of how to approach the curator.

"Fires are allowed in the picnic area," Ande grumbled. "If we'd been roasting marshmallows and not wearing wreaths…"

"Either way," Becca broke in, "we should rethink our strategy before next summer."

"But what about now?" Marcia eyed the last slice.

"Yeah, maybe another circle would be useful," said Becca, unaware of the reaction her response would provoke. "I keep thinking that if we could work a summoning, maybe we could find a way through this mess. And, I know we've had our differences, but Trent and Larissa have practiced the craft longer than any of us. Maybe their presence would make a difference."

"*No!*" Laurel howled, ears back, from beneath the kitchen table.

"Becca, is something wrong with your cat?" Marcia ducked her head to peer at the disgruntled feline.

"*Yes!*" Laurel's assent sounded much like her negative reaction to human ears, and soon Ande was looking under the table as well. "*Silly humans!*"

"Laurel, what is it?" Becca addressed the feline calmly, almost as if she knew how well she understood.

"*Not Larissa!*" Harriet, on the sofa, lent her voice to the protest. Soon, even the kitten was joining in. "*Don't they know?*"

Only Clara kept her mew at a reasonable level. "*Sisters, please,*" she pleaded. "*You're upsetting Becca.*"

"Laurel, Harriet, what's wrong?" Becca reached down to scoop up the offended seal point, who abruptly stopped her caterwauling with a little *urp*. "Are you going to have a furball?"

"*No, silly.*" Laurel's voice was softer, although it still had the distinctive Siamese whine. "*You just squeezed my middle.*"

"She seems calmer now." Ande sat back, eying the cat in Becca's arms warily.

"*It's Larissa.*" Clara did her best to send her thoughts toward Becca. "*For a witch, she's particularly insensitive to cats."*

What she didn't want to say—couldn't say—was that the idea of any human having more power than a cat was offensive.

"If I didn't know better, I'd say they were reacting to the idea of a circle." Marcia looked up, a slightly confused look on her face.

"Thank you." Laurel glanced over appreciatively.

"But, Harriet, when they meet, there are always cookies." Harriet, Clara had noticed, did not appreciate Laurel getting all the attention.

"Oh, right." Harriet settled back down. *"But that nasty Larissa and her stinky tea..."*

"They haven't made that in a while," Clara pointed out. In truth, since Larissa had ceded control of the coven, many of the small group's rituals had become more pleasant, from the switch to peppermint tea to the shortening of the otherwise somewhat lengthy invocations. But Harriet was no longer listening. Becca, still cradling a comforted Laurel, had stepped away from the table, and the big marmalade, with an athleticism she rarely displayed, launched herself onto the table, grabbing the remainder of Becca's slice as she slid across the surface.

"No!" Ande reached for the slice as Becca turned back. But her initial look of alarm soon faded to resignation.

"May as well let her have a bite," she said. "I've seen her eat worse with no ill effects. Thank Bast, I guess."

"I am the manifestation of the goddess." Harriet swallowed the last bit of stringy cheese that she had managed to get off the slice before Ande grabbed the crust.

"You're the manifestation of something," Laurel, still safe in Becca's embrace, ventured.

"Please, sisters." Clara looked from one to the other. *"Did you forget about the sapphire? Becca is trying to understand what happened."*

"Why bother?" Harriet set about grooming, one paw wiping at the orange grease on her chin. *"It's here, where it should be."*

"But it's not safe." Clara lashed her tail in frustration. Sometimes her sisters could be so simpleminded. *"Someone out there is willing to kidnap a person to*

get it. They threatened Mr. Butters, too."

That stopped her sisters. And as Laurel squirmed to be released, they gathered in the living room to touch noses. *"You're right, Clown,"* said Laurel, in a rare moment of acquiescence. *"That handsome gentleman deserves better."*

"It is time," said Harriet, in her most regal tone, *"for us to act."*

"Look at them now," said Marcia, a smile spreading across her face. "You'd almost think they've got a coven themselves."

Chapter Thirty-Two

By the time her friends left, they had decided to reach out to Trent and Larissa to at least see if they were interested in convening. As she texted Larissa, who controlled the couple's calendar, Becca caught sight of the time. She'd been planning to call Hallowell, the better to gauge his reaction. But eleven o'clock was too late, especially on a weeknight. With a sigh, she started to text instead.

"I don't even know if this is his cell," she muttered to herself as she typed. *Becca from Charm and Cherish here. I was thinking of visiting the museum Friday and was wondering if we could meet.* "Does that sound too forward?" *Maybe we can discuss Kali's gifts.*

The suggestion—she couldn't really call it an invitation—for the day after tomorrow wasn't ideal. She wanted to speak to the man as soon as possible, in person, but saying she was going to come by tomorrow not only meant rearranging her work schedule with Elizabeth, it decreased the chance that he'd be available to plan time for her. One thing she knew for sure: She didn't want to wait for the weekend, even if her own friends would be free then. For all Becca knew, the curator worked nine-to-five, Monday through Friday. Besides, suggesting a meetup on a weekday would sound less like she was interested in him personally, an impression she was particularly grateful for as she realized Jerry Keller had left a voicemail.

"Hi, Becca." From across the room, Clara heard the kind vet's voice and came to rub against Becca's shins. "My presentation went well today, and I've been getting some great feedback. Looking forward to sharing with you—and the kitties, of course—when I'm home. How does dinner on Saturday sound?"

"Bother." Becca frowned, and Clara glanced up in alarm. "I can't believe I keep missing him," she said, looking down at her pet. Almost, thought the calico, as if she knew how much her cats understood.

"Don't be silly." Laurel's voice reached her, even as she stared into Becca's eyes. *"Humans are adorable, but they're not cats."*

Clara purred her agreement, despite her own questions. Becca, after all, had begun to accept some of her cats' more magical behavior—such as Clara's ability to pass through solid walls—as normal. And her senior colleague at Charm and Cherish, Elizabeth, certainly seemed aware of Clara, even when she was sure she was shaded. Still, Laurel had a point. Which was why Clara and her sisters needed a plan. As long as Becca had the sapphire, she was in danger. And none of her pets should be comfortable with that.

"Is she going to wait until the vet comes home?" Laurel hadn't initially approved of Becca's beau, and Clara eyed her now with suspicion. *"What?"* Laurel stared back. *"I know she's fond of him, but..."*

Clara held back, knowing full well what her sister's half-closed eyes meant. Laurel had picked up enough from her younger sibling to know that Hallowell had a certain sense of style that Jerry Keller lacked. Plus, he dressed better.

"Never mind all that." Harriet plopped down between the two. *"I want to know what we can do with that pretty blue stone. If I wore a collar—"*

"It would still be dangerous," Clara dared to interrupt. *"If only we could get rid of it."* Harriet glowered but said nothing. Her powers extended to summoning objects—not making them disappear.

* * *

The next morning, Becca woke with a start. Her phone, plugged in to recharge, was buzzing, and she stumbled out of bed to read the incoming text.

"Love to catch up," she read aloud. *"Shall we meet at the museum, say, 10 a.m.?"*

"I'll be there," she typed back. That prompted a flurry of activity so out of the ordinary that her cats could only stare wide-eyed.

"What's going on?" Harriet's head had popped up from her nest of blankets as their person began pulling clothes from her closet.

"She's got plans." Clara yawned, looking over at Laurel, who had already begun her morning toilette. *"She's already thinking of tomorrow."*

"Not before..." Harriet could move quickly when she wanted to, but her fears were soon assuaged. As if suddenly hit by a realization—Clara looked at Laurel with suspicion—Becca paused her furious closet searching and headed to the kitchen, where she promptly laid out breakfast for the four felines.

Although her sisters were soon snout-deep in their plates—while the tortie batted at hers—Clara kept her ears up for any signs of what might be bothering Becca.

"I'm super curious to see this museum," she said. But even as she answered her pet's unspoken question, the device in her hand pinged. "But I hope he doesn't think it's a date."

"Told you." Laurel looked up from her breakfast long enough to blink at Clara.

* * *

Fifteen minutes later, Becca was at Charm and Cherish. "Hello," she called to the Bast set high on her shelf. "And to you as well," she greeted Elizabeth, who today was quite resplendent in a red and gold robe.

"Good morning." As she turned, the gold reflected the sunlight shining in the front window. "You have a visitor."

"I do?" Becca brightened perceptibly as Elizabeth gestured toward the back room. When Shira stepped out, though, her expression changed from one of excitement to curiosity.

"I'll leave you two to it." Elizabeth retreated to the back as the two younger women eyed each other.

"Shira, what brings you here?" As Becca spoke, Clara stepped forward to sniff at the visitor, who was dressed in her dark blue MGH uniform. Picking up Mr. Butters' scent, she remembered the ginger tabby's words: *"Shira's my friend...she would never do anything to hurt us."*

Becca didn't seem so convinced, as she regarded the shorter, stockier woman with a look that would do Laurel proud.

"I know you had more questions." Shira raised her hands and mugged. "I mean, I know I can't be looking too good to you right now."

"It's not that." Becca shook off the suggestion, clearly disarmed by the other woman's admission. "It's more that I'm curious if you saw something or even heard something that could shed some light on what happened."

"You mean with Trina?" Shira shoved her hands in her pockets and leaned back against the edge of a bookcase.

A nod as Becca crossed her arms and then, as if aware of how confrontational that might look, uncrossed them, consciously relaxing against the register counter. "And with the sapphire."

"Which you still have, right?"

Becca stiffened, a shift that was noticeable to her cat if not the woman facing her. "It's in a safe place," she said. "I've been in contact with the curator."

Shira raised her brows. "I'm sure he's gratified."

"Are you implying something?" Becca leaned forward.

Now it was Shira's turn to shake her head as she looked down at her black uniform shoes. "Not really. It's just that his job is probably on the line as well. Though that might be more of a status thing than a necessity for Hallowell."

Becca raised her brows, silently urging Shira to continue.

"You've seen what he drives and how he dresses, right? He used to sport a diamond pinkie ring, too, when I was first hired. He's got to have family money. I mean, the museum has an endowment, but it can't be that huge. And after the robbery..." She shook her head again. "The whole place is on shaky footing anyway."

"Oh?"

Shira's eyes rose to meet Becca's. "I'm not supposed to know, but you hear things, you know?"

Becca nodded, and Clara could tell she was holding her breath.

"Hallowell was always talking about money—about the Fallenburg's money, that is. The budget. Like, they probably weren't going to replace people when they retired, and I know they had accountants in, looking at the books. I know they have someone stationed in the gem room all the time now, too, so I guess they did some hiring, but I didn't know the guy who was there the day Trina and I visited. Some tub of lard who looked past it, to be honest, so I bet they're paying him less than they paid me.

"Sometimes I think that's really why they let me go." She shrugged again and stared out the store's front window. "What can you do?"

The question was clearly rhetorical, but as Becca took this in, Clara sensed she was weighing something in her mind, almost as if she were considering an answer. To her pet's surprise, she dropped the subject, moving instead to what she and her friends had discussed the evening before.

"Would you tell me what happened the day of the robbery?" she asked. "Even little things that you think might not have any meaning."

Shira nodded, her gaze turning inward again. "It was a Friday evening. I wasn't supposed to work that night, but I came in to collect my paycheck, and I saw Freida, the receptionist, was freaking out about something. I asked her what was going on, and she told me that one of the guards—Nick Roswell—hadn't shown up. Friday's our late night, and we get a decent crowd. Hallowell had been pitching it as a 'date night destination' on social media, and he was complaining that nobody was there to work the floor.

"We're short-staffed anyway, so the fact that Nick was the only one scheduled didn't totally surprise me," she continued. "And when I checked the roster, sure enough, I saw his name listed—but with a scribble on it. I thought it said 'special projects,' but I couldn't be sure. At any rate, Frieda was sure he wasn't on the floor. I'd left my uniform in my locker, so I changed and went to make the usual rounds."

"You didn't have a supervisor or someone you could check with?"

Shira shook her head. "We did, but he'd left a few months before, and the position hadn't been filled."

Becca took this in, nodding slowly. "What about Hallowell?"

Shira blew through her lips. "I wasn't going to bother the curator of the museum with a staffing question. And, I mean, we trade shifts all the time. I figured the important thing was that the museum have coverage."

"So, there's only one guard on at a time?"

Shira's brows went up again. "Budgeting," she said. "But we make the rounds. We're basically there to make sure nobody touches the art and to direct visitors to the restroom."

"Fair enough. So what happened then? Did you have a lot of 'date night' visitors?"

"No. It was kind of weird." Shira was once again staring off into space. Or, Clara realized, focusing on the multicolored dream catcher that hung in the front window. "The gem room was closed. Roped off. Maybe because of the shortage of security, I don't know. But that's always one of our biggest draws. I did walk through there—that's part of the security route—and I didn't see anything. Granted, the lights were off, but I would have noticed if the glass for any of the cases had been broken."

"You didn't check?"

"Why would I? Besides, it was right about then that I heard Nick."

"So, the guy you were covering for was there."

"Yeah." Shira clamped her lips shut. "I remember thinking that I wouldn't be able to put in for the shift. But since I was there, I figured I'd help him."

"Help him?"

"I'll admit, I was thinking of justifying a few hours," said Shira. "He said he didn't need me, though. That he was going to do the rounds, but before things got busy, he was working in one of the storage rooms, off the exhibit area, packing up some pieces for deaccession."

"Wait—deaccession," Becca interrupted. "You mean 'selling'?"

Another nod. "Just small stuff, like some prints that we had multiple copies of and some minor antiquities, mainly Indigenous pottery. That's trickier, of course, because provenance is an issue. But we've had a ton of donations over the years, and a lot of the pieces are delicate and need special care, so they cost us a fair amount to maintain them."

"I see." Becca's eyes strayed to a ceramic figurine set deep onto a shelf above Shira, and Clara knew she was thinking of her own blue-and-white bowl. "I can imagine how breakable pottery is."

"It's more than that." Shira warmed to her topic. "We have climate-controlled cases and, of course, climate control in our inventory storage rooms, and that's expensive, especially as energy costs go up, and so we're spending an awful lot on a very few pieces. Plus, Hallowell wants to install special cases in the display areas that will minimize vibrations, not just if there's an earthquake but from things like trucks passing by. So he's been prioritizing moving some money around for that."

As if reacting, a soft alarm went off. "Oh, man." Shira looked at her watch and straightened up. "I should get going."

"Wait, please." Becca reached out to touch her arm. "I don't understand. You said Nick was there, but you were the one singled out as a suspect?"

Shira shrugged. "He was on the schedule, and I wasn't. Plus, he's been there forever, and I think he's pretty tight with Hallowell."

"He wasn't the one who died..." Becca struggled to recall the name. "The guard who had a heart attack after the robbery?"

"No, that was Matt Robbins. Another old-timer. He was about to retire, and we'd already been told he wasn't going to be replaced."

Becca nodded, her expression growing thoughtful as the other woman headed toward the door. "One last thing, Shira," she called out. "Why did you come here today?"

The other woman turned, fixing Becca with a sad smile. "I thought it was pretty obvious. You suspect me of being involved. Trina tried to hide that, but I don't need to be a rocket scientist to see your doubts. I've already been through this once, with the cops. I want to clear my name."

✳ ✳ ✳

As soon as Shira had left, Becca called Maddy and filled her in on the visit.

"I don't know, Maddy." Becca sighed. "I'm not sure what to believe. The articles I've read have only said that a security guard was questioned and released. But the case is still open, and I know the authorities don't like to file charges until they have a good case. For all I know, Shira might have misread the schedule. Or she might be lying, either to make an excuse for why she got fired or, I don't know, to cast blame elsewhere. Plus, the fact that she showed up at the store is kind of weird. Especially because she asked about the sapphire early on. She knows I hung onto it."

Clara sat by her feet, her ears attuned to Maddy's response.

"Becca, this is just getting worse and worse." Even without her feline sensitivities, she would have heard Becca's aggrieved friend. "I know you want to help that other girl—Trina—but can't you drop it?"

Becca's sigh was answer enough.

"At least you've turned the sapphire in."

More silence.

"You have, haven't you? Becca?"

Maddy knew her friend.

"I'm going to." Becca sighed. "I wanted to. Only, there's been a hiccup."

"A hiccup? You know it was stolen from that museum."

Becca nodded, as if her friend could see her. "It's a long story, Maddy, but basically at this point, I'm afraid that the cops are going to think I'm involved."

Clara could almost hear Becca's friend holding her breath.

"It's—well—there may be a licensing issue with my witch detecting." Maddy started to speak, but Becca cut her off. "Besides, I have additional information that I can act on. I mean, don't you think it's interesting that the Fallenburg is getting rid of items?"

"According to one former employee."

"That's just it, Maddy. I need to find out more."

Maddy was still sputtering as Becca signed off with promises to be careful that even her cat didn't fully believe. When she started poking at the device, Clara expected to hear another voice. Ande's, perhaps, or Marcia's. Instead, Becca was soon staring at the device, her face knotted up in concentration, as Elizabeth swanned back in.

"Was your visitor helpful?"

"Maybe." Becca tucked the phone into her pocket. "I was just confirming something."

The older woman's bushy brows rose in question.

"The theft at the Fallenburg," said Becca in response. "There's not a clear timeline. The authorities say it probably occurred after the museum was closed. But there wasn't a break in, per se, so there's no real way of telling."

"Are you sure?"

"Hang on." Becca fished the phone back out again. "Yeah, they do have a statement from the curator saying that he checked on the exhibit before he left for the night. Still…"

"You're still wondering if Trina's roommate might be involved."

Becca tilted her head, acknowledging the truth of Elizabeth's assertion. "I don't know what you heard, but she was in the building when she wasn't supposed to be. And, except for Hallowell, she's probably the last person to see the sapphire." She stopped there. "Except that she didn't see it."

"Oh?"

"She didn't see anything," Becca explained. "The exhibit was closed, and the lights were off. Supposedly."

"Supposedly?" Elizabeth's dark eyes drilled in, and Becca could only sigh.

"Maybe I'll get some more answers tomorrow, after I meet with Hallowell. Because right now, I don't know, Elizabeth. I don't know who to believe."

That seemed to satisfy the older woman, whose vigorous nod set her gray curls bobbing. "That's the best way to approach a mystery," she said, and, for a moment, Clara was sure those piercing eyes were directed at her. "That is, if you can't consult your cat."

Chapter Thirty-Three

"*She can see me, I'm sure of it.*" Back in the apartment, Clara was trying to explain Elizabeth's odd glance to her sisters.

"*Maybe you forgot to shade yourself?*" Laurel, bathing, did not share her sister's concern.

"*There are times, when I've just eaten, that I find magic a bit taxing.*" Harriet, already lined up at the door, cast a quick glance at Clara. "*Did you have treats there?*"

"*No.*" Clara modulated her tone with care. It wouldn't do to argue with her sisters, so she tamped down her worries as Becca approached. The three could hear her footsteps and turned to each other as these slowed.

"*That neighbor,*" Clara hissed softly. Of the three, she had the most direct experience with Deborah Miles. In response, Laurel's ears went back, and both she and Harriet turned on their youngest sibling.

"*Do something.*" The lashing tail said it all, and so, without any plan, Clara slipped through the door once more. Sure enough, the downstairs neighbor was standing on the landing, as if waiting for a confrontation with Becca.

"Good evening." Despite her best intentions, the tension in Becca's greeting was enough to raise the fur on Clara's neck.

"Becca." The other woman's heavy makeup couldn't disguise her disapproval.

"Is everything okay?" Clara sighed. Becca's good heart was keeping her out here and making her vulnerable as well.

"It would be if I could get any rest." A hand to her brow might have seemed overly dramatic to anyone else, but Becca—always empathetic—hesitated.

"The noise," Deborah explained. "I don't know what kind of menagerie you're running upstairs, but the constant thumping is insufferable."

"I'm sorry." Becca cast a worried look up the stairs. "I know my cats can be rambunctious."

"That's one word for it." Deborah's mouth compressed into a scowl. "My lawyer advised me to get a decibel meter to measure the cacophony."

"I'm really sorry." Becca was looking increasingly uncomfortable. "I could get another rug."

The other woman snorted, but as she was about to respond, her phone pinged. Distracted, she waved Becca away, dismissing her.

"Wow," Becca sighed, letting out her tension as she headed up to her own door, Clara leaping once more ahead.

"Hello, kitties." Becca's face lit up as she opened the door to her assembled cats—and turned to take in the tortie, who was tumbling over herself in her rush to join the crew.

"Good work, Clown." Laurel leaned over her sister, apparently washing her ear.

"Thanks." Clara ducked her head at the unaccustomed praise. Besides, Laurel's tongue tickled. *"I wasn't sure I could make it ring, but I had to try."*

Harriet looked over, tail lashing. But before she could tell Clara how she would have handled the situation, Becca reached down and scooped up the kitten.

"I think you're the one causing all the trouble, kitten." The way she was peering down into the tortie's green eyes almost made Clara jealous. "You'll grow up soon, I know. But is there anything I can do in the meantime to get you to calm down?"

"I knew we had to take a firmer hand with that animal." Harriet's growl was barely audible. Becca must have picked up something, though, because she put the kitten down and addressed the assembled clowder.

"I've got to figure out a way to keep you all entertained while I'm at work. I know that," she said. Even as she did, her gaze went to the living room, where several books lay splayed open on the floor. "Something to keep you from knocking everything onto the floor. At least, while Deborah Miles is at home."

With a sigh, she shrugged off her bag and headed toward the kitten. "Maybe," she said as she reached for the cans, "someone in the coven will have some ideas."

"Why does she ask them?" Like any child, the kitten was full of questions. *"We could do whatever she wants."*

"I know." The thought made Clara purr. *"But they want to do it themselves, and they think that with all of them here, they'll have more power."*

Indeed, the calico could have explained, while Becca's desire to practice magic had gotten her into scrapes, it had also given their person a sense of purpose. And so while the young woman hastily picked up her apartment, scraping the crumbs off the table and giving the furniture a quick brush, her pet did her best to stay out of the way. If she could have calmed her siblings, she would have. As it was, they were showing their displeasure at yet another disruption of their routine in their own ways. Laurel by zooming: She had nearly managed to trip Becca three times by Clara's count. Harriet, by positioning herself stolidly in their person's path, specifically in the kitchen doorway, where she did her best to stop the disposal of those crumbs. *"No,"* she howled, as Becca managed to step around the sizable feline. *"I could eat those!"*

More than the loss of those crumbs—or the general disruption of Becca cleaning—it was the imminent arrival of Becca's full coven that was upsetting the other cats, Clara knew. Harriet and Laurel were well socialized. They all were, despite their feral origins. Before she sent them into the humane trap that had brought them to the shelter and, ultimately, Becca, their mother had taught them about humans, specifically which kind should be avoided and which kind could be trusted. Service to people—the right kind of people— was a large part of their mission, she had explained. And because she had foreseen that they would find someone to love and who would love them back, her admonitions about scratching and using the litter box were stressed with the kind of stern love—part nips and hisses, and part purrs—that only a mother cat could provide.

That maternal guidance would be useful now, Clara couldn't help but think. As the youngest, she had little or no sway over her siblings. But the way they were acting just now was adding to Becca's stress as she rushed to get ready. Not because of Ande and Marcia, the calico knew. They had grown into the kind of friends who didn't notice a messy kitchen, or didn't mind if they did. But tonight's gathering was going to re-introduce Larissa and Trent, the founders of their particular coven—and a troublesome pair from the start.

As could be expected, the irksome couple were late. Ande and Marcia were already at the table, the tea steeping and the cookies plated. The treats, brought by Marcia in a bakery box tied with a particularly intriguing length of string, were intended for after, but Becca had brought them out to the table for safekeeping, to Harriet's dismay.

"It's like she doesn't trust us," the fluffy marmalade had muttered in a voice that sounded awfully close to a growl.

"I can work on that." Laurel closed her eyes to concentrate, while Clara wisely held her tongue.

"Do you think we should start without them?" Marcia reached for a cookie, breaking off a bit to hold under the table.

"Let's give them a few more minutes." Becca, glancing over to the door, didn't seem to notice as Harriet scarfed up the scrap, rubbing her body along Marcia's shin in thanks.

"It worked." Laurel, perched on the back of the sofa, smirked, her blue eyes closing in triumph. Clara, coiled on the cushion below, refrained from commenting. At least Laurel was using her powers of suggestion for benign ends. Besides, all three cats had felt the vibrations. Laurel's ears went back as Harriet licked up the few crumbs she had dropped. Even Becca seemed to sense something, although Clara attributed that to her person's nerves.

"Here we are!" Larissa threw open the apartment door, arms raised as if to take them all into her embrace. Dressed in black palazzo pants and a flowing gold and black top that matched the turban covering her brassy hair, she stepped into the apartment like a diva about to sing. "It's been too long."

"It has." Becca was the first to greet the prodigal witch, giving her a hug and nodding to the man behind her. Tall and slim, with a sleek black beard that made him look like some TV warlock, Trent smiled back in a way that accentuated the lines around his eyes, making him look older than his thirty-two years. He and Becca had almost had a romance, back before Becca had learned that he was not only involved with Larissa, he was also financially dependent on her.

"Hey, Becca." His subdued greeting seemed to acknowledge their rocky past, but Becca reached for him anyway, giving the tall, dark man a hug as well.

"It's about time." Ande stood back, her arms crossed. She'd had a run-in with Trent, too, back in the day, which could have explained her reticence. But something had changed. Maybe it was the way Trent hung back, sheepishly. Maybe it was that he had aged visibly. It wasn't just those lines, Becca realized as she'd hugged him. The coven's one male member had lost weight and now felt almost gaunt. As if in recognition, Ande relented, too, unfolding her arms to beckon the pair in to where Marcia waited, a curious look in her eyes.

"Hello, darling!" Larissa reached out to the coven's remaining member, turning the full wattage of her smile on the short Sox fan. "I know," she said, shaking her head. "I missed your wedding. But I hope you felt the energy we were sending your way from Tempe."

"You've been in Arizona?" Becca ushered the newcomers over to the table, while her cats gave them a wide berth.

"Back when…" She flapped her hand, as if Marcia and Luz's wedding had happened in the prehistoric past. "This month, we've been on the Cape."

"Of course." Becca's quiet aside earned a grin from Ande, as they all found their places around the table.

"Shall I?" Waving her big sleeves aside, Larissa reached for the teapot. Becca was faster, however.

"I've got it," she said, softening the words with a smile. The older woman was used to being in charge, after all. "We've introduced some changes since you two last joined us."

Larissa's unnaturally dark brows went up toward her turban as she peered around the table, taking in each member of the coven in turn.

"We start each meeting with a quick catch-up now," Marcia jumped in, holding out her cup for Becca. "And we discuss any issues we might want to bring up for our circle."

"Also, we've found that mint tea is most conducive to conversation—and invocation." Becca reached for Larissa's cup as Trent leaped up to hold his own out. "And during the circle, we all have a chance to speak. If we want to, that is."

"How egalitarian." Larissa's smile was looking strained. "But we do have a lot of news."

Ande cut her off. "Since the rest of us have already had a bit of a chat, I move we go straight to the invocation," she said, as the three reached out to take each other's—and the newcomers'—hands. Although their most recent gathering had been quite casual, Clara could sense tension in her person. Becca had been disappointed at that last circle. This time, her pet knew, she was hoping for more, which explained the formality with which Becca recited the ritual call to summon the coven's energy and open the portals. Determined not to miss any ceremony that might help, she then led her fellow witches through a cleansing ritual, which seemed to relax Laurel. After that, she looked over at Ande, who led her own invocation to African deities, raising Larissa's brows once again. Only then did the group break hands.

Becca, visibly relaxed, took the lead. "Blessed be, Larissa. Would you like to share what you've been up to and how you've used the craft?"

The older woman's mouth opened and closed as Becca spoke, and she took a deep breath before replying. "Trent and I have been communing with nature at the Cape's end," she said, giving her partner a significant glance. "It's been most restorative. The moon over Cape Cod Bay—"

"We did participate in another solstice festival," Trent chimed in. "Although, honestly, it was more of a party."

"Parties are good." Becca smiled at her onetime wannabe beau.

"Especially with the members of the Cape End Arts Society," said Larissa. When nobody responded, she continued. "It's a very exclusive group," she said. "Very aware."

Becca nodded, smile still in place if a bit strained. Under the table, she kicked Ande, who was rolling her eyes.

"Becca's been hired for another case." Marcia jumped into the gap. "It started with a missing cat, but it's evolved to involve a kidnapping and a jewelry heist."

"A jewelry heist?" Trent's deep voice tightened, even as Larissa was shocked into silence.

"That sounds more dramatic than it is," Becca blushed slightly. Not, Clara hoped, because of Trent's interest. No, rather because her instinct was to downplay her role, her pet decided, as her person caught the couple up. "Anyway, I'm going to be meeting with the curator, Brian Hallowell, tomorrow," Becca concluded.

"Someone's moving up in the world." Larissa's painted eyebrows, already dramatic, inched up as she and Trent exchanged a loaded glance.

"What do you mean?" Becca couldn't keep the edge out of her voice. Or didn't want to, her pet realized. It had been a long day, and the older witch enjoyed her gossipy insinuations a bit too much.

"We see him in Provincetown," explained Trent, clearly hoping to moderate between his over-the-top girlfriend and their host.

"He's a member of the Society," said Larissa, accentuating the final word with a nod.

"Good for him." Ande cut that short. "Shall we?"

Marcia looked at her curiously, but whether the shorter witch had something to share or had thoughts of her treatment of Larissa, Becca couldn't be sure. Instead, she nodded her approval as Ande began the ritual that would formally invoke their circle.

Moving the cookies just a bit, she placed a mirror on the table and, beside it, a small open dish of salt. (*"Is that one of our dishes?"* The kitten had sidled up beside Laurel on the sofa's back to observe. *"No."* Laurel was unusually terse when she was concentrating. *"She has special dishes for this."*)

"As the full moon approaches," Ande continued, "we seek the light. As she shows her face, may all truths be revealed. May falsehoods be laid bare and secrets revealed."

"May I suggest something new?" Once Ande had finished, Becca spoke up, looking around at her colleagues.

"I know it sounds a little crazy, but I was thinking of my cats and, well, I'd like to try an invocation to Bast."

"Bast?" The name of the goddess seemed to stick in Larissa's throat, while Trent's eyes went wide.

"Yes." Becca nodded enthusiastically. "Like I said, I know it sounds odd, but I've been getting the feeling that my cats—or maybe all cats—have a link to the unseen."

"There's certainly precedent," Ande chimed in.

"Why not?" added Marcia. Larissa and Trent exchanged a look, but even he was smiling,

"Let's do it," he said. "Becca, it sounds like you know what you want to say."

"Not really," she admitted. "But I was thinking something like: *"Bast, great mother, see justice done."*

"I like it," Marcia piped up. "Bast, great mother, see justice done," she repeated as the others joined in.

As the humans chanted, Clara felt a warm hum. Closing her eyes, she concentrated, adding her purrs to those of the Great Mother.

"Bast, great mother, see justice done..."

Becca sat up straight, her eyes closing in concentration. In the desire to bring together the concerted powers of five would-be witches. Humans, yes, her devoted pet thought. But colleagues. Friends, even, in an alliance that might finally be able to break through the barriers that had held them back. Almost as if they were cats…

"Bast, great mother..."

It was no use. Becca sighed, her focus shot. Maybe it was Larissa talking about Brian Hallowell, but she kept picturing him as she'd first seen him—a nice-looking man in a good suit, turning to beep the alarm on a fancy car. He had a certain flair, she admitted. Despite the bald spot, he was an attractive man. Not as sweet or generous as Jerry Keller, but something about him kept drawing her attention. Most likely because of the case. Because of the sapphire.

"Becca?"

Becca looked around and realized all eyes were on her. Even her cats—well, Laurel, Clara, and the kitten—were staring from their perch on the sofa.

"I'm sorry." She shook her head as if to clear it of its cobwebs. "My mind was wandering."

"Was it?" Ande fixed her with a stare, her dark eyes particularly intense. "Or were you channeling something?"

"Your face went kind of slack," Marcia added.

"No," Becca admitted. "I was just caught up in the case."

Ande and Marcia exchanged glances, while even Larissa looked thoughtful. To everyone's surprise, it was Trent who spoke up.

"Those two aren't mutually exclusive," he said, his deep, smooth voice reminding Becca of why she had almost fallen for him once. "Is it possible you were thinking of the case because we were channeling the moon? Clarity and light and all that."

"That's a great idea." Becca hated to disappoint them. "But I wasn't getting any answers. There was no great light shed. I just keep going over the same questions."

"Why don't you share them with us, dear?" Larissa leaned forward.

"Shouldn't we finish the circle first?" Now she felt embarrassed for hijacking the ritual.

"Perhaps this is its purpose." Ande spoke solemnly, but her eyes sparkled. "And, hey, we adapt these traditions to our needs as well as our times."

Becca looked around at her friends. Even Larissa and Trent were on board, she realized, their former position as disrupters abandoned. Beneath the table, she felt the brush of soft fur.

"What are you doing?" Harriet glared at Clara as she rubbed up against their person.

"Encouraging her." Clara touched her wet nose to Becca's bare ankle.

"Encouraging her to make this all last longer," her sister grumbled, settling into a pose Clara privately thought of as 'peeved meatloaf.' *"And I heard that."*

"Sorry." Clara ducked her head, even as she pricked up her ears, anxious

to keep up with the conversation above her.

"I'm just distracted." Becca shook her head. "I keep thinking of the first time I saw Hallowell."

"What is it exactly about that first appearance that's bothering you?" Ande was clearly trying to establish some order.

"I don't know." Becca's brow was furrowed with concentration. "The clothes. The car, maybe. I mean, it was a Jaguar."

"You can't discredit someone for wearing nice clothes," said Larissa, fluffing out her sparkling sleeves.

"I'm not discrediting him." Becca sounded thoughtful, rather than antagonistic, but Larissa raised one of her unnaturally dark brows anyway. "It's that it doesn't fit. His museum is broke, and he's flashing so much money?"

"He may have money privately," said Marcia. "I mean, who becomes a curator anyway? It sounds like one of those jobs for wealthy people."

"He did seem to have his own resources," added Trent. Becca thought she saw him glance quickly at his older mate, although she couldn't be sure.

"Plus, part of his job is representing the museum, right?" Ande didn't seem to expect an answer. "So, he has to look good."

"Yeah, you're all right." Becca nodded thoughtfully. "But I want to find out. I think I need to ask him straight out about the museum's finances. Maybe even about his salary."

"Whoa." Marcia put her hands up. "How are you going to do that?"

"I'm not sure." Becca smiled once more, her eyes lighting up for the first time all evening. "But I'll figure it out."

Chapter Thirty-Four

By the time her friends had left, Becca was humming. Tunelessly, to be sure, but to her pets, who knew her well, it was a sign that she was happy—and that she was making plans.

"That was successful." Harriet preened. Not only had she received more cookies before the guests left, but Larissa had praised her coat and coloring.

"I'm not sure a compliment from that wrinkly thing is a good thing." Laurel, bathing, gave her sister her trademark side eye.

"You're just jealous because you wanted to grab one of those sleeves."

"How was that a success?" The kitten asked, her head tilted at a quizzical angle. *"They didn't work any magic."*

"Our person did something better, kitten." Clara smiled down at the tortie, her eyes closing in satisfaction. *"She resolved something in her mind."*

With that, the calico jumped up onto the table, where she had a good view of Becca, who was elbow deep in suds.

"The key," her person was saying, apparently addressing the mug she was rinsing off, "is how to ask him about money without letting him know what Shira said about the museum's finances. After all, it's possible that Shira was wrong—or lying for her own reasons."

Two mugs later, she seemed to have reached a decision. "That works," she said, as she reached for a dish towel. With her tail lashing in concern, Clara could only hope that her person's plan would not put her at risk.

The next morning, Becca leaped out of bed, eager to start her day.

"What's going on?" Harriet, still snuggled near where Becca's feet had been, looked over with half-open eyes.

"It's the curator." Laurel sat up from her own blanket nest, intrigued. *"I'm going to make sure she dresses properly."*

Since "properly," in Laurel's lexicon, usually meant something designed to attract the opposite sex, Clara followed after her as the slinky seal point jumped down and sauntered over to Becca's closet.

"It's an investigation, not a date." She phrased her objection as softly as she could, dipping her head as her sister turned and glared.

"I know that," Laurel spat. She could be cranky in the morning. *"But the proper outfit will give Becca an edge."*

Clara didn't respond. Becca had already laid out the cats' dishes and begun to dress. But, thanks to Clara's intervention, Laurel had been distracted enough to not do too much harm. In fact, when Becca tied a feather-light blue scarf around her neck and reached for a straw hat she'd bought on a whim two summers before, Clara could only approve.

"You see, Clown?" Her sister's voice sounded in her head. *"I can do tasteful, too."*

Still, it was with a whisker-bristling hint of apprehension that Clara followed her person out the door and onto the street toward her rendezvous with the dashing curator.

The plan, her cat knew, was to meet Hallowell at the Fallenburg Museum. Or, as Becca had put it, "the scene of the crime." Although her friends had blanched at that description, Becca had laughed off their concerns.

"It's a public space," she had said. "What can happen?"

In truth, her cat realized as she watched Becca prepare, her person was excited about the outing. To the best of her knowledge, Becca had never been to the museum, which was located somewhere her person had referred to as "the suburbs." That sounded ominous to the cat, but after all the hoopla at Charm and Cherish, Clara was just as happy to see her person heading out to a neutral location. If she enjoyed the visit, so much the better.

That didn't mean the trip was easy, and Clara's concerns grew as Becca proceeded into Central Square with her cat, shaded from view, trotting by her side. Pedestrian traffic was light this morning. Much of the city appeared to have abandoned it for cooler climates or the Cape. Becca did turn at least one head, however, and Clara didn't think it was because of her pace. No, that outfit—the scarf, the hat—set off her person's particular beauty, even as the walk brought color to her cheeks. But her cat worried about other reasons for onlookers to be interested in her person. Was Hallowell involved in the theft? Would he have confederates ready to snatch Becca, as Trina had been grabbed? If only her person would be more aware, she fretted, ears twitching back in distress and then upright to pick up any telltale sounds. If only Becca cared for herself the way her pets cared for her.

Becca did slow down as she entered the Square, to her cat's great relief. Like her pet, she appeared to be scanning the sidewalk. A bit late for those commuters who weren't on vacation and early for the lunch crowd, who would pour into the Square looking for outside dining in the fine weather, the sidewalks were relatively quiet. Instead, the pedestrians who, for the most part, strolled at a leisurely pace in the growing heat, appeared uninterested in the young woman who now stood still on the corner, letting them pass her by as she watched with interest.

Was she scrutinizing them as thoroughly as her cat did? That's what Clara asked herself as she eyed a heavy-set man in an Army jacket, who ambled, hunched, and mumbling, toward Becca. Bracing for an attack, Clara was relieved to see Becca step aside. More relieved still to watch the man pass, still grumbling about some private demons, as he made his way up the street.

Clara watched him walk away, almost missing that her person had made an abrupt turn to trot down a set of stairs that led underground. They were descending into the T, her cat knew. An infernal machine that would carry them under the city, the dreaded subway was both loud and odoriferous— and terrifying to a feline. Still, for the great love Clara felt for her person, she inched her way forward, standing with Becca as she waited on the platform. And when the wild beast drew up, she leaped into its gaping maw, taking up a guard position beneath Becca's feet as she sat and the car set out once again.

"That wasn't so bad." Becca might have been echoing Clara's thoughts when she disembarked some twenty minutes later, having already changed one monstrous car for another. Then again, her pet realized, Becca might have been referring to the time spent—and to the fact that as they began their ascent to the street, they were clearly outside of the city as Clara knew it.

The change was in the air. Even as she bounded up the last few steps, Clara smelled the moist greenery. And while she was certainly familiar with birdsong, the cacophony of calls that greeted them here nearly distracted her as Becca turned and began walking down a tree-shaded sidewalk. Although the pedestrian traffic here was almost as thick as it was in the city, the pace was different. Maybe it was the cool shadows—or those heady scents—but the people Becca passed on the sidewalk seemed more relaxed. An older woman, her white hair in a neat bun, even paused to smile at Becca, who grinned back in return.

"How lovely." Becca paused after a block, and Clara—almost drunk on the summer scents around her—had to scramble to keep from running into her. Looking up to see why her person had stopped, she saw a set of steps that led to a small portico, its white columns dappled by the shadows of the mature maples that lined the street.

As Clara sniffed at the air—the aroma of leaves here cut by a faint scent of dust—Becca started up the three steps, pulling open one of two large glass doors to enter a large, well-lit space within. After the moderate bustle of the street, the museum felt unnaturally quiet, as if it were removed from the world outside by more than just a glass door.

"Welcome to the Fallenburg." An older woman dressed in a blue blazer greeted her from behind a gleaming wooden counter. "Are you here for a tour?"

"No." Becca approached, her shoes tap-tapping on the polished floor. "I'm supposed to meet with Brian Hallowell."

"Ah." The woman nodded. "I'm afraid he's not in yet. Would you like to take a look around while you wait?"

"I'd love to." Becca craned around. "Is it possible to visit the gem room?"

At this, the woman sighed. "Yes, it's open. I'm afraid it's become our most infamous attraction."

"Because of the robbery?" Becca softened her voice, and the other woman smiled as she nodded.

"Can't be helped, I guess." With that, she fished out a folded map and pointed Becca toward one of three arches. "Down and to the left."

"Thanks." Becca took the map. Her cat, sensitive to her moods, could almost hear the words she wanted to say—that the missing sapphire would soon be home. But Becca kept quiet as she set off down the hall, pausing at the arch to admire the detailing in its woodwork.

"This looks in pretty good shape," she said to herself, letting one finger trace the carving. "They haven't made any cutbacks in upkeep, at any rate," she noted as she continued down the spotless walk.

The gem room, when they reached it, was a disappointment—at least for Clara. While the sidewalk in front of the museum had been rich in sound and scent and the lobby of the big house perfumed with wood polish, the gem exhibit itself felt sterile and still. While Becca walked slowly around the small and dimly lit room, peering down into glass cases, Clara found herself growing bored. Stones, after all, are only as interesting as the soil they sit in to a cat. And although Becca oohed and ahhed as she walked from one display to the next, her pet couldn't see the appeal.

"Oh, my." Halfway around the display, Becca had paused. Although Clara couldn't make out the signage, she could see that red velvet covered one case. "So this is where it was."

With that, Becca stepped back, taking in the room's two exits. One led back to the hallway, from which she had entered, while the other was blocked by a closed door. "Staff," Becca read.

"This all seems pretty much like Shira described it." Becca might have been speaking to herself, but her pet took note. "Except that the museum doesn't look like it's hurting for money. They certainly haven't stopped taking care of things."

At that, Becca made one more round, nodding at the multicolored specimens before heading back.

"Any sign of Mr. Hallowell?" The attendant looked up to respond, but just then, Becca glanced out at the street. "Never mind," she called out and pushed open the door.

Hallowell, dressed in light blue seersucker, was climbing out of a ride share.

"Becca!" Raising his arm, the curator hailed Clara's person. Becca waved back, quickening her pace. "I'm sorry I'm late. My car's in the shop again."

"Not a problem." At her side, Clara could feel her person pause, though whether it was something about the curator's appearance or his mode of transport, she couldn't tell.

"Something isn't right." Staring up at her person, Clara did her best to project her thoughts. *"You know it. Trust that instinct."*

How much of that got through to her human, the calico couldn't tell. But as Becca trotted down the steps to meet the curator, she felt as much as saw her person hesitate, her steps slowing as she hit the sidewalk. Only then did Becca notice movement on the curb alongside the museum. A black sedan, its windows heavily tinted, was pulling out of a space several cars behind Hallowell and now inched up, moving slowly along the curb.

Much slower, in fact. Which was probably why the red Honda behind it honked and then honked again.

What happened next unfolded so quickly, Clara barely had time to react. That first honk got both Clara's and Hallowell's attention, and as the latter looked, the cat could see the scowl forming on the curator's face as he turned back to scold the offending driver.

Becca, for her part, seemed more surprised than annoyed, her eyes growing wide—and then wider, causing her pet to whip around. As she and Becca watched, the black sedan drew up beside the museum, within feet of Hallowell and Becca, both of whom appeared frozen in their respective spots.

For a moment, the world stood still. All the surrounding pedestrians seemed to disappear as the car's passenger door slowly opened to reveal a heavy-set man clad in black jeans and T-shirt. Adjusting the oversized dark glasses that shielded his eyes, he stepped out onto the pavement, making up the ground between the car and the sidewalk in two large steps.

"You!" Becca spoke up, the movement breaking through. "You're the man who was with Trina."

She was right, of course. As Clara blinked up at the stranger, she caught a whiff of his scent—that strange mix of glue and sweat. But as she readied herself to jump, Hallowell stepped in front of her, shielding Becca with his body.

"What are you doing?" He raised his arms, as if his summer suit could somehow stop the black-clad bulk of the man. "This is not—"

But before he could finish, the hulking man had taken hold of his left arm, twisting it in a way that made Becca wince and brought Hallowell to his knees.

"Enough." The big man's voice was a growl as he turned his gaze on Becca, and Clara hunkered down, her hindquarters twitching as she waited for the optimal moment to leap at the attacker. His face, she decided, might be too high for her to reach. But those bare arms would make a good target for both claws and fangs.

"No!" Becca's yell stopped her, just for the moment, and she turned toward her person in time to see her adjusting her stance so that she stood, feet apart, and effectively blocked the sidewalk. "Stop it!"

The big man smiled, turning down to look at Hallowell, who was still crumpled on the sidewalk. He took a step toward her.

And stumbled as the prone curator grabbed his ankle with his good arm. Becca stepped back as he fell toward her, those big forearms flailing as he hit the concrete sidewalk.

"Are you okay?" Behind her, a woman her mother's age put a reassuring hand on her back. "I've already called the police."

"Stand behind me." Another bystander, a dreadlocked man in a lab coat, stepped forward to put himself between Becca and danger.

"Thank you, but I'm okay." She smiled up at the man and ducked around him. She was too late. Black T-shirt was scrambling to his feet, and while the growing crowd of onlookers had begun to surge forward, one growl sent them back as he dived into the car, which sped off, leaving the crowd buzzing.

"Mr. Hallowell! Are you okay?" The woman from the front desk appeared and was fluttering around Hallowell as a very pink man in running clothes helped him to his feet.

"Yes, yes." He withdrew from the runner with a grimace, which could have been provoked by the sweat dripping from the man's headband but which turned into a startling rictus as he righted himself. Only then did Becca notice how awkwardly he held his other arm—the one black T-shirt had twisted.

"Someone call an ambulance." She looked around. Several people in the crowd had their phones out, and she hoped they weren't simply filming. "Never mind," she said to no one in particular as she pulled her own phone out.

"I'm fine," Hallowell reiterated. "I don't need an ambulance."

"Yes, you do," she said, eying his arm. "And I'm going with you."

* * *

The EMTs, when they arrived exactly six minutes later, agreed. "That's not good," said one, a stout woman with a motherly air. "Would you lie down, sir?"

Hallowell had turned a bit green around the gills by then, Clara noted. And so, as much as she dreaded riding in an ambulance, she jumped in, waiting for Becca. There was no way she was letting her person go alone.

"Mr. Hallowell." With the crisis over, Becca returned to a more formal mode of address. "May I ask you a few questions?"

Considering that the curator was strapped to a gurney, Clara thought her person had a good chance of finally getting some answers. She hadn't counted on the maternal medic.

"I'm sorry, Miss. You can't be doing that here." Her tone was noticeably cooler than when she had been addressing Hallowell. "This man is injured, and he may be in shock. We let you ride along because we thought you were his friend or partner."

"We were meeting for breakfast." Becca's answer was noncommittal.

"Well, unless you're taking his order, I would suggest you be quiet for the rest of the ride."

Their arrival at Mass General wasn't any better. Hallowell was whisked off for X-rays, leaving Becca to wait. Undecided as to what step to take next, she called Maddy.

"I know, Maddy. I was half convinced that he was behind it too, but he actually got injured trying to protect me." A pause, and then Becca clarified. "Yes, really. The EMT said he had probably dislocated the joint, so they took him for X-rays. Which was all for the best, though it did mean I lost my chance to question him."

With all the beeping and other noises of the waiting area, Clara wasn't able to hear how Becca's friend had responded. Her ears did prick up as Becca began nodding, however.

"Yup, this is where Shira works. I might just reach out to her, Maddy. If nothing else, I'd like to see how she responds when she hears her former boss has been brought in here."

Chapter Thirty-Five

"Hi, Shira. I don't know if you're working today, but I'm at Mass General." Becca was standing beneath a sign asking visitors to "refrain from or limit cell phone usage," but nobody else in the crowded waiting room seemed to care. "There's been an incident with Brian Hallowell. I'm down in the Emergency Department, if you have a moment."

Clara's person had spent several minutes deciding what message to leave for Trina's roommate, not wanting to say too much or too little. "I'd love to watch them interact," she'd told Maddy before they hung up—and before she'd noticed that sign. "I don't know what would happen, but throwing them together might be interesting."

However, as the hours passed with no reply, Becca began to despair of getting any response at all. Spending the morning in a hospital waiting room was not what Becca had planned. And although Clara made the best of it, curling up beneath Becca's orange plastic chair for a nap, her person wasn't so easily occupied. Without her laptop, Becca realized, she couldn't even read over her notes, and the talk show host yelling out of the overhead television wasn't conducive to thinking either. Still, she tried, closing her eyes to run through everything that had happened since Trina had rushed into Charm and Cherish, panicked about her cat.

Her thought process was interrupted by a gentle hand on her shoulder, and she looked up to see the Emergency Department gatekeeper leaning over her.

"I'm sorry to wake you, but you had been asking about Brian Hallowell?" Out from behind her desk, the woman in the blue scrubs seemed smaller somehow, as well as friendlier.

"Yes, I came in with him." Becca quickly shed her sleepiness. "May I go in to see him now?"

The nurse shook her head, even as she gave a close-lipped smile. "He's been sedated for a procedure. I'm afraid I can't tell you more, but please, don't worry. It's not life-threatening. I just didn't want you waiting here all day. You might check back in about four hours, though."

"Thanks," Becca managed to smile back. "Is he going to be admitted?"

"I don't imagine so, but please, check back later today. That is, if he doesn't call you first." Her smile turned into a full-fledged grin, and Becca realized she'd taken them for a couple. It dawned on Becca that this misconception could be useful at some point, especially if Hallowell was admitted to the hospital, and so she widened her own smile as she thanked the nurse.

"I just have to touch base with a friend," she offered up her phone. "Is that okay?"

As the woman nodded, Becca started to type. *Don't know if you got my voicemail. I'm still at MGH but may be taking off soon*, she wrote. *If you get this, would you let me know?*

A row of dots appeared, causing Becca to hold her breath. But then they disappeared, and with them, her reason to stay.

Once outside the hospital, Becca breathed a sigh of relief. Even though she wasn't a patient and the man she came in with didn't seem to have been seriously hurt, the atmosphere in the waiting room had been tense. Outside, the day had blossomed into a perfect late August day: a warm sun set in a sky so deep and clear blue that it hinted at the cool of autumn to come. It was the kind of day that made summer seem all the more precious.

To Clara, the weather was a mixed blessing. A desert creature at heart, she loved the hottest days and would have enjoyed basking on the windowsill at home, if that were an option—and if Harriet allowed her any room. For now, however, she made the most of the day's warmth. Maybe, she mused as she trotted alongside her person, her appreciation of that glowing orb and the heat it provided was because of her family's near divine heritage. The priestess her ancestor had served, the one who had bestowed such powers on her feline aide, had worshiped a great goddess with myriad powers. Maybe one of them gave her servant's loyal felines the ability to convert solar power into, if not energy, then happiness.

It was true, Clara noted, that other cats enjoyed warm windowsills. Thanks to her ability to shade herself and pass through solid objects, she'd been out in the world more than her siblings, at least since those first days of kittenhood, when they'd survived on the street with their mother. In her wanderings, she had witnessed other cats basking in the sun. Some openly outdoors, even, stretched along stone walls or rowhouse stairs.

That thought made her think again of the kitten. Despite her coming from an unknown family, the tortie had displayed powers of her own. Knocking things off high shelves seemed a very kittenish action, at least as far as Clara could remember. But doing it without physically being on the shelf? Apparently, manipulating those objects with a simple flip of her one peach-toed paw? That reeked of magic. And while Clara knew how upset her siblings had been at first—referring to the young female as an "it" was particularly nasty—she had also noticed how they had come to accept that the tortie could communicate with them as freely as they did with each other. Even Mr. Butters, a quite common tabby, had possessed the power of speech, to Clara's surprise.

Perhaps, she wondered, there was more to these powers than she or her sisters had realized. Perhaps there was more to these cats. An idea began to form in the back of her mind, like a tickle at the base of her ears. Only just then, she picked up a change in Becca. Her person had straightened up, her relaxed posture switching into high alert, and her pet followed suit.

Looking ahead, Clara saw what must have caught Becca's attention. A figure, halfway down the block, with long, stringy hair, its color a kind of dishwater blonde. When she turned, showing a hawk-like nose and tired, heavily shadowed eyes, Clara was sure. This was the woman who had come into Charm and Cherish on a specious search for gems—and who had then reported to someone inside a black car with shaded windows.

"Excuse me!" Becca sped up, but the blonde was already turning the corner. "Miss? Wait up."

The blonde head swiveled, but didn't appear to see Becca in the crowd and, with a shrug, turned down a side street. At that, Becca broke into a run, Clara loping by her side. Catching up to her quarry, Becca reached out and gently touched the woman's arm, prompting the woman to spin around. Startled, no doubt, Clara assumed. But there was something more to this woman, she quickly ascertained. Something wrong.

It started with her scent. The woman smelled, a strong scent for a human, with an aroma that reminded her of when Becca had last cooked onions. Blocking the memory of Laurel and Harriet running wild, agitated by that smell, Clara focused in. Sweat, she realized, with an undertone of something chemical and so harsh it made her pull back, the black leather pad on her nose twitching. Looking up, she saw that Becca must have picked up this strong scent too. Unless, she reasoned, Becca was responding to the woman's appearance. Humans were less gifted in the senses, she reminded herself. Even her beloved Becca couldn't quite match a cat for discernment. But the look of fatigue or, no, defeat on the woman's face as she turned toward Becca would have alerted even someone less astute.

"Excuse me?" The blonde echoed back Becca's words, but fatigue—or something else—had her slurring them into one.

"We met at Charm and Cherish." Becca spoke quickly, as if aware that this woman's attention would not be held long. "You came in looking for jewels but then left rather abruptly."

"I'm sorry." The woman ducked her head, letting her lanky hair fall over her face. When she raised it to speak again, her eyes seemed clearer, if still tired. "I remember. That was rude of me."

"You were fine." Becca's tone softened. "But I was curious. When you left the shop, you spoke to someone in a black car. It looked like he— they—handed you an envelope?"

The blonde raised her hand to brush back her hair, or to hide the blush that was flooding her pale face with color. "He did," she nodded in acknowledgment. "I also—I made a call for him that I probably shouldn't have."

"The call about Mr. Butters. The missing cat." Becca explained, when the blonde's face scrunched up in confusion. "Trina had said it was a woman."

The blonde nodded. "I'm sorry. I've hit some hard times recently. I'm trying to stay clean."

"Good for you." Becca leaned in, giving the blonde woman's arm a gentle squeeze. "Is there anything I can do to help?"

For the first time, the blonde smiled, and her graying teeth couldn't hide her pleasure. "You're so kind, but no. I'm heading to a meeting now." She nodded over to a church up the block.

"I won't keep you then. But, first, do you mind telling me about the man in the car?" Becca's voice dropped. "Was he a dealer or something?"

"No." Another smile. "I am done with dealers. In fact, I thought it was a bit of payback, me helping the authorities and all."

"The authorities?"

"Yeah. I was kind of wondering if they were investigating you. Like, maybe your store was a front for something."

"We're not." Becca's smile was back.

"I figured as soon as I walked in. Nice place, truly. I'd have stayed, but I was supposed to report back, and I wanted to get paid."

Becca caught on that last word. "The police paid you to check out Charm and Cherish?"

"Private, not police. But they both had uniforms that said 'Security,' and they had that air about them. You know, like they were used to bossing people around."

"I think I do," Becca looked thoughtful.

"Anyway, I should go."

"Of course. Hey, if I can help you in any way or if you just want to browse, please come back. I'm Becca Colwin." She held out her hand.

"I'm Delia, Delia Crown," responded the blonde woman, giving Becca's hand a quick squeeze. "I will definitely drop by."

Becca stood on the sidewalk as the blonde—Delia—trotted up to the church and watched as she greeted a man standing outside the door, smoking. "Security," she said to herself, and Clara knew she was thinking of Shira. "I should have asked what the uniform looked like," she said, unaware that her pet was wishing the same, as she turned to continue the walk home.

193

Chapter Thirty-Six

"Trina, is Shira around?" Even before she'd made it to her apartment, Becca was on the phone. "I've got a few more questions for her."

"I'm sorry. She's working this afternoon." From the noise in the background, it sounded like Trina was rearranging furniture—or maybe just playing with Mr. Butters. "Is there something I can help you with? Does this have anything to do with the police?"

"Not exactly," Becca hedged. *Afternoon...*her pet could almost hear her thinking. When she'd gone to the hospital with Hallowell, it had been morning. Still, it was interesting that Shira hadn't gotten back to her by the time she'd left. "You haven't heard anything more from the police, have you?"

"No, it's strange." The bustle ceased, and Trina's voice grew more thoughtful. "I thought they'd follow up with me, you know?"

"Yeah." Becca squirmed, dragging out the word, and Clara, at her side, wondered if she was going to tell the other woman what had—or *hadn't*—happened. "Trina? I've got something to tell you. But, first, may I ask you a few questions?"

"Sure, do you want to come over?" The unmistakable sound of a cat's plaintive mew broke through. "I'm just hanging out with Mr. Butters, and you are like his godmother now."

Becca paused to take in her surroundings.

"Why not?" She might have been talking to herself. "I'm not that far away. I'll be over in a few."

Within fifteen minutes, Becca was climbing the stairs to Trina and Shira's apartment, Clara at her heels. As she trotted, the calico gamed out the situation before her. Mr. Butters might have the power of speech, but he surely couldn't shade himself as Clara could—or pass through solid matter. Then again, Mr. Butters wasn't likely to be able to communicate directly with his person. If the ginger tabby acted odd, Clara reasoned, the humans in the room would simply chalk it up to kitty weirdness, as they do so much of feline activity.

"Hey, what's up?" The Trina who opened the door looked happy, if flustered, as she brushed her dark hair off her face.

"I have a confession to make." Becca sighed heavily as she stepped into the room. Beside her, Clara stepped forward carefully, peering around for Mr. Butters.

"A confession?" Trina's easy smile wavered in confusion. Coming up beside her, Mr. Butters reached out to touch noses with Clara.

"Welcome," said the ginger tabby, his voice little more than a purr.

"Thank you." Clara dipped her head. *"You can see me?"*

"Of course. You opened your house to me." Mr. Butters gave the equivalent of a cat smile, his eyes closing as his whiskers went back. Clara felt a low purr begin in her belly, even as she tuned back into what the humans were saying.

"So, I didn't turn the sapphire in." Becca was leaning forward in her seat, her hands clasped, as Trina stared, eyes wide.

"You didn't…" The dark-haired woman shook her head. "I thought that was the point."

"So did I." Becca gave a rueful smile.

"Is it because of the stone's power?" Trina's voice fell to a hush.

"Not exactly." Becca shook her head. "I mean, yeah, I do want to be careful about it. There's something strange going on with this sapphire. Well, you know."

Trina nodded.

"And some of it is that the police aren't taking this seriously. They don't seem to believe that you or Mr. Butters were kidnapped. And if they don't believe that, what are they going to make of us having the Cat's Eye Sapphire?"

"You think they'll blame Shira again."

Becca nodded, close-lipped. "And they'll think we were in on it. After all," she continued, as Trina inhaled in surprise, "you had the stone for a long time. And I—well, I have some history with the local cops. In fact, I'm worried that they may prosecute me for another reason: practicing as a private investigator without a proper license."

"But you've helped them out. I've followed your cases."

"I'm not sure it matters." Another sad shake of her head. "They see me as a meddling amateur. They've warned me off before, but I thought that was just because they were concerned with my safety. Now I have reason to believe that they think that by advertising myself as a witch detective, I'm breaking the law. It would be one thing if I'd turned the sapphire in right away, but since I didn't…"

"They're going to assume that either you're involved or you're trying to play some angle for yourself."

"Exactly," Becca said.

The two women sat in silence for a moment, mulling over the situation.

"So what are you going to do?" Trina spoke first.

A shrug. "That's where things get complicated," said Becca. "I'd like to figure out what happened and deliver everything to them with a neat bow on top." She laughed, but it was a sad, little laugh. "Unfortunately, I'm more confused than ever, so I'm just kind of stuck."

The two sat there for a moment longer, until Trina broke the silence. "You said you had some questions for Shira?" Her voice sounded tentative. "Is there anything I can help with?"

"I'm not sure." Becca sighed before continuing. "I ran into the woman who came into Charm and Cherish. The one who was sent to see if we had the sapphire. She said that she was hired by someone in a security uniform."

"You can't think that Shira—"

Becca held up her hand. "I don't. Or, I don't want to, but there's something going on. I reached out to Shira earlier today, and I never heard back. Maybe she was getting ready for work or on her way in, but it makes me wonder. Maybe Shira's not involved, but I can't help but think maybe she knows more than she thinks she knows. You know?"

This time, it was Trina who shook her head. "This is all a mess, isn't it?"

"Yeah."

"What can we do?" Mr. Butters had been observing his person and now turned to Clara to comment.

"Watch out for our people." It was the best advice Clara could come up with, even if it didn't lay out a plan for either cat.

Becca, meanwhile, seemed to have come to a decision. "Maybe I just have to give up on trying to figure out what happened," she said. "The longer this drags on, the more trouble it makes."

The other woman leaned forward, her voice lowering. "Do you think you should try a scrying spell? I've heard they're good for finding things, but maybe they'd be useful for discovering the truth as well."

Becca shook her head and sighed. "I have, with no luck. But thanks for believing in me. To be honest, my coven got together, and I was hoping that with all of us concentrating, but… nothing. That's one reason I was hoping to ask Shira about the other people who worked security. Maybe if I could talk to that one guy she mentioned, the one in charge, I could get a new lead. If I'd been able to talk with Hallowell, I bet he would have put me in touch with him."

"Shira's friend, Nick? I have his number." Trina popped up from her seat on the sofa. "He called Shira a few weeks ago about her last paycheck. Hang on."

Dashing from the room, she came back with a Post-It note and an expectant look on her face. Taking a deep breath, Becca nodded—and then dialed the number.

"Hi, this is Becca Colwin from Charm and Cherish." Making a face, she mouthed the word *'voicemail.'* "I'm a friend of Shira's who used to work with you, and I was hoping you could answer a couple of questions for me. Would you give me a call back?"

"Excellent. I bet he'll get back to you. It sounded like you might be calling about a job reference, and I'm sure he'd give her one." Trina sounded buoyed by the exchange. Grateful, Clara realized, to have something to contribute.

"So what now? Do you want some lunch?"

"Thanks, but I think I ought to hit the road." Becca didn't seem to be quite as cheered. "Honestly, I'm about ready to just turn the sapphire in and deal with the consequences. I don't know if I've been fooling myself, telling myself I could solve crimes as a witch detective. Maybe it's time I give it up. Every time I try to make headway on this case, I run into another dead end, and I just keep on digging myself in deeper and deeper."

"Well, *I* believe in you."

Becca responded with a sad smile.

"Are you going to the cops now? Do you want some company?"

Becca shook her head. "I've got to get the sapphire first."

The other woman waited, eyes wide.

"It's back at Charm and Cherish," confessed Becca. "Hidden in that tray of semiprecious stones."

Chapter Thirty-Seven

To Becca's surprise, Trina responded with a resounding guffaw that startled Mr. Butters into a jumping position, ears back and eyes alert.

"What was that?" The cat choked out.

"Perfect," his person hooted. Once she noticed her pet's distress, however, her laughter stopped, and with some coaxing, Mr. Butters settled—with Clara, unseen, by his side—beside Becca's chair. Glancing to make sure her pet was comfortable, Trina continued. "Didn't you say that that woman—Delia—had taken a look at that tray?"

"Yeah." Becca might have been a bit taken aback at Trina's reaction at first, but now she chuckled along. "But I downplayed what was there, and it worked: hiding in plain sight. Kind of like when it was around Mr. Butters' neck."

"Better." Trina wiped her eyes. "Maybe those stones will protect it—or even amplify its power."

That gave Becca pause. "Can you tell me more about the Cat's Eye Sapphire's power?" she asked, reaching down to fondle Mr. Butters' ears.

"Just what I've told you: protection," Trina was quick to speak up. "And clarity. Though what that means, I'm not quite sure."

"You know a lot about the sapphire." Becca kept rubbing around the base of the cat's ears, but Clara picked up something in her tone. Mr. Butters must have, too, because he abruptly pulled away.

Trina shrugged. "I've been doing my research."

Clara looked at her person, waiting for a response. Becca only smiled and reached for her jacket.

"I guess I should be off."

"Can I join you?"

For a split second, Becca appeared to waver. "Sure," she said, at last.

"I'm going to text Shira, too," the other woman added, seemingly oblivious to how Becca suddenly stiffened. "She's probably got the biggest stake in this of us all."

"My person isn't sure about this," Clara quietly mewed in Mr. Butters' ear.

"I know," responded the ginger tabby. *"But you'll keep her safe. You'll keep all of them safe."*

It wasn't exactly what the little calico had meant, but with Becca already heading out the door, it was too late for her to explain.

"So, you just left the sapphire in the tray?" As they walked, Trina started pestering Becca with questions.

"Yeah," Becca admitted.

"So now it's in theshop?"

Becca nodded. "Charm and Cherish is closed today, but I have the keys and the alarm code."

By the time they reached the shop, Becca was clearly on edge. Clara, shaded as always, even dropped back to keep an eye on Trina. But even as she eyed the dark-haired woman, she wrestled with her own doubts. Mr. Butters might not be a magical cat, but he was a feline, and Clara was inclined to trust feline instinct and intuition even over her darling Becca's. Surely, the orange tabby couldn't be that wrong about his person—or about Shira, who sounded like a second pet parent to him. Unless—the thought momentarily froze Clara in her tracks—Mr. Butters was deceiving her.

Would a cat deceive another cat? The question was too profound for the calico to even consider. Certainly, her sisters didn't trust other felines—or not completely. Clara could all too easily recall the way Laurel had scoffed at the kitten. And while neither Laurel nor Harriet had gone so far as to be cruel or—she paused again—deceptive, they had both been dismissive of the little tortie. And of Mr. Butters as well.

Was it possible that the tabby was exacting revenge? Or acting out of some kind of misguided loyalty to his human?

"You welcomed me into your house." The echo of the ginger tabby's declaration rang in Clara's ears, distracting her until a loud honk startled her out of these thoughts. With everything going on, she had let her shading fade. Plus, she was in a crosswalk. A driver, his window open, was leaning out the window.

"Crazy cat! You're going to get yourself killed." From the strain around his eyes, Clara could tell the man was more frightened than angry, and she shook herself. If she had been shaded…she didn't want to think about what might have happened.

"Sometimes, we have to trust the universe."

The memory of Elizabeth's words shook the little cat, even as she bolted for the sidewalk and once more cloaked herself in a gray haze. Making out Becca and the taller woman a half a block away, she exhaled in relief. Clara was lucky, and she knew it. Not only hadn't she been hit, she also hadn't been spotted unshaded by her human. Becca had enough to worry about, Clara knew, without her supposed house pet appearing suddenly on a city street.

"You've got to be more careful, Clown." As she raced to catch up with her humans, Clara heard Laurel's voice in her head. This time, she was sure, it wasn't a memory.

"Laurel?" Careful, this time, to stay focused, Clara queried the air around her.

"We're with you, silly." Harriet, this time. *"But there's only so much we can do."*

"Thank you." Clara did her best to express her gratitude as both a thought and an emotion. *"But... what are you doing?"*

"Becca may be in trouble, silly." Laurel picked up the conversation—and their older sister's epithet. *"We're not going to leave you two alone."*

Closing her eyes ever so briefly, Clara felt warmth like a purr flood through her body. In an uncertain world, she knew she had her sisters to rely on. And Mr. Butters? Well, that question would be answered at a different time.

* * *

By the time she caught up with Becca and Trina, the pair were nearly at Charm and Cherish. Dashing past the alley that bordered the little store, Clara managed to slip inside the door just as Becca unlocked it, gesturing for the other woman to join her.

"Wow, I'd forgotten how cool this place is." As Becca relocked the door behind them, Trina looked around the shop, craning her head as if she'd never seen its shelves packed with books, candles, and statuary. Pausing just inside the door, she turned first to the front window display, where three crystal prisms refracted the afternoon sun into colorful beams, and then to the empty counter where the register stood. "It looks like business has been good," she said, pointing to the bare space.

"Not particularly." Becca shook her head as she proceeded toward the back. "Honestly, we're barely getting by with the online lessons. But we are careful with putting things in the back when we're closed. This is a pretty safe neighborhood. The foot traffic helps, but any losses would really hurt—even with insurance."

"Gotcha." Trina turned to follow Becca, pausing at the doorway. "I didn't realize that the great Charm and Cherish was on such fragile footing."

"I think this is typical for a small business." Becca spoke from the back room. "But the owner—Elizabeth's sister—wants more. She keeps threatening to turn the space into a craft store or something."

"That would be a pity." Trina stopped to admire the statue of Kali, the duplicate of the one Hallowell had bought. "Hey, did you tell anyone else we were going to be here?"

"What?" Becca's head popped out of the backroom, the tray of colored stones in her hands. "No."

"Maybe this guy didn't know you were closed today." Trina nodded toward the sidewalk, where a slender, balding man with his arm in a sling stood in front of the shop, looking around. Dressed in jeans and a button-down shirt, a bit frayed at the collar, Becca didn't recognize him at first. Then he turned up his face towards hers, and she recognized the curator.

"Oh, that's Brian Hallowell." Becca's voice broke with relief. Placing the tray in its usual spot by the register, she went to unlock the door. "I've never seen him so casually dressed. But of course, he must have just gotten out of the hospital."

"Shira's old boss?" Trina followed behind as Becca stepped outside.

"Mr. Hallowell," she called. "Brian." At the sound of his name, the slender man started, before turning and fixing a smile on Becca.

"Becca. I'm so glad you're here." Without waiting for an invitation, he walked past her into the store, nodding to Trina as he did.

"How are you? I wasn't sure when the hospital would let you out. Are you okay?"

"Oh, this?" He looked down at his sling, wincing slightly with the movement. "I'm fine. I'll be fine," he corrected himself with a lame laugh. "There's a dislocation, but I'm not going to need surgery."

"I'm glad of that, but I'm sorry." Becca was holding back from touching him, Clara could tell. Instead, she clasped her hands together. "May I ask what the police said?"

"The police?" He must have jolted his arm as he spoke, because he winced again. Trina, meanwhile, looked on with growing interest.

"They came to talk to you, didn't they?" Becca pried gently.

"Oh, yes, of course." A slow nod. "I gave them a statement before I went home to change. I gather they'll follow up."

"Do you think I should I talk to them?" Becca paused before answering her own question, turning to Trina for confirmation. "I should. When I go in today, I'll tell them about the attack."

"Wait." Hallowell raised his good hand. "What are you going to tell them?"

"Well, how you saved me, of course." Becca looked down at the ground, and Clara had the distinct impression that she was blushing. "I mean, those thugs were after me."

"After you?" Hallowell blinked as Trina's eyes went wide.

"It's—well, it's a long story." Becca's color had definitely pinked up, as both Trina and Hallowell waited for her to continue. "But you know that someone kidnapped Trina, right?" Hallowell looked over at the other woman but before he could comment, Becca started to explain. "They thought she had the Cat's Eye Sapphire. I mean, she did at one point. Like I said, it's a long story. But by then, I had it. Anyway, I think those two men figured it out and that they were actually trying to grab me." She finished with a smile. "Only you stepped in."

"Oh." The curator had the grace to look embarrassed, staring at the ground as a slight wash of pink rose to his cheeks.

"Anyway, today I'm finally going to the police, and I'll be sure to tell them the whole story. Including your part."

"Thanks." He looked up at her, but then quickly turned toward the window.

"You think they're going to come after me again?" Becca's head swiveled, and Clara, who had taken up a post beside the gemstone, leaped silently to the floor. She wanted to watch over the sapphire, but keeping an eye on the street outside took precedence if Becca's safety was concerned.

"I don't know." Hallowell scanned the street, his face looking increasingly drawn.

"Do you need to sit down?" Becca must have noticed something, too, her cat thought, and she turned toward the other woman. "Trina, would you get the chair from the back room?"

"I'm fine." Waving her off with his good hand, Hallowell protested. "Really. I just want to be careful."

"Of course." Becca bit her lip in thought. "You probably have a little PTSD from the attack."

"What? Oh, maybe." He was so focused on the front window that Becca went to look. Clara glanced up at her, willing her to understand that her devoted pet was on guard.

"Anyway, I'm protected," she continued, eying the traffic outside. "At least, I think I am. The sapphire has its own magic."

"Excuse me?"

"Didn't you know? The Cat's Eye Sapphire has powers of its own."

"Uh huh." He nodded, but Clara got the distinct sense that he wasn't listening or that something was off..

"Supposedly, it also provides clarity. Though in this case, I'd say it has done everything but. Trina could probably explain more." She looked around. "Where is Trina? She was supposed to be getting a chair for you, Mr. Hallowell. I think you need one. You've gone positively white."

With that, she turned toward the back room, and Clara sat up with a start. *"Watch out, Clown!"* Laurel's words rang in her head as she raced after Becca. *"The danger isn't coming from the front..."*

Clara whirled around—too late. Readying to leap, she nearly rammed into Becca, who had stopped short in the doorway. As Clara peered past her, into the breakroom, she saw why. Two masked men, both wearing black, stood there—and one was holding Trina with an arm around her waist and another over her mouth.

"Where's the stone?" The man holding Trina had a deep, raspy voice that Becca recognized.

"What are you doing? Let her go!" Becca yelled in response, stepping toward the dark-haired woman, who had gone white with fright.

"I wouldn't do that if I were you." The other man stepped forward, the wide and lethal-looking hunting knife in his left hand plain to see. As he took another step toward Trina, she whimpered, her voice muted by the gloved hand over her mouth.

Becca stopped short and turned toward Hallowell.

"Brian?" He only shook his head as she stared at him, her face falling.

A loud belly laugh caught her attention as everyone—including Clara—turned back to the man with the knife.

"Is he your knight in shining armor?" The ridicule cut through his mask, and while Becca stared, confused, Clara turned to see the curator's face going a blotchy red as he hung his head.

"He defended me," Becca responded weakly, prompting another bitter laugh.

"So that's what you think. Brian sure knows how to spin a story, doesn't he? Like the one he spun about the sapphire going missing overnight. I think the cops might have bought that one, don't you, Brian."

The curator didn't raise his head, and the black-clad man laughed again.

"Brian didn't tell you what was really going on, did he?" His deep voice held the edge of that cruel laughter in it. "He let you think we were going for you, I bet. In truth, he's the one we wanted—and would have gotten, too, if you hadn't gotten in the way. Why don't you tell the nice lady why, Brian?"

The curator only shook his head, his eyes still fixed on the floor.

"He owes us—owes my group, that is. Has for years, running up the expenses with his fine clothes and fancy car. We took the wheels a while ago, but that barely put a dent in the total. Right, Brian?"

Becca inhaled sharply, her head snapping back to the shamefaced curator.

"Is this true. Mr. Hallowell? Your car—you said it was in the shop."

Another laugh. "Oh, that's a good one. And are the silver cufflinks and Rolex in for repairs as well?"

Becca took in the curator, seeing his jeans and worn shirt anew. "Mr. Hallowell…"

The curator looked up at the sound of his name. "I'm sorry," he said in a voice barely above a whisper.

That provoked another bark of laughter. "Not as sorry as you're going to be. He didn't tell you how he was going to settle his tab, did he?"

Becca shook her head, the truth dawning on her in the moment of silence that followed. Clara, for her part, had figured out what was going on moments before. That didn't help the calico make a plan, but it did give her an edge as all the humans turned toward Hallowell.

"The sapphire," Becca broke the silence, her voice flat and low. "You promised them the Cat's Eye Sapphire."

"Bingo!" Another cruel laugh. "He promised to deliver it, and when he lost it, we had to take matters into our own hands. But now he's found it—or found you, at any rate. Which amounts to the same thing."

Becca turned to Trina, whose wide eyes held a wordless plea.

"Let her go first." Becca's voice faltered, but she got the words out. "Then I'll take you to it."

"Take us to it? No." The man with the knife shook his head. "You've already told us it's in this store. Mixed in with the cheap stones by the counter."

"They're not —"

But before she could finish her thought—a defense of the semiprecious gems, Clara suspected—a sound from the front of the shop silenced her. A jingle of bells, and a familiar voice calling. The front door, her cat realized with a start. Becca hadn't locked it again after letting Hallowell in.

"Hello?" A familiar voice called.

"Shira." Becca breathed out the name of Trina's roommate, her face falling further. "I thought, for sure…" She swallowed hard. "I wanted to trust her."

Becca looked at Trina, but all that the other woman's face showed was panic. It was time, Clara told herself, to act. Steeling herself, she squatted down, hindquarters quivering. She'd go for the man with the knife, she decided. It would be difficult to attack while still shaded, but if she concentrated, she could do it. The element of surprise—the sudden pain of teeth and claws ripping through his gloved hand—would be worth whatever happened to her next as he shook his hand in pain and disbelief, undoubtedly sending her flying across the room.

"Hello? Is anybody here?" Shira again, her voice hesitant. Becca took a breath, and Clara put her ears back, readying herself. In front of them, the two masked men exchanged a glance.

"Go get her." Raspy voice—the one with the knife—held it out, pointing to the front room. "Bring her back here, but if you say anything…" He looked over at Trina and then back to Becca, who nodded her acquiescence.

"Shira?" Becca's voice broke as she called the other woman's name. "Is that you?"

The man with the knife nodded, gesturing for her to go. "Bring her back here," he whispered, and Clara followed as her person stepped into the front room. As much as she wanted to bite that man—to feel her claws ripping into his flesh—her first duty was to her person. Besides, Clara had no idea what new threat awaited Becca back in the shop.

"Becca, hi." Shira sounded a bit confused. "I got your call and went to look for you, but you'd already left Emergency." She looked around, gesturing back toward the door. "I thought the store was closed today."

"We are. I just came in to clear some things up." There was a hitch in her voice, and Clara could only hope the other human couldn't hear it. With her acute feline senses, however, she could smell that Becca was sweating. If only she could comfort her! But the little cat kept her distance, waiting until she could aid her human in a more material way.

"Would you come back with me while I finish up?"

"Oh, I don't want to bother you. I just remembered something about the investigation. It's probably not important, but since you'd asked if there was anyone else…" Shira left the sentence hanging.

Becca, who had started to move back toward the door, paused. She wanted to ask the other woman to continue, Clara could tell. But from her quick, anxious glance toward the backroom, it was clear that she was also worried about Trina—and that knife.

"You remembered something?" Becca's tongue darted out to lick her dry lips, even as she glanced back over her shoulder once again.

"Yeah." Shira nodded, apparently oblivious to the danger waiting—*or unconcerned*, Clara thought. "I remember because it really made Trina angry, the way they shifted the blame onto me."

Becca was about to follow up when a strained voice called from the storeroom. "Shira, is that you?"

"Trina?" Shira started toward the backroom.

"You were about to tell me what you remembered." Becca stepped in front of her.

Shira stopped, looking at her curiously. "What's going on here?"

Becca inhaled, and Clara braced, waiting for what her person would do next, when Trina once again called out.

"Shira, can you come here?"

Pushing by Becca, the security guard plowed into the backroom only to stop suddenly as she took in the scene before her.

"I'm sorry," Becca, behind her, said under her breath.

"What?" Shira shook her head, as if to clear her vision.

"Glad you could join the party." This time, it was the man who held Trina who spoke, his voice tight and strained. "We're waiting for your friend Becca to deliver."

"Becca?" Shira whirled around.

"They want the sapphire," she said, her face unreadable. "That's what they've been after all along. And Brian Hallowell is helping them."

"I'm not—" The balding man started to speak, his protest falling off.

"He owed these guys," Becca continued. "And the sapphire was supposed to pay it off."

Shira spun around, and as she did, the man with the knife stepped closer to Trina, who whimpered and closed her eyes.

"Only they have a problem now." Becca's voice was firm, though her cat could hear the effort that held it so. "You see, when they grabbed Trina, they had a hold over me. But now you're here too. And for all that he's complicit, I doubt very much that Brian Hallowell is going to get involved in bloodshed."

"Do you really want to risk that?" The taller man pulled Trina away from his partner, pressing the large knife to her throat.

"No, no. Of course not." Shira held her hands out in a placating gesture. "Though I should have known, Nick."

Becca turned, her face questioning.

"That's what I came to tell you," Shira said, her face now set in anger. "When I was taken in for questioning, all the investigators asked me about was, why was I there? Why had I come in to work at the museum on my day off? They kept asking me about that. Well, that and how long I'd spent in the gem room."

She paused and looked at Trina, who nodded almost imperceptibly.

"It was Trina who pointed out what I was missing. That whenever I tried to tell them about how I'd been told that nobody had shown up for the shift, they told me I was lying. They pointed out that Nick Roswell had been there all along. It was Trina who realized that Hallowell must have been lying. That he never admitted that he had told the front desk that the shift needed coverage.

"He set me up to take the fall, and I didn't even realize it."

Becca turned toward the curator, who had gone pale. When he didn't speak, she cleared her throat and spoke again, facing the masked men. "So, what are you going to do? We know who you are. Are you going to kill all of us?"

At that, Trina whimpered again, tears starting in her eyes, but Becca's eyes had gone to the curator—as Clara was carefully gauged her next move.

Shira, however, remained the wild card. "Becca," she said, stepping forward to take the other woman's arm. "What are you saying?"

It happened so quickly Clara didn't even have time to react. As Becca watched, Hallowell stumbled—or appeared to—stepping away from the black-masked thugs.

"Get him!" The shorter man called out. Raspy voice—Nick—turned and Becca made her move, lunging for Trina as soon as the knife had been pulled away.

"Run," she yelled over at Shira, throwing herself at the masked man. But the other woman didn't heed her call, instead adding her substantial bulk to the pile up, pulling at the arm that restrained her roommate.

"Trina!" At that moment, something in the captive woman roused, and she bent forward, pulling her captor off balance and, at the same time, kicking backward. With a cry of pain, he loosened his grip, and Becca and Shira pulled the girl free.

"Well, good for you." They looked up to see that their raspy-voiced adversary had grabbed Hallowell, his knife at the curator's throat.

"I gather you don't like this mutt much right now," said Nick Roswell. "But do you really want to see him die?"

Chapter Thirty-Eight

Becca had no response, and when the other two women looked to her for guidance, all she could do was shake her head.

"Well, then." Even with the mask, Clara could make out Nick's smile. "Shall we, ladies?"

Without removing the knife from Hallowell's throat, he nodded toward the door, and Becca led the way, walking slowly, as the group of six crowded into the front room. As they walked, she leaned slightly toward Trina.

"I don't think he can afford to let us go," she said, her voice barely above a whisper. In response, the dark-haired woman gasped and then nodded before shuffling over to share Becca's realization with her roommate.

"Enough chitchat," Nick called out as Trina leaned in to whisper to Shira. "Unless you want blood all over your pretty little shop."

Trina and Shira exchanged a look as Becca stepped up to the register. Despite her fears, she was holding herself steady, her pet noted with pride. If only she could find a way to help her. If only, the little calico thought, her sisters were here with her.

For a moment, Clara thought Becca had heard her. Something about the way her person paused, her mien defiant as she looked back over the heads of the others to directly address Nick and the terrified man he held close.

"Let him go," Becca said, her voice tight. Only Clara could hear the tremor she was holding back. "Let Brian Hallowell go." Hallowell, his face drawn and white, glanced up at her with something akin to hope, and Clara began to plan. One jump. The men were standing close enough together that maybe she could claw them both…

"The sapphire first," said Nick. Gesturing with his chin, he motioned his companion up toward Becca, while he stepped back, pulling Hallowell with him and ruining Clara's admittedly sketchy scheme.

"Got it." Becca stepped back toward the counter, as Trina and Shira both stepped aside, letting the shorter masked man through. Glancing at the tray that lay there, she shook her head. "You should be aware, Nick, that the sapphire is not what you think it is."

That made the man coming toward her pause, but Nick simply laughed.

"Do you think using my name is going to make me relent, *Becca?*" There was a coldness in his words that made Clara shiver. "Let me guess, the stone's got an ancient pharaoh's curse on it."

"Not exactly." Becca glanced at the masked man at her side but continued to address Nick. "But it does have certain powers—powers that do not bode well for someone who takes it by force or violence."

Another cold laugh, about as jolly as a stone. "It also has the power to make me very rich—and to save your friend here's life." The knife ticked up a notch, its point digging into Hallowell's throat as the curator gulped nervously. "And enough of the stalling. Rich?"

Becca couldn't read anything in the shorter man's eyes, the only part of his face exposed by the black balaclava he still wore over his head. Clara, however, could sense his reluctance in his increased perspiration as well as the slight hesitation as he reached out to take Becca by the arm.

Pulling free, Becca turned and reached for the tray. As the others watched, she scooped the multicolored stones on display down toward her and began to work her finger under the velvet at the other end. Flipping it up, she reached in to reveal a large blue stone.

"So that's where it's been." Trina was the first to speak, as Becca lifted the sapphire for all to see. "I couldn't imagine you had it in with the others."

"No." Becca turned with a sad smile. "I couldn't risk someone wanting to buy it. Despite its powers."

"Enough." Nick's gruff bark interrupted them. "Rich? Get the stone."

Only Clara saw the slight tremor in his hand as he reached out, and it took the cat's sharp feline hearing to catch the invocation that Becca mumbled under her breath as she slowly reached forward, the blue stone cupped in her hand.

"Bast, great mother, see justice done..." It wasn't the entirety of the spell that the coven had tried, more a prayer than a summoning of power, but something about the words—or maybe it was the desperation in Becca's voice—made the fur rise along Clara's back.

"Bast, great mother..." Becca's face was turned up now, addressing the Bast statuette that had watched over the shop for days now. Even as she released the gemstone, letting it fall into Rich's open palm, her voice gained strength, energizing the crowded space with a crackle that made her cat think of the air after a thunderstorm. *"See justice done!"*

"Shut up." Nick's raspy voice had grown even more hoarse, as if he were choking, and he grew pale as he backed up against the bookcase, pulling his hostage with him. "Shut up or I'll cut him."

"You were always going to cut him anyway." Becca's voice rang with authority, her gaze falling from the cat goddess's statue to meet his. "You can't let any of us go."

"Nick?" Rich, confused, turned to face his partner. And in that moment, it happened.

Afterward, Clara couldn't be clear on the sequence of events. One thing she knew for sure: As if struck by Becca's words, Nick jerked back, his head hitting the shelves behind him. And in that moment, Clara saw a paw—black, daubed with pink—as if it were reaching down from above, reaching from the top of the bookcase. Or, no, she realized, *above* the case, as if from Charm and Cherish's pressed tin ceiling. And either that paw or the jolt of Nick's head caused the case to jostle, ever so slightly, upsetting the Bast statuette that sat on top and sending it down to strike the knife-wielding thief on the head.

"Now!" Clara didn't know whose voice gave the command, but as the masked man stumbled, loosening his hostage, she didn't hesitate, leaping to sink her fangs into the arm that held the knife.

Even as her claws sought purchase, digging into his shirt and reaching up to puncture the thin fabric stretched over his face, she heard more voices joining the fray.

"Trina!" This time, it was Shira who yelled as she plowed into the second man. Trina jumped a split second later, wrapping her arms around the ruffian as the two brought him down to the floor.

Becca, meanwhile, had not wasted any time. Kicking Nick's hunting knife into a corner of the shop, she kneeled above the prone man, the statuette raised above his head. "I told you the Cat's Eye Sapphire had power," she said. "Bast protects her own."

Chapter Thirty-Nine

"*H*ow did you do that?" Clara, still shaded, bowed her head before the cat goddess. *"I mean, thank you. But would you explain?"*

A warm vibration, reminiscent of a purr, enveloped her, and she let her query go. There was too much else happening for her to stand in the way.

"Yes, we've had a break-in. The perpetrators were armed, but we've managed to disarm them." Becca was talking on her phone as Trina finished knotting Nick's wrists behind his back, using the yarn from a dreamcatcher that had been broken in all the commotion. Stripped of his balaclava, he was staring at his own knife, which Shira held close to his eye, even as she kept her seat on the back of Rich's neck.

"Watch it." Trina nodded over to the other man, who was struggling.

"I can't breathe," he wheezed out.

"Don't be a baby. I'm not that heavy," said Shira, who shifted slightly, allowing the prone man to take a deep breath.

"Yes, we'd like some assistance." Becca rolled her eyes, and—with her hand over the phone—turned toward her colleagues. *"Finally,"* she mouthed.

"Done." Trina moved onto the other man, and Shira rose, still holding the knife.

"I can't believe you set me up, Nick." The betrayal seemed to rankle more than the theft for the big woman. "You were my mentor."

"I can't believe you betrayed the public trust." Becca was looking over at Brian Hallowell, who had collapsed on the floor, his head in his hands. "And worse than that, you allowed those men to threaten us."

"I know, I know." The voice that emerged was muffled with tears. "I need help."

"The time for that is past." Everyone turned as Elizabeth swept into the room. Although her orange and yellow pattern shone as bright as the August sun, the scowl on her face more closely resembled a thundercloud, making Clara recall that strange moment when Becca had invoked the goddess. "Justice is owed."

"Elizabeth, you wouldn't believe what happened." Becca paused, a half-smile lighting up her face. "Or maybe you would. Though I'm not sure if it was Bast herself or the sheer coincidence of Nick here banging his head back on the bookcase that allowed us to get the upper hand."

"Good things happen when we work in concert," said the older woman, her face softening. "That's why we join together in a coven. Why we join with our sisters." Her eyes shifted momentarily to the space where Clara, still shaded, sat watching. "And sometimes, we have to trust the universe."

The police arrived soon after, and, what with all the humans stomping around, the shaded calico took refuge in one of the bookshelves, wedging herself into a cozy spot right by *Spells for Change.* It seemed to take Becca an unusually long time to explain what had happened in the little store, and by the time she handed over the blue stone—which she'd retrieved from a downcast Rich as Trina had tied him up—the little cat was dozing. She'd stirred only to hear Becca say something about "tomorrow."

"Yes, I'll make a statement," she continued, as Clara blinked herself awake. "Just please make sure someone other than Detective Newsom is there. I tried to explain what was going on to him days ago, and he was a bit threatening."

The officer she was speaking to scribbled in his notepad as she spoke, raising his brows at this last bit. "Threatening?"

"Yes, I don't know if I was supposed to hear what he was saying, but he clearly thought that I was acting as a private investigator without a license. I believe he was considering charging me." The adrenaline must be wearing off, her cat realized. After the scare and all the excitement, Becca was settling into a funk. "That's why I didn't turn the sapphire over right away."

The officer's eyebrows went higher at this, but he kept his thoughts to himself. Soon after, the police left—with all three men in handcuffs—and Becca collapsed on the floor.

"Are you okay?" Trina rushed over.

"Yeah." Becca nodded. "It's just been a lot."

"I'll say." The two turned as the bells announced their latest visitor: a dumpling of a woman whose swath of red lipstick was stretched in a broad grin.

"Margaret." Becca greeted the store's owner without getting up.

"Sister." Elizabeth dipped her head, much like Clara would to her siblings.

"I hope you're not angry." Becca struggled to her feet, brushing off her jeans as she rose. "I didn't mean to involve the store."

"Not involve the store?" Margaret's eyebrows, as bushy as her sister's, rose in alarm. "That would have been terrible!"

"Excuse me?" Becca looked from one sister to another, taking in Elizabeth's enigmatic smile.

"You're all over the web." The store's owner leaned over, as if her stage whisper couldn't be heard out to the street. "People are saying you found the Cat's Eye Sapphire through magic. Our online traffic is through the roof."

Chapter Forty

"What a day." Becca was already dialing Maddy as she collapsed on the sofa. "I don't know if I have any magical powers, Maddy, but I'm pretty sure my job is safe."

Even as she lay there, she was eying the shelf where she had tucked the shards of the broken blue-and-white bowl days before. "I guess I'm good publicity for the store," she explained. "Plus, it turns out that Margaret was wrong about the PI license."

Maddy's response was inaudible to the calico who sat, grooming, on the rug.

"What I do isn't considered 'private investigating.' In part, I gather, because I use the craft. But when we went into the police station to tell them about Trina being abducted, they weren't talking about me being in trouble for what I do—they, well, Newsom, was saying that I was going to get *myself* into trouble. I guess he's right, I do. But I also solve cases, and he knows that. That's why he was willing to start the paperwork on the kidnapping. He trusted me. He just didn't want me investigating alone."

This time, Clara could hear Maddy's agitated response. Becca, however, seemed quite calm. "I know, Maddy. But how could I refuse to help someone who had lost her cat?"

Maddy went on for a while after that, but Becca's attention was clearly focused on those broken pieces once more.

"Now if only…" She shook her head. "Never mind, Maddy. It's just another spell I've been trying."

Just then, the doorbell rang.

"Maddy, I've got to go." Becca sat up. "I lost track of the time."

She raced to the door and opened it to see a beaming Jerry Keller.

"Hey, sweetie. I missed you." He handed over a bouquet even as she pulled him close.

***

When the two left for dinner, Jerry listened with widening eyes as Becca filled him in, the cats of the household had a chance to catch up.

"How did it go down?" Laurel was circling, sniffing at her sister.

"You haven't thanked us yet." Harriet plopped herself down in front of the calico, her ears tilting ever so slightly back.

"Thank you." Clara dipped her head—and then raised it, the question apparent in the curl of her tail. *"But...what happened? I thought I saw something..."*

Harriet glanced back at Laurel, who had paused to wash. *"That must have been a manifestation of our will. We were sitting on the windowsill, concentrating on Becca. And you, of course."*

Sleeping, Clara said to herself before quickly dismissing the thought. Instead, she focused on the brief vision that had preceded the Bast statuette's fall onto Nick Roswell's head. *"Did either of you manifest a paw?"*

Harriet's eyes betrayed her, as with a flick of those golden orbs, she looked at Laurel and then back at Clara. *"Of course."*

"That was one possibility we considered." As smooth as her fur, Laurel broke in, giving cover to Harriet's lie. Or, Clara allowed, exaggeration.

"What?" Harriet swatted at Laurel. *"It was."*

"And I am grateful." Clara wasn't going to get in the middle of this. Harriet might not mean to hurt either of her sisters, but she was a large cat, and a swipe from one of her paws could sting. That didn't mean Clara didn't have doubts about her sister's claim, but it had been a very long day, and she desperately wanted a nap. As respectfully as she could, she bowed her head one more time, all the while watching Harriet's big white mitts.

That's when it hit her.

"Where's the kitten?" Her energy suddenly renewed, Clara leaped to the back of the sofa. From her perch, she saw the little tortie, curled into a fuzzy disc and deep in slumber.

"Kitten." Clara reached down carefully. *"Kitten, wake up."*

The tortie woke, yawning so widely that her eyes closed and she once again rested her multicolored head on her paws.

"Wake up," Clara mewed, directing her urgent thoughts toward the younger beast.

"What is it?" The tortie roused, blinking up at her.

"Your paw. Let me see it."

The kitten stretched out her left front leg, revealing a paw as velvety black as those on her hind legs.

"No, the other one." Her own fatigue was taking its toll, as Clara began to lose patience. *"The pink one."*

The kitten stared up at her, fully awake. *"You mean my peach toe?"*

"Yes." Clara did her best to tamp down her restlessness. The tortie was young and untrained. A kitten still. And yet she couldn't help but remember a paw reaching down, one pink toe extended.

"You're remembering correctly." The voice of the kitten filled her head as she stretched out her other foreleg, revealing a black paw with one peach toe.

Clara gazed at the paw with growing confusion, even as the little tortie curled up once again. *"Why do you think I'm so tired?"*

"But wait, I don't understand." As Clara spoke, a soft thud to her left alerted her to the arrival of Laurel, while a heavier one, to her left, signaled that Harriet had ascended to the sofa back as well.

"Oh, very well." The kitten struggled to her feet and, with the help of her claws, clambered up to the sofa's top to join the other felines. *"You called for help. Well, you specifically called for your sisters, but with only two of them here, their powers were limited."*

Harriet opened her mouth to object, but a quick hiss from Laurel made her close it again.

"Those two are so connected to you, it was easy for them to locate you and do the channeling. I simply looked down and saw the goddess. She did the rest."

"Bast?" Clara thought about the statuette. Made of some stone composite and shaped by a mold, it was one of dozens that Charm and Cherish stocked. Sleek, yes, and graceful, but would the goddess really manifest herself through such a thing?

"She manifests through all of us." The kitten's green-eyed gaze was so intense that Clara found she couldn't break away.

"Who are you?" Laurel's distinctive yowl broke the spell.

"Don't you know?" With a leap, the kitten landed on the floor, and soon Harriet, Laurel, and a very confused Clara were on the rug facing her.

"Let's assume we don't." Laurel's tone was a little defensive. A sign, Clara realized, that her sister was as bewildered as she was.

"Yes. Let's." Harriet clearly was as well.

Cats don't roll their eyes. But the kitten looked up at the ceiling with a sigh, in what Clara recognized as the feline equivalent of the human response. Or, she realized, the kitten could be invoking the feline goddess herself.

"I would have thought you, my sisters, would recognize me." The kitten's voice took on an authority that Clara had never heard her use before. *"I am Tadibastet, but you can call me Tadi."*

"Tadibastet?" Laurel and Harriet exchanged a glance, but Clara remained as perplexed as ever. *"It means 'daughter of Bast,' Clown,"* Laurel explained.

"But you're not a daughter of Bast," complained Harriet. *"We are."*

The room had begun to spin for Clara, as the scenes Harriet had once shared with her whirled through her mind. Their ancestor, a tawny desert cat, coming to the aid of a temple servant, ridding the House of Bast where she labored of rodents—thus allowing the poor girl to more easily pull together the tribute due the holy place. With the cat's help, the serving girl became a priestess herself, elevating the cat to a position of reverence before ultimately revealing herself as a manifestation of the goddess Bast and then, to the sand-colored cat's amazement, granting both nobility and power to the feline. Hereditary power, the priestess explained, that would pass down all her line.

"Exactly." Harriet had regained her composure and, with it, her air of superiority. *"Our line."*

"Wait." The hint of an idea was forming in Clara's mind. *"You called us 'sisters'?"*

The kitten slowly blinked, an expression of contentment Clara had never seen in the little tortie. *"Indeed,"* she mewed. *"Although our mothers' mothers' mothers were still far removed from that original site."*

"Our mother's mother's..." Clara paused to think, recalling the warm memory of the dam who had nursed her and licked her before sending her three kittens into a humane trap—and the shelter that would bring them to Becca. It had been just Harriet and Laurel with her then, their mother purring encouragement and reminding them all of their obligations to the person who would choose them for her own. To Becca.

But then she thought of Mr. Butters, who had been able to speak as well as either of her sisters. Of the kitten who stared up at her now. And she thought back to that temple. To the blessing bestowed on the tawny cat—and all her offspring, stretching through time. *"We're related,"* she said at last, her mew fading even as she spoke.

"Exactly," said the kitten, Tadi, Clara corrected herself, even as images of that first cat opened up to include her with her first litter of kittens, and then her kittens' kittens, and those kittens' kittens, on and on through generations of domesticated cats. All of whom, she realized with growing astonishment, were the favored offspring of that first beloved cat.

Chapter Forty-One

y the time Becca got to work the next morning, the line at Charm and Cherish ran down the block. Even Margaret came down to help, cackling with glee as Becca and Elizabeth answered questions—and rang up sales. Three times Clara had to change her perch among the books as eager hands reached up for primers on the craft and the history of Wicca, before finally finding a calm place to nap up on the top shelf, where the statuette of Bast once more stood guard.

Only once the shop closed for the day did the humans have a chance to catch up.

"The statue of Kali. It was blue, so he thought that the sapphire could have been hidden inside." Becca's eye went wide as she pieced together the clues for the sisters and for Shira and Trina, who had come by later in the afternoon. "Hallowell said he was looking for antiques, but he really just meant second-hand items, didn't he?"

Elizabeth only smiled.

"He told me he was considering a special exhibition, but that was only an excuse to go poking around." Becca exhaled, as if her own credulity exhausted her. "He was desperate to find the sapphire."

"The museum is private, but the board that runs it was already looking into possible embezzlement," Shira chimed in. "I didn't know that until this morning, but the accountant I'd heard about? She wasn't helping with the budgeting. She was a forensic accountant hired by the board to look at the books."

"Hallowell must have panicked." Becca took it all in. "I bet she'll find he was selling smaller items and pocketing the funds, but he couldn't keep doing that. He had to have a big score to pay off Roswell. But he wouldn't have been able to sell the sapphire right away. Part of the deal must have been that Roswell would get the sapphire, but for all their safety, he had to keep it quiet for a while. I don't know whose idea it was to disguise it with some plaster and paint, but it was a good one. At least, until Robbins—another 'old-timer' and Roswell's buddy—died. Robbins must have told them he'd hidden it as a 'blue charm,' but neither Roswell nor Hallowell had any idea what kind of charm or what Robbins' family did with it. Hallowell must have visited every metaphysical store and botanica in the state."

"Try in New England," said Shira. "Remember those break-ins in New Hampshire?"

"Those break-ins—and there have been a couple of store closures too. I'm betting we'll find that Robbins' family sold the charm to one of them, and Hallowell found that out somehow."

"It wouldn't have been difficult," Shira mused. "A few simple questions during a condolence call."

Becca nodded. "There's still the question of how the charm ended up at a flea market. But maybe the proprietor had a stall there—or she was liquidating her assets. At any rate, you bought it."

Trina nodded vigorously. "And that's why he didn't find it."

Becca paused, mouth slightly open and eyes wide.

"You called it, Elizabeth." She turned toward the older woman, a new appreciation in her eyes. "You said that he didn't find what he was looking for that very first day he was in the shop."

"I also pointed out that Kali is both a creator and a destroyer."

"But why..." Becca ignored her mentor's comment. "If you knew, even then, why didn't you say something?"

"I didn't know. Not for sure." Elizabeth continued to look at Becca, her gaze soft. "Knowledge is set. It's sure. More often, reality is in flux, with many possibilities in the offing."

Becca shook off her words. "You knew enough. You at least suspected. If you had told us, we could've avoided so much. Trina's apartment being broken into and her being kidnapped. Mr. Butters on the streets…" The enormity of the last few days seemed to fall on her then, and she sighed again, looking up at the older woman for an answer.

"Perhaps," said Elizabeth. For a moment, Becca and Clara both thought she was going to leave it at that, especially as she started to turn, today's caftan wafting out around her like a jewel-toned cloud. "But then where would you have been?"

Becca started to answer and then caught herself. Looking at her kind, open face, Clara didn't need her sister's powers to read some of what was going on. Her doubts about Detective Newsom—and her own calling. Her work finding Mr. Butters that had not only brought the handsome cat home but had introduced her to Trina and Shira. Even the tensions that had arisen in her coven had served a purpose, testing and reinforcing the bonds between them.

"Exactly." Elizabeth spoke as if she had read Becca's—or Clara's—thoughts herself. "There is value in doing the work. Especially when we work together," she said. With that, she turned toward Clara and winked. And the calico, bowing her head as she would toward an older sister, gave her the slow blink of love and appreciation in return.

* * *

When Becca returned home that evening, she was ready to collapse. That didn't stop her from feeding her cats—and herself—and texting Maddy about the success of the day. By the time she had put down her phone, the cats were all apparently asleep, curled together on the sofa, each within a paw's reach of the other. Smiling at the peaceful scene, she rose slowly and headed for the kitchen, where she dug around in a junk drawer until she found some Elmer's glue. With that in hand, she began poking along her bookshelf, seeking the shards of the blue bowl that had been broken days before.

That was when she found it. The blue bowl, back in its original shape, its cloud-like pattern stretching unbroken along the delicate surface.

"I don't understand." She spoke softly, unaware that her cats were listening in. "I didn't—I didn't think I could…"

Raising her head, Clara turned to face her oldest sister.

"*Harriet?*" she called softly. "*Did you summon a new bowl while we were out?*"

"*Who me?*" The big marmalade slowly kneaded her special pillow, the one that had started everything,

"*Yes, you.*" Laurel blinked drowsily at her big sister—or, more accurately, at her tail, which she clearly wanted to swat.

"*Will it last?*" Clara blinked at the older cat to soften the implication inherent in her question. "*No offense, but sometimes…*"

"*Yes, yes, I know.*" Harriet closed her eyes again. All three of the older cats knew too well that often the things Harriet had summoned—cat treats and toys as well as that gold-trimmed pillow—had a tendency to resolve back into the ether once Harriet stopped paying attention. "*But this is different. For starters…*"

Clara waited while her sister started to gently snore,

"*She didn't do it,*" the tortie—Tadi—chimed in. "*Becca did. It just took time.*"

"*Well, we helped. While you were out.*" Harriet roused herself, only to settle in for a deeper sleep. "*But that's what we do, right?*"

Clara could feel Laurel and Tadi looking at her, and so she bowed her head, both in recognition of her sisters' combined powers and the inevitability of the collaboration to come.

"*Always,*" she purred.

Acknowledgments

So many friends and readers helped bring this series to life. Karen Schlosberg, Brett Milano, and Lisa Susser were early readers, and Sophie Garelick, Frank Garelick, and Lisa Jones have always been incredibly supportive. My former agent, Colleen Mohyde, got this book its first publisher, and my current agent, Anne-Lise Spitzer, found a new home for my witch cats with Level Best Books. A big shout-out to Nicole Williams, whose generous contribution to the Writers for Trans Rights auction resulted in Mr. Butters taking over the role of the guest cat in these pages. Last but not least, Jon S. Garelick not only read multiple versions, but put up with some very late dinners, too. Thank you all, my dears. Purrs out.

About the Author

Clea Simon is the *Boston Globe*-bestselling author of three nonfiction books and more than thirty mysteries, including *World Enough* and *Hold Me Down*, both of which were named "Must Reads" by the Massachusetts Center for the Book. A graduate of Harvard University and former journalist, she has contributed to publications ranging from Salon.com and *Harvard Magazine* to *Yankee* and *The New York Times*. Visit her at www.CleaSimon.com.

AUTHOR WEBSITE:
  http://www.CleaSimon.com

SOCIAL MEDIA HANDLES:
  https://www.facebook.com/CleaSimonAuthor/
  https://x.com/Clea_Simon
  https://bsky.app/profile/cleasimon.bsky.social
  https://www.instagram.com/cleasimon_author/

Also by Clea Simon

Mystery series:
    Theda Krakow cats and crime and rock and roll mysteries
    Pru Marlowe "pet noir" mysteries
    Dulcie Schwartz academic mysteries
    Blackie & Care dystopian black cat mysteries

Standalones:
    World Enough
    Hold Me Down
    Bad Boy Beat
    The Butterfly Trap

Nonfiction:
    Mad House: Growing up in the Shadow of Mentally Ill Siblings
    Fatherless Women: How We Change After We Lose Our Dads
    The Feline Mystique: On the Mysterious Connection Between Women and Cats